lies like
wildfire

lies like
wildfire

JENNIFER LYNN ALVAREZ

DELACORTE PRESS

Text copyright © 2021 by Jennifer Lynn Alvarez
Jacket art copyright © 2021 by MISHKO

All rights reserved. Published in the United States by Delacorte Press, an imprint of Random House Children's Books, a division of Penguin Random House LLC, New York.

Delacorte Press is a registered trademark and the colophon is a trademark of Penguin Random House LLC.

GetUnderlined.com

Educators and librarians, for a variety of teaching tools, visit us at
RHTeachersLibrarians.com

Library of Congress Cataloging-in-Publication Data
Names: Alvarez, Jennifer Lynn, author.
Title: Lies like wildfire / Jennifer Lynn Alvarez.
Description: First edition. | New York : Delacorte Press, [2021] |
Audience: Ages 14 and up. | Summary: When Hannah and her best friends
accidentally spark an enormous and deadly wildfire, their instinct is to
lie, but as the blaze roars through their rural town, Hannah's friends
begin to crack and one ends up missing.
Identifiers: LCCN 2020032253 (print) | LCCN 2020032254 (ebook) |
ISBN 978-0-593-30963-6 (hardcover) | ISBN 978-0-593-30964-3 (library
binding) | ISBN 978-0-593-30965-0 (ebook)
Subjects: CYAC: Best friends—Fiction. | Friendship—Fiction. |
Wildfires—Fiction. | Missing persons—Fiction.
Classification: LCC PZ7.A4797 Li 2021 (print) | LCC PZ7.A4797 (ebook)

The text of this book is set in 11.75-point Adobe Jenson Pro.
Interior design by Andrea Lau

Printed in the United States of America
10 9 8 7 6 5 4 3 2 1
First Edition

For good people who do bad things

lies like wildfire

part one

The Lie

1

August 11

Time: 11:10 a.m.

I'm not dressed to find a body. I'm wearing cutoffs and a thin white tank top. The mosquitoes are going to suck me dry, and my new Vans are going to get trashed. I'm dressed for summer, not for crawling around in the woods, searching for one of my best friends with a bunch of overcaffeinated volunteers.

I hope we don't find her. I want Violet to be alive. We just graduated high school, and we're going to college soon. Getting kidnapped or murdered or committing suicide, or whatever happened to her, was not scheduled for today. What *was* scheduled was shopping for bedding and other dorm supplies.

So no, I'm not dressed or prepared to find Violet Sandoval's dead body. Besides that, I believe she was murdered, and I'd like to let that sleeping dog lie. Why? Well, why would *anyone* want

3

a dead girl to stay missing? Because they don't like her? Maybe (but not in this case). Because they want a shot at her boyfriend? Perhaps. Or because they helped kill her? Now that's a reason. I just got out of the hospital, and I don't know what happened to Violet and I don't want to know.

Only one thing is certain: it all began with a flame.

2

As I reach into my Jeep, I hear quick footsteps and feel the back of my bikini top snap against my skin. I whip around to see the gleeful face of Nathaniel James Drummer, my main best friend out of my four best friends, smiling at me from my driveway. I aim a kick at him. "What are you, twelve?"

He dances out of my striking range, cloaked as usual in faded jeans and a too-tight T-shirt. Grizzled, spiny trees surround us, rearing toward the sky, and a hot summer wind gusts off the Sierra Nevada mountains. "What's in the bag?" he asks. "And you better not say homework."

"It's summer, idiot." I snatch my backpack and sling it over my shoulder. I did make the long drive to the library to check out books on criminology, nothing wrong with getting a head start, but it isn't technically homework—not until I leave for college.

Drummer eyeballs the heavy pack, and his smile deflates. "Come on, Han, don't waste the time we have left reading."

I laugh. "That's exactly why I'm going to college and you're not." But when I meet his gaze, my stomach lightens. Drummer has no idea I fell in love with him in the sixth grade. It happened fast, like sliding off a cliff. One moment he was my sharp-kneed, slightly smelly best friend, and the next he was golden-skinned and handsome and a million miles out of my league. I cross my arms so he can't see the gigantic Drummer-shaped hole in my chest. The thing about love is, unless your best friend falls too, you fall alone.

Drummer hooks his finger around a loop in my jeans and tugs me closer, his deep voice making my eardrums vibrate: "I came to get you. Everyone's meeting up at the Gap for a swim. Want to go?"

"Everyone?"

"Yep, all the monsters. And Mo's bringing beer."

Our group—Mo (short for Maureen), Luke, Violet, Drummer, and me, Hannah—are the kids he's referring to when he talks about the "monsters," a nickname we received when we were seven years old.

It was at the community center. Our parents had signed us up for a low-budget daycare-in-disguise summer production of *Where the Wild Things Are*. The director asked who wanted to be a wild thing, and since none of us wanted to play the human, our hands shot into the air. After that, she called us simply the monsters, and we've been the monsters and best friends ever since.

I bump my hip against his. "Let's ride the horses there."

He and I have moved into the shade and are now leaning against my Jeep in the driveway. My bloodhound, Matilda, watches us from the family room window, her big ears cocked.

Temperatures will soar into the hundreds today, with afternoon winds blowing from the east. Humidity is at 11 percent and dropping. I know because Red Flag Warnings started pinging on my phone at 8:00 a.m. Drought caused an early fire season this year, and the electric company plans to shut off the power at noon. When you live in California, in a tinderbox called a forest, you know more than you ever wanted to about wildfires.

Drummer slits his eyes. "I'm not riding that colt that stomped on you."

"Sunny didn't stomp on me; he *stepped* on me. Not his fault he weighs a thousand pounds."

"Another reason I'd rather not ride him." His gaze shifts to the tank top covering my bikini, and his eyes burn straight through it. "You're the only woman on this damn earth who can get me on a horse, you know that?"

My voice falls an octave. "I know it." Drummer flirts with everyone, it means nothing, but my stupid, traitorous heart soars when he looks at me like that.

His pretty blue eyes slide up to my face. "All right, Hannah Banana, have it your way."

A half hour later, we're saddled and on the trail. Drummer's horse, my fourteen-year-old Appaloosa barrel racer named Pistol, hops at every shadow. "He's bucking," Drummer complains.

"That's not bucking. Sit up and relax." Drummer obeys and Pistol settles.

We emerge from the pines and there's Gap Lake, a sapphire oval sunk in its mountain crown. Steep, unshaven peaks surround it, and the wind creates ripples that blow across the water, making it shimmer like wrinkled satin. Underground springs feed the Gap all summer, and rainwater and snowmelt replenish it in winter. Pine trees and noble firs surround the shoreline like undecorated Christmas trees.

The Gap is a pit, really, a hole full of fresh water with no shallow end, its sheer edge skidding straight down into a black abyss. Scientists say the lake was formed by shifting tectonic plates back in 480 CE. Ancient peoples claim that it was carved out during a volcanic battle between gods. The citizens of Gap Mountain don't care how it came to be. We care that (according to new measurements) it has surpassed Lake Tahoe as the deepest lake in California, and we care that if you drown in the Gap, your body will never be recovered.

Violet spots us. "Over here," she calls, waving.

Our group is sprawled on a piece of dusty shoreline we call "the beach," the only area where you can climb out of the Gap. There are no other kids here, which means everyone else is at the river. Mo is digging into her hot/cold bag that I know will be filled with cut fruit, sandwiches, chips, homemade muffins or cookies, and beer, while Violet lounges on an oversized towel, humming a tune. I don't see Luke.

Drummer and I guide the horses to the beach and slide out of the saddles.

"Hannah!" Violet leaps to her feet and hugs me before I can tie them up. A heady cloud of designer lotions and perfumes wafts from her hair and sun-darkened skin, tickling my sinuses. She smiles up at me—sable eyes shining, dimples popping. She's short and curvy and bright, and I feel like a giraffe standing next to her—tall and wiry with huge eyes and a long nose, camouflaged to *blend*.

She kisses each of my cheeks in her continental way. "Tell me who sings this?" Violet breaks into some new song from the radio and, as usual, I guess wrong.

"Close," she cries, generous as always.

Violet is the only monster who doesn't live in Gap Mountain. She comes up from Santa Barbara each summer to visit her rich grandmother. Sometimes her older brother comes too, but this year he's in the Maldives with his new wife, so we get Violet to ourselves. She nods toward Drummer, grinning. "I can't believe you got him on a horse."

"It tried to buck me off," Drummer calls out.

"He did not," I protest.

Mo slides her sunglasses down her freckled nose. "You guys hungry?"

"Hell yeah." Drummer helps himself to her bag.

"Take off those boots—you're getting dirt on the blanket."

Mo jabs his ribs with her bare foot, but Drummer doesn't listen, just starts snacking on muffins. Mo hands me a bottle of sunscreen. "Lather up."

"No thanks, that stuff's worse for you than the sun."

"I believe that's a conspiracy theory, Han, but whatever." She goes back to jabbing Drummer until he removes his boots.

"Where's Luke?" I ask.

Violet nods toward the tree line. "Sulking, as usual."

Drummer licks his sticky fingers and grabs Violet's hand. "Let's swim." He drags her toward the Gap while she protests about her hair, which she flat-ironed this morning.

Drummer isn't having it. "Don't come to the Gap unless you plan to get wet," he teases. "Totally soaking *wet*." He picks her up, tosses her into the water, and dives in after her.

Mo shouts at them, "Get a room."

"He wasn't—they're not," I start, and then shut my mouth. In the sixth grade, our group made a pact: *monsters don't date monsters*. It was my idea to sign it in blood, and so far, we've stuck to it.

I pull off my tank top and slide out of my jeans, revealing the same faded-orange Walmart bikini I wore last year. "I'll take a muffin," I say to Mo.

She opens a plastic container and hands me a blueberry muffin, still warm from the oven. Then she pulls out two bottles of Bud Light. "My brother got us beer. You want one?"

I shake my head. My dad is the county sheriff, and his deputies patrol the lake sometimes. The last thing he needs is for his daughter to get hauled into the station for underage drinking.

Besides that, I lost my mom to a drunk-driving accident that happened when I was six.

Strangers freak out when they hear this. They pat me and say *poor thing*, and single women flirt with my dad—the stoic widower raising a motherless girl. We hate that, Dad and I, but we let them fawn, since it's better than hitting them with the punch line: my mom *was* the drunk driver.

She didn't die right away, but the driver of the other car did. Yeah, my mom got convicted of DWI *and* murder. My dad was still a deputy when he arrested her—*The law is the law, Bug*—and Mom died in prison two years later of inflammatory breast cancer. But I don't blame the illness for taking her. No, I lost my mother, and in some ways my father, the night of the accident.

So it's not that I don't drink—I do sometimes—but I know better than to get caught. It's why I'm going into law enforcement. I'd rather *drive* the police cruiser than ride in the back, and maybe that's the difference between my mom and me, and maybe it's the only one, but it's probably the most important.

Mo returns the extra beer to her bag, pulls out an ice-cold bottle of lemonade, and presses it against my leg, making me squeal. She nods toward Sunny. "You probably shouldn't drink and ride a horse anyway, huh?"

Laughing, I open the lemonade and take a long swig. "Probably not."

We squeeze onto the blanket together and watch Drummer and Violet swim. The cell signal here sucks, so Mo and I take dozens of photos and videos to post later.

Luke finally shows up, stomping out of the trees like a yeti, his clothing wrinkled and his face screwed up tight. "Fucking assholes," he says.

"Who?" Mo asks.

"Everyone." Luke skips a stone across the water, almost striking Drummer and Violet, who raise their hands in protest.

"I wouldn't throw rocks if I were you," Drummer shouts, recalling Luke's vandalism last spring. He's on probation for throwing rocks at his neighbor's house after they harassed him about his loud music. He broke six windows and caused two thousand dollars in property damage. After a beat, we all bust up laughing.

"You're the assholes," Luke says, and then he pulls off his shirt, kicks off his shorts, and stands at the edge of the Gap in his underwear. He lifts weights obsessively, and his body is thick and pale and ripped with muscles. Luke was a happy kid, but that changed in middle school after his mom left his dad. Since then, he's moody and sad and he won't let any of us in except Mo.

"Afraid to get wet?" I yell as Luke paces the shore like a dog wondering if it should jump in.

He gives me the finger and then dives headfirst into the water, which is cold even during summer. When he pops back up, he whoops and shakes out his hair, flinging water droplets in an arc around him.

My eyes slide back to Drummer. He's cradling Violet in his arms as she floats on her back, and my heart dips to the pit of my stomach. She's so relaxed, so happy, and she's headed to

Stanford in the fall, no need for financial aid or a scholarship, the whole world at her pretty feet.

Violet has no idea I applied to Stanford too, or that they rejected me. She doesn't know how hard I work at home, cleaning stalls, mending fences, and training my horses myself because I can't afford to hire help. Her grandmother pays twelve hundred dollars a month to board each of Violet's imported show horses—animals so expensive she's not allowed to ride them on trails, only in carefully engineered arenas with perfect footing so they don't slip or trip.

I squint at her. It's the luck of genetics, of being born to the right family. Violet has everything: beauty, money, brains—and maybe Drummer too. We all love her, but she's not like us. She's an outsider. I slide on my dark-tinged sunglasses. Looking at Violet is like looking at the sun: it hurts.

Mo ties back her dark red hair and calls out: "We've got to plan the rest of summer. We can't come *here* every day. I made a list." She withdraws a pen and a pink spiral notebook from her bag. "This is what I have so far: swim at the Gap, duh, day trip to hike the Vernal Fall trail in Yosemite—"

"No way," shouts Luke. "Too touristy."

"Just let me finish," Mo says. "Movie night at Violet's, shopping trip to Reno for clothes and college stuff, Escape Room—I'm going to make one—the rodeo in August, a spa day—that's just for the girls—and a hunting trip for the boys."

"I like to hunt," I protest.

"But do you want to?" Mo asks. "Really?"

Do I want to spend a couple of nights in a tiny hunting cabin with Drummer? Uh, hell yeah, but I let it go.

"Anything to add?" Mo asks the group.

"Camping in Death Valley," Drummer calls out.

"As long as someone else drives," Mo says. "There's still dust in my dad's truck from last time."

"I've got an idea," Luke grumbles. "Let's do something *unplanned.*"

Mo frowns at him. "I— That's not something I can write down."

He splashes her from the water's edge, and Mo narrows her eyes. "If it weren't for *me,* you all would starve and die of boredom."

Drummer and Violet have emerged from the lake and Drummer tackles Mo. "I doubt that very much." He nibbles on her arms and then her tummy, sending her into gales of laughter.

Then Luke swims ashore and flops onto the blanket, exhausted because he smokes at least two packs of cigarettes a day and can hardly breathe. Violet and Mo dig into the snacks while my horses graze on the tall, dry grass behind us.

Is this our last summer together, I wonder? Mo is leaving first, to attend Fresno State's nursing program. Violet is going to Stanford to study biochemistry, I'm going to San Diego State to study criminal justice, and Luke and Drummer will work full-time somewhere.

I wonder if Violet, Mo, and I will get jobs next year at school and stay over the holidays? Will we come home only when our parents beg us? Will geography be all that separates the monsters, or will it be education too? A shudder rolls through me at the thought of leaving Gap Mountain, of making new friends, of moving on. . . .

The wind kicks up and blows off Mo's hat. "I'll get it," I say.

Drummer squints at the sun beating down on us, his lashes creating spiked shadows on his cheeks. "This is fire weather."

"Don't say that," Mo warns, as if his words alone could call up a fire.

Other than the wind, which is really gusting now, the day is perfect. Our futures expand before us like the Gap, beautiful and unknowable, and I vow not to forget a single moment of this summer.

That's when Luke stands up, pulls a bag of weed out of his pocket, and says the words that will change our lives forever: "Who wants to smoke?"

3

July 7

Time: 3:00 p.m.

"Why can't you vape like a normal person?" Mo asks, groaning. "Go away. I don't want that nasty smell on me." Her cheeks have turned red in the heat, and her lips are chapped.

"It's too windy by the water anyway." Luke snatches his backpack and heads toward the sheltered woods that meet up with the beach. Drummer follows. Violet watches them a moment, then pulls on her shorts, buttoning them low on her tiny waist, and slides on her Vans. "Be right back." She skips after them, fingers dancing, head cocked.

Mo rolls up her blanket and packs everything into her bag. "The party's over, I guess."

"Or just beginning," I grumble. "You know I don't like Drummer when he's high."

"Because he ignores you, right? You need to get over him, Han, there are other guys."

Heat sweeps to my cheeks. "Are there, though?"

She laughs and slings her bag over her shoulder. Her large hazel eyes flick toward the woods. "Crap, we should keep an eye on them."

"They're not babies."

She lifts her eyebrows.

"Fine." I pack my towel into Sunny's saddlebags, leave the horses tied, and follow Mo onto an animal path through the pine trees.

"Look, bear tracks," she says, pointing. "I wish you'd brought Matilda."

"Me too." My dog is old, but her bark is big enough to scare away bears. I haven't drunk much water today, and a wave of dizziness washes over me. It's hardly any cooler in the woods, and the dry wind reaches us between the branches, hot as devil's breath. The brittle grasses and undergrowth are parched from the hottest summer in Gap Mountain's history.

I glance at my phone. The time is 3:12 p.m. Pine needles rattle beneath my feet, reminding me to watch for snakes. I hear laughter ahead.

Mo and I find our friends standing in a small clearing. Luke and Drummer are gossiping in low tones about someone they both don't like while Violet leans against Drummer, gazing up at him as he inhales off Luke's pipe. I notice his arm slung casually around her waist, his fingers splayed over the rear pocket of her shorts. My heart stutters. This is not fucking cool.

Mo notices too and glances at me. "The pact," I mouth, but she shrugs as if to say, *We were in sixth grade. Does it still count?*

My spine tightens in answer. Of course it still counts. We all agreed that *monsters don't date monsters*. I stare at the pine needles. God, I'm still twelve years old inside, just taller.

Drummer passes the pipe to Violet, and she takes it, sucking deeply through her kiss-shaped lips. His fascinated gaze lingers on her face in a way that's familiar—not because he's ever looked at me that way, but because I've witnessed it with a slew of girls over the years. Drummer and Violet are both single this summer, and this flirting—it feels dangerous. If he starts something with her, it won't last. Violet could get hurt.

When Drummer notices me watching, he breaks apart from Violet and slides his arm back to his side—looking guilty as hell, I might add. I know my disapproval isn't fair. Drummer doesn't belong to me. What we have is some twisted thing that sucks, mostly for me, but sometimes for him too.

The pipe has gone out, and Luke pulls a book of matches out of the tin he keeps in his backpack.

I gape at it. "Hey, you can't light a match in the woods."

He glances at me, his eyes bloodshot and half-lidded. "Uh, yes I can."

"Not on a Red Flag day."

"I'm being careful," he argues, and Drummer giggles.

I shake my head. "Why don't you use a lighter? Who uses matches anymore?"

"He's not old enough to buy a lighter." Drummer giggles harder because Luke is still a minor.

Luke nods. "But I can buy a shotgun."

"Hell yeah!" Drummer cries, bumping Luke's fist.

No one is looking at me. No one is listening. "You seriously shouldn't smoke here, not today. I know; my dad's the sheriff."

"*My dad's the sheriff*," Luke repeats—in perfect imitation of me—and they all laugh louder.

Fury rises and swallows me whole. "Fuck all of you."

Luke flinches. "If anyone needs a hit, it's you, Han Solo." He strikes the match, lights the weed in the pipe, and takes a long hit. Then he blows the smoke in my face.

It's meant as a joke, I know, but my brain switches fully off and the sky turns blinding red. I grab Luke's arm and dig my fingernails into his flesh. He's strong, really fucking strong, and he yanks his arm free. The lit pipe and the matchbook fly out of his hand, and the flaming red embers scatter across the dry grass. My voice rings like a gunshot. "I said stop!"

"Shit, Hannah, calm down." Luke turns in a circle. "Anyone see where the pipe landed?"

Everyone stops laughing. "This is exactly how fires start," I mutter.

"You're the one who made me drop it," Luke snarls.

"You're the one who lit it," I return.

We drop to the ground and search for the pipe in the long yellow grass. "If we can't find it, you owe me a new one," Luke says. "I just bought that pipe."

"Guys," Violet calls a few moments later. "I smell smoke." We stand up and spin around, hunting for it. "There!" She points to a trail of white smoke and a series of small spot fires that are gobbling up the fallen pine needles and spreading west, pushed by the wind.

For a brief moment, we stare at it, the thing we've been taught to fear since birth but have never seen in person: wildfire.

"Oh my god, put it out!" I yell.

We fly into action, ripping off our shirts and beating the flames, but the motion just adds oxygen and life to the fire. Luke grabs fistfuls of dirt and throws them, but the fire skirts out of the way. One blaze splits around a tree, creating two horn-like prongs, and we chase them. "Head it off, make a firebreak!" Drummer yells.

We charge ahead of the fire and start yanking weeds and clearing the brush. "Do you have anything in your bag, Mo, any water?" I ask.

"Yes." She rips it off her shoulder and pulls out a half-full bottle of water. She tosses it on the flames, and they shrink away, sizzling angrily, then leap over the moistened grass.

"That's all you have?" I shout.

"I have some beer left." She opens those and pours them on the flames, but the blaze has grown too large to be doused. Mo drops the bottles.

"I'll get water from the Gap!" Violet cries. She grabs Mo's sun hat to use as a container and takes off running. The wildfire reaches our break and leaps right over it, buoyed by the wind. Embers flutter ahead, starting more fires. The dancing orange flames speed west, climbing trees and swallowing shrubs. They spread faster than we can run. Large weeds and pine cones pop and send sparks that glide on the wind. Where they land, more fires ignite, hungry and newborn and squalling for fuel.

"Shit, shit, shit," says Luke.

Violet returns with the sun hat, sees how wide and far the fire has already traveled, and starts to cry. The water she collected dribbles impotently out of the hat.

Drummer swipes back his hair, panting. We're all breathing hard, starting to cough.

Mo pulls out her inhaler. "We can't stop it. We have to get help," she wheezes.

Luke yanks out his phone. "Fuck, I don't have a signal."

None of us do.

Behind me, the horses whinny and I have an idea. "Drummer and I can ride the horses to the fire department."

Violet shakes her head. "No, I'll go with you. I'm a better rider; I can ride fast."

It's true. Like me, she's been riding her entire life. We run toward the horses, but then I skid to a halt and turn to the others. "Mo, pick up all those bottles, get rid of everything that says we've been here."

For a second, no one understands. Then Luke nods. "Yeah, we didn't do this."

"What?" Mo asks. Her red hair has come undone, and it whips around her face.

"You heard Luke—*we* didn't do this. We weren't here. Don't talk to anyone. Just head to my house! Violet and I will warn the town." I nod to Violet and she stares at me, confused and terrified and high on weed.

We jog to the horses, slowing when we get near so as not to spook them. Sunny prances and rears, but Pistol looks more curious than upset. I pull their slipknots, and we stick our feet in the stirrups, fling our legs over the saddles, and gather up the reins. "Give Pistol his head," I instruct Violet. "You take the lead. Sunny likes to follow."

Violet and Pistol trot onto the main trail that leads from the lake and into Gap Mountain. The fire burns behind us on the ridge, gobbling brush, beginning to roar. Pine cones roll downhill, flinging hot pitch, starting more fires. Thick, pale smoke rises in a plume, and I bet the volunteer fire department has already seen it. We urge the horses into a gallop and race toward town.

All the way to Gap Mountain, laws and penalties I've heard about from my dad flash through my mind: It's illegal to start a fire, even accidentally. Reckless arson is a *misdemeanor* in the state of California. Bodily injury caused by reckless arson is a *felony* in the state of California. Death caused by reckless arson is *murder* in the state of California. We have to stop this wildfire before anyone gets hurt.

I kick Sunny in the ribs. "Yah!" Both horses lower their necks and run faster.

4

Violet and I gallop the horses into Gap Mountain proper. There is one main avenue, called Pine Street, and the volunteer fire department is located there.

I guide Sunny onto the street, and his hooves slide across the asphalt. The horses whinny, upset by the fast ride and the tang of smoke in their nostrils. The wind at our backs blows their tails forward, and Pistol prances ahead of me. Violet steers him with one hand and grips the saddle horn with the other. She glances back, her eyes glassy and red-rimmed.

"Violet, get on the sidewalk!" I call to her.

She nods but pulls too hard on Pistol's reins, and the

Appaloosa rears at the same time a car turns onto Pine Street, driving straight toward them. The brakes shriek and Violet leans up Pistol's neck, as if they're going to jump over the car, but then Pistol drops to all four hooves. He snorts at the little Honda and its shocked driver.

"Get off the street!" I shout at Violet, but she's already guiding my horse to the sidewalk. The Honda drives slowly away, the driver shaking his head.

I catch up to Violet. Her thick hair is matted to her forehead, her face is soaked with tears and snot, and her eyes are swollen. "You look terrible, V. Let me talk to the firefighters, okay?"

"All right." We glance at the mountain where the pale smoke has turned brown. It rolls out of the trees and spreads across the sky.

I cluck my tongue at Sunny and guide him down the sidewalk to the fire department, but they've already spotted the plumes. Their double garage doors are up and the red engine is out, lights swirling. Firefighters scurry into their gear. Gap Mountain's brand-new hi-lo sirens, which were installed for emergencies like this, sound from the trucks.

Citizens spill out of the Wildflower Café, the hair salon, and the general store and line the streets, eyes fixed on the mountains that hunch over us.

All at once, every cell phone in Gap Mountain pings, and the people on the street, including Violet and me, stare at the incoming Mono County sheriff Nixle alert:

> **Vegetation fire on Gap Ridge.**
>
> **Firefighting resources deployed.**
>
> **Residents of Gap Mountain, prepare for possible**
>   **evacuation.**

I gape at my phone. "Evacuation? Seriously?"

"Hannah, this is bad!" Violet cries. She's sitting on my spotted horse in the middle of downtown with her eyes closed, looking high and scared and guilty.

I have to get her out of here. "Violet, look at me."

She opens her eyes, and her lower lip trembles. "We did that," she whispers, glancing at the smoke billowing out of the forest.

"Shhh, don't say that." The fire truck streaks past, startling Sunny. "See, they know. They're on their way, and they'll put it out fast. Let's get the horses to my house. There's nothing more we can do."

Violet nods and we trot south on the outskirts of town. Just then a police cruiser slams to a halt beside us. The car door opens, and out jumps my father. Shit. The afternoon wind is really gusting now, ruffling his silver-blond hair. His sharp blue eyes flicker with worry. "Why are you two riding horses in town?"

I fiddle with the reins so I don't have to look at him. "We saw the smoke and came to report it." If my dad knew I helped start the fire, he'd be obligated to arrest me, just as he arrested my mother. I can't do that to him.

Dad pats Sunny and glances at the flaming mountain. "Good, but we've got this now, and Cal Fire is coming to help. Get these horses home, Hannah. If we have to evacuate, head to Bishop. Here." He thrusts his credit card at me. "Use this to book a room, and grab some clothes for me and get your mother's pictures."

My back stiffens. "You mean *my* pictures."

He sighs. "Yes, your pictures."

Did I mention I was in the car when my mom drove drunk? Dad says she was too young for marriage and children, but that's bullshit. She was seventeen and he was eighteen, and I was unplanned. It happens all the time. I think it's simple: she was selfish and couldn't be bothered to raise her little girl. That's why the pictures are mine and not hers. Nothing is hers anymore.

My dad's radio blares at him, and I recognize Deputy Vargas's voice: "We're closing Gap Lake Road to traffic."

"On my way." Dad squints at Violet, taking in the tears and bloodshot eyes, the fact that she's not dressed for riding, and grows curious. "Did either of you see what started the fire? Or anything unusual, like unattended campfires or kids messing around with fireworks, anything?"

I open my mouth. I should probably tell the truth, but I can't. *Monsters don't rat on monsters*, another of our pacts. Confessing should be a group decision.

Violet speaks, making the choice for all of us: "We didn't see anything, Sheriff Warner, just the smoke. That's why we rode here."

My stomach tightens uncomfortably, like I'm on a roller coaster that just picked up speed, zipped around a fast corner, and is heading toward a drop.

Dad glances again at the flames, still miles away on the mountainside. "Ninety percent of wildfires are manmade," he says. "It was probably the damn electric company." His radio babbles at him again. "I gotta go." He dips into his car, answers his radio, and squeals his tires as he pulls away.

"Oh god," says Violet with a loud exhale. "I just lied to your dad. I feel sick."

"You're fine, V. It's the weed and the heat. Give me your reins, and I'll lead you back."

She shakes her head. "No, I have to check on Grammy and the poodles." She starts to dismount.

"I'll go with you. My dad's just being cautious. The fire won't reach Gap Mountain."

She looks at me doubtfully.

—

Twenty minutes later, we're almost to Violet's grandmother's house—trotting on back roads, passing families standing on their front lawns. They're either staring at the mountain or watering their roofs or packing their cars. A new Nixle alert pings on our phones:

Vegetation fire approaching Gap Mountain.

High winds a factor.

Firefighting resources on-site.

Prepare to evacuate.

I whirl Sunny around and peer back the way we came. "Oh god," I whisper.

"What is it?" Violet turns and sees what I see.

The fire, *our* fire, has grown into a ferocious wall of groping orange flames. It's crossed the ridge, and it's toppling trees, snaking toward town like a dragon. Smoke billows in endless jets toward the sky, and ash has begun to fall like snow.

"It's coming!" Violet cries. Pistol feels her tension and breaks into a canter. I kick Sunny and we catch up to her, hurrying to her grandmother's.

When we reach Elizabeth "Lulu" Sandoval's house, a white three-story Victorian modeled after the mansions in San Francisco and surrounded by forestland, we find her packing her SUV. She's wearing scuffed cowgirl boots, a T-shirt with a faded rainbow across the chest, and old jeans, with her gray hair tied in two long braids. You'd never guess she was rich by looking at her, but the Sandoval lumber fortune is immense. "Violet, Hannah," Lulu calls when she sees us. "Are you girls all right?"

Some sense of self-preservation has overcome Violet on the way here. She wipes her eyes dry and pulls herself together. "We're fine, Grammy. What are you doing?"

Lulu's eyes dart east toward the fire. "I'm evacuating. What does it look like I'm doing?" The smoke drifts, blocking the sun, and the sky has gone from blue to muffled gray, like someone threw a blanket over it. Gusts of wind tug at my clothes, and bright embers streak down like comets.

"The fire won't reach us," I promise.

Violet's grandma sighs. "Honey, it already has."

"What?"

"It won't be the flames that set this town on fire. It'll be the embers."

I notice the red ashy particles landing around us. They can't ignite her property because Lulu keeps it as firesafe as possible. Her immaculate lawns are green and moist, gutter guards keep debris away from the roof, and she's tilled a wide firebreak between her home and the woods, but few people in Gap Mountain are so careful. The leaves that fell last autumn still clog gutters on homes throughout town, cords of firewood are stacked on paint-chipped porches, and dry lawns are littered with pine needles. Gap Mountain is primed to ignite.

Violet and I dismount and help Lulu load up her Lincoln Navigator with boxes of photos, her medications, a suitcase, her important papers, a case of bottled water, snacks, and her three standard poodles. The big dogs leap gracefully onto the backseat.

Next, Lulu sends Violet upstairs to pack some clothing. When Violet returns, she tosses two carry-on suitcases into the cargo area.

Lulu glares at her phone, her impish face pinched. "I can't reach your parents."

"They're in the middle of the South Pacific, Grammy," Violet says, reminding me that her parents chartered a private yacht cruise from San Francisco to Australia this summer. "Don't worry, we'll be safe in Bishop," she adds.

"Pet food," I blurt out. "Did you pack pet food?"

Lulu snaps her fingers. "Good call, Hannah. I'll get it." She walks briskly back to her house, her braids bouncing against her back.

"We've got to get our stories straight," I whisper to Violet when Lulu is out of sight. A hot ember lands on my skin, sizzling the fine hair on my arm.

Violet's half-closed eyes begin to clear. "Why?"

"Because we lied to my dad," I say, shouldering the blame with her. "Because Luke's still on probation, and because you guys drank and smoked weed. No one can know we were at the Gap when this started." I motion toward the flames.

Her olive skin pales before my eyes. "But it was an accident."

"Doesn't matter, V. It's still arson, and Luke didn't light that pipe by *accident*." I wipe my face and start pacing. "We could go to jail."

Violet gives me a pained look.

"Our stories have to match—yours, mine, and the others. We need to meet up and figure this out." I pull out my phone and start a group text: **Are you guys at my house?**

Seconds later we hear from Luke: *The fire freaking took off! Yeah, we're at your house.*

Me: *Stay there. We have to meet up. All of us. Delete this thread.*

Mo: *What about evacuating?*

Me: *STOP TEXTING*

When Lulu returns, we persuade her to let Violet help me return the horses and pack my stuff. "I'll drive her to Bishop as soon as we're done," I promise.

"I'll follow you," Lulu offers.

"It's fine," says Violet. "We're heading away from the fire, and the roads are going to be jammed. We'll be right behind you."

Lulu eyeballs her poodles and then climbs into the Navigator with a nod. "I'll call ahead and book rooms at the Holiday Inn. I'll get one for you and your dad too, Hannah."

I thank her and then Violet and I mount the horses and urge them into a lope. As we ride south, the wind increases, driving smoke and ash toward us. We lift our shirts to cover our mouths as the sky darkens.

For the first time since I saw the flames, real fear slithers through my body. The fire is down the ridge now and chomping the trees and brush, gliding toward the north side of town. The homes there are old and sprawled on quarter- and half-acre lots. The north is where most of our elderly citizens live.

Violet and I cross the road and spot a caravan of Cal Fire trucks speeding toward us, lights on, sirens blaring. Sunny loses it and bucks hard, throwing me off his back and into the brush. I land on my back. "Whoa!" I cry, grabbing at his trailing reins, but he whinnies and bolts into the trees.

Pistol wants to follow, but Violet wrestles him into submission. "Ride with me, Han," she says. My back muscles throb as I climb up in front of Violet, and we ride Pistol double to my house.

Our phones ping with another Nixle alert:

> **Uncontrolled vegetation fire has reached Gap Mountain.**
> **Structures under immediate threat.**
> **EVACUATE NOW.**
> **Fire 0% contained.**

Violet and I ride in shocked silence, picking our way down side roads and avoiding downtown. Soon, the first explosions reach our ears: propane tanks. Sirens ring out across the Mono County valley, and smoke spans between the peaks as if a nuclear bomb has gone off.

Guilt settles neatly between my shoulder blades. I shouldn't have grabbed Luke while he was holding a lit pipe. What an idiot move! So what if he mocked me? Why couldn't I brush it off like Drummer or Mo would have? We all make fun of one another. Why am I always the one who gets mad? Is this wildfire my fault or his?

I steer Pistol up my driveway, and there's my house, an old two-bedroom cabin nestled in the pines. Everyone is sitting on the porch when we arrive: Drummer, Luke, and Mo. My palomino, Sunny, found his way home too. Someone, probably Drummer, pulled off his saddle and locked him in the paddock.

All eyes turn to me as Violet and I mount the stairs, and I release a pent-up breath. "Everybody inside. We need to talk."

5

"We are so fucked," Mo says as she passes out water bottles from my fridge.

We grab seats around the scuffed farm table in my kitchen. Dishes are piled in the sink, and Matilda lies at our feet, whining because we're ignoring her.

The refrigerator light didn't turn on when Mo opened the door, and a quick glance around my small house tells me why: the electricity is out. This means my well isn't operational. If the fire comes this way, I don't have water to fight it. My cabin is in the southern quadrant of Gap Mountain, and the fire is heading northwest, but that doesn't mean we're safe. Hot ashes are falling all around us. We need to go, but we also need to talk.

Luke slams his fist on the table. "No, *I'm* fucked. I'm on probation." His alabaster skin looks bloodless against his dark hair and eyes; his face scrunches with anguish. "I'm going back to juvie."

"No one is going anywhere as long as we keep our mouths shut," I say.

"God, I can't believe I lied to the *sheriff*," Violet adds. Shadowy circles have appeared below her eyes.

Luke's gaze meets hers. "You talked to Hannah's dad?"

She nods and I explain: "He saw us by the fire department and asked if we'd seen how the fire started and we said we didn't." The repercussions of this sink in with the others. A lie is a commitment—one we haven't fully discussed, one that will bind us together.

Luke frowns. "That's good, I guess. Look, we saw two empty hunting lodges catch fire on the way here. This shit is out of control. The electricity's shut off and the wells don't work. No one can get water. We don't want our names on this."

"You saw two lodges burning?" I ask.

"Yeah, empty ones." Luke won't look at me, still pissed about our fight.

"Tell her about the bears," says Drummer. He's amped and twitching, unable to sit still. He throws opens a cabinet door, retrieves a box of Frosted Cheerios, and starts shoving fistfuls into his mouth.

Luke casts his eyes toward my kitchen window. "The wildlife is coming down the mountain. We passed right by a bear, and it just ignored us. And we saw some deer, and a coyote too, all running away from the fire."

I lean back and think. Property damage ups our crime to a possible felony, and that's no exaggeration. California doesn't fuck around when it comes to fire. Luke is correct: we are screwed if anyone finds out what we did. Besides ending up in prison, Mo, Violet, and I could have our college acceptances revoked. My heart races faster, and my guts twist unhappily. We need to get ahead of this.

I glance at Violet and silently thank God she lied to my dad. "Listen, we aren't suspects, not yet and maybe never. We just need to get straight what we're going to say if anyone asks where we were, which they probably won't."

"You're right," Mo says and lets out a huge breath. Her inhaler is in her hand and her eyes are red from smoke and tears. She doesn't look good. "There's no reason to suspect us."

I've given my friends more hope than I meant to and dial it back. "There will be an investigation, Mo. Cal Fire will find the point of origin, which is near the Gap, so we just need to make sure no one knows we were there. Did any of you talk about our plans for today?"

"I don't know," Mo says. "Maybe? I can't think." Suddenly her phone vibrates with an incoming text. "Shit," she cries, reading it. "My mom says the fire's near Stony Ridge."

Luke bounds from his seat. "You're kidding!"

Mo trembles. "No—she says she can see flames. Oh my god."

Luke and Mo live in Stony Ridge, the neighborhood of older homes and mostly elderly citizens that I'm worried about.

Luke, who hates phones, checks his and curses. "I have three missed calls from Aiden! My fucking mother better be home. She better get my brother out of there." We all know Luke's mom is probably gambling and getting high at the casinos in Nevada, not minding eight-year-old Aiden.

"We need to get out of here too. We'll have to talk about our stories later," Drummer says, pacing.

Luke turns up his phone's volume, and it pings with a new message. "Shit, Aiden's texting. He says he's home alone and can't find our cat." His voice is strangled. "I gotta go."

"You can take my four-wheeler." I grab the keys off the hook and toss them to him.

"Can I go with you?" Mo asks Luke. "My parents are evacuating. I need to help them." She wheezes and sucks on her inhaler, gasping. "My room. What about all my stuff?"

Violet starts to cry, and we run outside together, with Matilda trotting at our heels. Luke jumps onto the ATV and starts it. Mo climbs on behind him.

Drummer grabs Mo's arm, yelling over the wind and the distant bang of exploding propane tanks, "You shouldn't be out in this smoke." Ashes flock the trees, the summer sky is nickel gray, and the winds have knocked over my bear-proof trash can.

Mo shakes her head at Drummer, tucks her inhaler in her bag, and circles her arms around Luke's waist. "I have to go home."

Luke squeezes the throttle and guns the four-wheeler onto my gravel driveway, the back end fishtailing, rocks flying. We watch as he and Mo vanish down the road, and then I turn to my friends: "Drummer, hitch the horse trailer to my dad's truck. Violet, get Matilda's leash. I'll be right back." I race up-stairs to throw some clothes in a backpack.

I don't know where my dad keeps important papers, so I just snatch some clothes for him too and grab our photo album. It depicts the slow death of a family, ending with pictures of an abandoned dad and daughter, but I can't leave it behind. I grab my phone charger and, on a whim, my yearbook.

"Hurry, Han, let's go," says Violet as I come downstairs. She's leading Matilda on a leash.

"I'm ready."

I bump into Drummer on the porch, and his defeated expression stops me cold. "Your trailer has two flat tires," he says "The horses have to stay behind."

Tears fill my eyes. "What if the fire comes this way?"

He holds up a can of spray paint from my garage. I groan but I know what I have to do to protect my horses. I have three in total: Stella, Pistol, and Sunny, the last one compliments of my neighbor's stallion that broke free and got Stella pregnant four years ago.

While Drummer holds them steady, I spray my phone number on the horses' sides. Once they're marked, Drummer and I turn them loose and watch them gallop into the forest. "This is my fault," I whisper.

Drummer pulls me into his arms and dries my tears with his shirt. "It was all of us." His heart knocks against my chest.

I wipe my nose. "No one can ever find out."

"I know. They won't. Where are your keys?"

I find them in my pocket, and then Violet, Drummer,

Matilda, and I load into my Wrangler and I steer the car down the driveway to the county road below.

We cough hard on the smoke, and the sky is almost black. I can't believe that tiny red pipe embers started all of *this*.

At the end of my road is Route 395, and when we reach it, I slam on the brakes. The two-lane highway is jammed with cars heading south. They inch past, the drivers like zombies, eyes round and mouths gaping.

Crammed into the cars and trucks are kids, dogs, cats in pet carriers, and birds in cages. People are towing horse, livestock, and RV trailers. We see truck beds loaded with suitcases, boxes, cases of water, and more pets. One pickup holds three young pigs that are covered in ashes. Another truck bed holds an entire family, huddled and coughing. The cars aren't letting us in, so I push the nose of the Jeep between two sedans and force my way into the southbound procession. A new Nixle alert lights up our phones:

**Structure fires in Gap Mountain between Summit Ave.
    and Windy Peak.
Streets closed.
Firefighters on-site.
Leave now!**

"That's the Stony Ridge neighborhood," Drummer says. His pupils have contracted to tiny points, and his blue eyes are wide and glossed. "Luke and Mo could get trapped."

"Maybe we can catch up to them." I throw my arm out the window as a warning to other cars and then whip the Jeep into the opposite lane, which is empty, since no one else is heading *toward* the blaze. The driver behind us lays on her horn.

"Oh my god," Violet cries in the backseat.

I press hard on the gas pedal, and we speed in the direction Luke and Mo went in. I veer onto a backstreet called Sanders, the same road Luke took, and drive straight into a wall of smoke. My headlights beam on, but I can barely see the road. "Shut the windows!" Drummer shouts. Then he cranks up my air conditioning, which helps clear the air in the Jeep.

"I don't like this!" Violet says, her hands pressed against the ceiling.

My mind flashes to all the old people living in Stony Ridge. How are they going to get out? I often hear the medical calls on my dad's radio. Some of those folks have walkers, and there's at least one resident who uses an oxygen tank. I know a few have dementia, and many don't hear well, and some don't have cell phones. Are they getting these Nixle alerts? Did my dad and Cal Fire get them out? What about kids like Luke's brother, who is home alone? What if one of them dies? That's felony murder. Shit! Tears sting my eyes. I don't want anyone to get hurt.

As we barrel into the smoke, I glance at Violet in the rearview mirror. Her glossy hair is tousled, her eyes shimmer like black glass, and she's grimacing so hard she looks like a corpse. Beside me, Drummer wipes his palms on his jeans. His blond brows are drawn tight, hooding his eyes.

I think I'm the first to realize that things between us will never be the same. This secret, this *crime*, will bind us in a knot so tight we'll never escape it—not at our weddings, not at our kids' Little League games, not in our nursing homes. Whether we get caught or not, it will follow us to our deaths. We are five separate souls on one fast-spinning plate, and if anyone loses their balance, all of us will fall.

I vow right then not to let that happen. I will keep this plate spinning. I will keep us out of prison. I will protect the monsters.

6

My Jeep bounces down the dirt road with the windshield wipers on, clearing the ash. We peer out the windows, looking for Luke and Mo on the four-wheeler, and the cabin is silent. I'm about to turn around and head back when the furious winds suddenly shift. The smoke rises and the view clears.

I accelerate, driving as fast as I can as the Jeep thumps over potholes and culverts. Everyone braces against the ceiling and doors, but no one asks me to slow down. We have to catch up to Luke and Mo and get them out of Gap Mountain. Embers drop and brown haze shrouds the sky. If this isn't hell, it's a damn good imitation.

"Watch out!" Drummer screams.

A bear lumbers onto the road, shuffling and confused. I

slam on my breaks, turn hard, and the Jeep slides for a second on two wheels. I glimpse Drummer, his chin tucked, his mouth gaping. Then the Jeep rights itself and halts with a jolt that throws us all forward, then back.

The bear stands just a few inches from my grille, a small one, maybe a yearling. She rears and chuffs at the Jeep. I crack open my door to shoo her away just as she turns and runs back into the woods. I return to my seat, clutching my chest. Then I think to ask, "Has everyone got their seat belt on?" I hear belts clicking and Violet muttering, "Oh my god, oh my god."

I shift into first and keep driving. "Watch the sides of the roads in case Luke crashed the four-wheeler. I'll watch the front."

My hands shake like mad as I shift into second gear. We cross an area the wildfire has passed through already and go silent. The landscape is black and charred. Small, industrious flames linger, eating up anything flammable. The road is covered with smoking branches and debris. I engage my four-wheel drive and steer the Wrangler around obstacles, sometimes driving off the road.

"Is that a deer?" Violet asks.

I hit the brake and we all stare at where she's pointing. The fire swept through so fast that it turned the deer and her fawn to ash right where they were standing. They remind me of the Bible story about the woman who looks back and is turned into a pillar of salt, except these two look more like pillars of pepper.

"If animals can't make it out, how can the people?" Violet asks, her voice tremulous.

Drummer reaches back to touch her, and I notice his eyes glimmering with tears. The last time I saw Drummer cry was when his dog got cancer. He refused to admit the dog was sick—because that's Drummer, ignoring the ugly shit—until the day he found it dead on his laundry room floor. He called me to come take care of it, and when I got there, Drummer wailed like he was being murdered. I had no idea how to help him, so I offered to dig a grave and bury the dog, but that made him cry harder. Now, watching him touch Violet, I realize what I should have done: I should have held him.

I try to calm everyone down. "The rescue workers will get the people out. Don't worry."

Ahead is downtown Gap Mountain, and we still haven't seen any sign of Mo and Luke. "Shit!" I cry. "There's my dad!" I slam the brakes again, but I can't hide my Firecracker-red Jeep Wrangler. Besides, it's the only car on the road that's not fire or police. Everyone else is gone or heading in the opposite direction.

My dad, two blocks away, sprints toward us, wearing an N95 face mask.

"Look, the post office is on fire!" Luke shouts.

I peek over the wheel. Behind my dad, orange flames lap at the office's wood siding like greedy tongues. A fire truck is on-site, and firefighters are trying to save it and the buildings around it. Embers must have started this fire, because the real blaze is still in the trees. The flaming dragon is now forty feet tall, miles wide, and, we later learn, traveling at three football fields a second with an ember cast of one mile.

When my dad reaches my window, I roll it down, and

smoke fills the cabin, making us cough. From her place on the floor of the Jeep, Matilda barks.

"Why aren't you heading to Bishop?" he asks fiercely.

Tears fill my eyes. "Luke and Mo took the ATV to try to get to their houses. We can't find them."

"Which road are they on?"

"Sanders."

My dad nods and speaks to his deputies through his walkie-talkie. "We'll find them," he says to me. "You guys turn around and get outta here. Now!"

"Dad, wait." His veins are bulging and his hands shake with adrenaline. "Is everyone . . . okay?" He knows what I mean—are the citizens of Gap Mountain okay? Has anybody died?

My dad grips the Jeep's windowsill. "Too soon to tell."

I believe he knows more than he's saying, and I'm terrified we've killed somebody. "Dad?"

He slaps the car door. "Turn around. Get to Bishop. Text me when you're safe." And then he's gone, running toward the blaze.

God, *he's* not safe. I grip the wheel. I can't breathe, and suddenly I feel utterly lost.

"Fuck, move over, Han." Drummer drags me out of the seat and switches with me as I dissolve into panic. "Take deep breaths." He slams the Wrangler into gear and whirls around, squealing the tires as he drives back toward Route 395.

The blaze reaches Pine Street just as the first airplane full of pink fire retardant roars overhead. Bulldozers churn past my Jeep, heading toward the forest to knock down trees and create firebreaks. I send a mental cheer to Cal Fire, but this isn't good news. It means our fire is massive and raging out of control. It means the cost of fighting it is skyrocketing before my eyes.

Drummer takes a side road to the highway while I text Mo repeatedly, getting no answer.

Violet checks her social accounts on her phone and starts yelling out what she sees. "The laundromat is gone," she cries. "Stony Ridge is"—she chokes on her words—"it's on fire, all of it!" Then her voice pitches higher. "Gap Mountain High School is burning."

"What?" Drummer yells.

"The high school is on fire!"

"This isn't fucking happening," I whisper. "This is going to kill Mo." We know how much she loves that school. She was on the leadership committee, student council, and dance team and was president of the culinary club.

Violet stares at her phone, her eyelids splayed wide, her mouth slack.

"Hey, we don't know what's true yet," I point out. "Go to a real news site."

"There's the highway!" Drummer shouts. He jerks the Wrangler onto another shortcut and then rockets down an embankment and onto the shoulder of Route 395, almost slamming into a Nissan Pathfinder. The driver honks his horn and won't let us in. The car behind him slows for us as Drummer pulls into traffic.

Both lanes are moving in the same direction now. No one cares that the left side is northbound and the right side is southbound—everyone is heading south anyway. Rescue vehicles will have to use the shoulder. "It's the fucking apocalypse," says Drummer.

Nixle alerts keep coming, and I read them out loud from the passenger seat. The last one makes the world slide out from under me:

> **Gap Mountain and surrounding areas—Evacuate now.**
> **Fire 0% contained.**
> **Numerous structure fires in Stony Ridge neighborhood.**
> **Possible fatalities.**

My breath stalls and Violet collapses into tears. The silence in the Jeep is like the eye of a storm. Drummer glances at me, and our past ricochets between us: running through sprinklers as kids, camping in the backyard, jumping on my ratty old trampoline, riding horses, swimming in the Gap—the memories swirl up and drift out the window. None of it matters anymore; our childhood just got squashed like Godzilla smashing Bambi. *Possible fatalities.* Have we killed people?

"We're going to hell," Violet says, her teeth chattering.

Suddenly, Drummer flips his head around, and his blue eyes round in terror. "Get out of the car! Get out!" he screams.

We all look back. The wind has shifted again, and the wall of flames has reached the road. The sky is dark, almost black, as the fire bears down on us, chomping cars and exploding them just a mile or so back. Since traffic has all but stalled and the fire is moving faster than the cars on the highway, people flee their vehicles and run. They pass my Jeep, carrying children, animals, and boxes. One lady has a lamb in her arms.

For one brief second, we're frozen, and then we fling our doors open. Matilda bays like a wolf and follows as we leap out, all but Drummer. He slams his door shut and rebuckles his seat belt. "I'm going off-road," he says. "If I can outrun the fire in the woods, I'll meet you all up ahead."

"No!" I cry. "You won't make it; you'll get trapped in there! You'll die!"

"We need a vehicle, Han. Run, I'll try to meet you up ahead."

"Don't go!" I scream.

He shakes his head, guns the engine, blasts out of the southbound lane, and disappears into the forest. The fire is traveling even faster between the trees than it is on the highway! The flames pass from limb to limb, and the embers shoot out and ignite spot fires that race ahead of their ravenous mother.

My heart slams. The smoke and ash sting my eyes. Flaming firebrands fall from the sky and explode on the asphalt. The fire marches toward us like a terminator, flinging cars out of its path as if they're toys. It wants *us*. It wants its creators.

"Come on!" Violet shouts. She snatches my sleeve, and we sprint down the highway, dodging cars and slower people. Matilda gallops beside me, already panting in the heat.

Toxic ash blankets our hair and skin, and we lift our shirts to cover our mouths. Violet and I are still wearing our bikinis under our clothes, but we are not the same girls who swam in the Gap hours ago. We are killers. *Possible fatalities.* God, it can't be true.

It's a hundred degrees today, but on this black pavement with the blaze chasing us, it feels much hotter. My arthritic dog starts limping and whining softly. Her red hair is brilliant against the blackened sky, recalling the deep russet of her puppyhood. I pull on her collar. "Come on, girl!" Matilda wags her tail, a weak thump, and tries to walk faster. Her brown eyes are apologetic, as if she's thinking: *I'm sorry I got old.*

I dare a glance back and see the wildfire gaining. A man dives into a ditch as the voracious flames pass over him. "Holy shit!" I cry. Fear floods my brain. I glance at Matilda; she's flagging.

"We can't outrun it!" Violet screams.

"Yes we can!" I scoop Matilda into my arms, and somehow we run faster. I struggle beneath the weight of the dog, my terror cycling faster than my blood. The fire bears down on us, and a sob fills my throat. Is this how we're going to die?

7

I quickly fall behind Violet, because Matilda weighs eighty-five pounds and I'm trying to run with her in my arms while wearing flip-flops. Violet glares at me. "Put the dog down, Hannah!"

"What? No!"

She whirls and grabs my arm, her fist a vice, her eyes like black stars. "You're going to die if you don't."

I pull back. "She's my *dog*."

"She's too heavy. You have to leave her."

"But I can't, V. I can't leave Matilda alone!" I shake my head.

"Hannah!" she screams, tugging on me. "Put the damn dog down and come with me. *I* need you!" The flames reflect in her dark eyes.

I heave a breath. "I can't."

Violet gapes at me, stunned, maybe hurt, and then drops my arm and runs, leaving me behind.

I set Matilda down, grab her collar, and try to encourage her. "Come, Mattie! Heel!" The approaching flames slow to lay waste to a minivan but then erupt again when they meet gasoline and the van explodes. I fall on top of Matilda, clutching my ears. She cries out when I land on her hips. "I'm sorry!" I pull her back onto her feet.

Next to us, a horse trailer has stalled. The animals neigh and kick inside as the owner races to the back. "Move your dog," he calls. "I'm gonna let 'em out."

I drag Matilda out of the way, my ears buzzing, the heat crinkling my skin. The man opens the trailer door, and four horses snap their safety ties and leap out. They gallop down the highway, skidding and whinnying and leaping over scattered belongings. One knocks a woman over, and people start screaming, warning others to watch out. Tears stripe the owner's ash-covered face, and then he bolts, chasing them.

Matilda licks my hand. "Let's go," I say, grabbing her leash and pulling. The wind gusts and embers strike us. The ashes are laden with chemicals, burned up cars and homes, photographs, plastic toys, and the bodies of animals and people. We're breathing it in, absorbing it into our bodies, and a coughing fit envelops me.

I pull hard on Matilda's leash, forcing her to run. She rallies but she's overheated, and her burst of speed doesn't last long. We trot down the yellow centerline of the highway, not moving fast enough. I'm Dorothy, she's Toto, and we just want to go home. Deep cries warble in her throat, and I imagine the arthritis in her hips is killing her on this hard pavement.

As the fire gains on us, I try to pick her up again, but she struggles and I can't hold a thrashing dog. Humans race past us, and most don't give us a glance. It's a stampede.

We jog about a half mile before Matilda halts and plops down. She turns her huge brown eyes to mine and wags her tail as if she's saying goodbye. "No," I whisper, a lump balling in my throat. "Come on. You can do it."

I try to pull her up, but she won't have it. She's done. The fire is coming, and when it arrives, sheer terror will force me to abandon my dog. Sobs shake my body. I bury my nose in her fur, inhaling the familiar dog scent beneath the smoke. "I love you, Matilda." She wags her tail and sinks her head into the crook of my neck.

The fire roars closer, heating my flesh. My tears dry before they fall.

Then the rumble of an aircraft's motor overcomes the rushing blood between my ears. I glance up and spot a huge fat-bellied firefighting aircraft. I wipe my tears as it zooms lower. Dozens of people stop and look up.

The plane flies to the edge of the inferno and dumps several tons of fire retardant on it. The bubble-gum-pink chemicals douse the nearest flames and coat the cars and road near it. Around me, people's voices rise in a cheer.

The fire roars and bites at the retardant but cannot cross over it. I sputter, gasping in amazement. The blaze's southern march is stymied, and my heart soars. The firefighters bought us time. They saved my dog.

I urge Matilda into a walk, and she lurches to her feet. After several yards, I spot a child's red wagon in the back of someone's abandoned pickup truck. I hoist it out, whisper a silent thank-you to its owner, and help Matilda into the wagon. Taking the handle, I pull her along and join the rest of the zombie herd on the long trek toward Bishop. The fire flickers behind us, trapped and angry, as its western edge enters the open woods and roars toward Yosemite National Park.

The folks whose vehicles didn't burn return to their cars, and the traffic starts moving again. We must look like refugees, half of us on wheels, the other half marching along the shoulder, carrying what we can: kids, food, photos, and pets. Drivers with available space stop and offer rides to families with young children.

A little blue pickup truck full of fishing and camping gear rolls up next to me. The driver leans out his window. "Need a lift?"

I glance over to see a young guy with an unshaven jaw and a baseball hat. He's in his mid-twenties and not anyone I recognize from Gap Mountain. He's soaked with sweat from the heat, and a thin layer of ash has collected on the outside of his vehicle. His eyes shift toward my dog. "He doesn't look comfortable."

"She," I say automatically. Matilda's paws are splayed wide, and her balance seems precarious in the toy wagon. I imagine dragging her all the way to Bishop and feel suddenly exhausted.

My feet hurt, my throat is parched, and my adrenaline is leaking out of my toes. I peer into the stranger's eyes. He looks safe enough. "Do you live in Gap Mountain?" I ask. "Are you evacuating?"

"No, I live in Bishop. I was just coming home from a fishing trip when this fire started. Here, I can slide this cooler onto the floor and make room for you."

"Okay, thanks."

I help Matilda climb into the small cab. She flops onto the passenger seat with a loud sigh and won't budge, so I end up sitting in the middle. The man tosses the red wagon into the truck bed and then slides into his seat and starts driving. The cab is cramped, and his leg is so close to mine, we're almost touching. His eyes flit toward my bikini, which is visible through my sheer, sweat-soaked tank top, and then back to the road. I cross my arms, cheeks flaming.

"I'm Justin," he says, a smile curving his lips.

"I'm Hannah. Thanks for picking us up." I glance at his glove box, wondering if he has a gun. A hysterical giggle rises in my chest. I can see the headline now: GIRL MURDERED WHILE FLEEING WILDFIRE.

"Good to meet you, Hannah. You all right? Here, have some water." He reaches across me, his bare arm rubbing mine, and collects a canteen off the floor. "I filled it earlier but haven't drunk off it yet. I promise," he says.

"Thanks." I don't know if I believe him, but I'm so thirsty I don't care. I guzzle the fluid, then pour some into my palm for Matilda. Water spills onto the seat. My eyes flip to Justin's. "Sorry."

He grins. "It's just water. Nice-looking hound you got."

I pat Matilda's soft head. "She's the best but getting old."

He shakes his head at the unfairness of that, and suddenly I'm fighting back tears. I wipe my eyes and try to breathe normally.

"You can cry," Justin says, adding a wink. "I won't tell."

His dashboard blurs as the tears fall. The time is now 7:18 p.m., and it's summer, so still light out. The sky hangs over us, a ceiling of swirling ash. My throat burns, and I can't stop coughing once I start. I feel sick. Then my phone pings with a new Nixle alert that makes my stomach churn:

Stony Ridge area closed to traffic.

Fire and medical personnel on site.

Uncontained structure fires pose immediate threat.

Do not return home.

God, I hope Luke and Mo are safe. I'm grateful when Justin turns the radio up, a country station, and we ride the rest of the way to Bishop without speaking. "Where can I drop you?" he asks as we pull onto North Main Street.

"The Holiday Inn."

He finds the hotel and parks at the curb out front. "Here."

He scribbles a phone number on an old receipt and hands it to me. "Call me if you need another ride, or anything at all."

His gaze lingers, and my stomach flips because he's at least twenty-five years old. His body is much thicker than Drummer's, filled out and mature, and I feel a blush storm my cheeks as I grab his number. "Okay."

He helps me lift the red wagon out of the truck bed, and when his hand grazes mine, I pull away. "Thanks for the ride." I wave goodbye, heave Matilda back into the wagon, and hurry toward the hotel. Justin idles, watching me walk away.

The first thing I notice is that wildfire evacuees are all over Bishop, driving their ash-covered cars or walking with whatever possessions they didn't drop on the way here. Across the street is a Travelodge, and there's a line of people waiting for rooms. We're all dirty and smell like smoke. In contrast, the citizens of Bishop are clean and hydrated and scurrying like ants to help us.

A woman approaches me out of nowhere with water bottles and a bowl for Matilda. "Hi, honey, I'm Giselle, from Christ Church," she says. I stop as she fusses over Matilda and me, giving us water and wiping the mucous from Matilda's eyes. Then she walks alongside us, just as Jesus would, I guess. "Do you have a place to stay?" she asks. "Our church has beds and food."

I nod toward the Holiday Inn. "Yes, here." My voice comes out in a rasp. "My friend's grandma booked me a room earlier today."

"Oh, that's good. Most of the hotels are full." She walks with me toward the lobby. On the way, I glimpse my dusty Jeep

Wrangler in the parking lot and relief washes over me. Drummer made it. He outdrove the fire.

Giselle stays with me until I'm issued a keycard and I've received permission from the manager to keep Matilda in my room. "Thanks," I say to the woman.

"You're welcome," she says, adding a sympathetic smile and a pat on my shoulder. "God didn't start this fire, honey, but he'll see you through it."

I gape at her because, yeah, I know God didn't start it.

Satisfied, she leaves me as the elevator door opens and then closes around me. I bend over and release a huge agonized sigh into my hands. Matilda snuffles my face, trying to lick it.

When I reach the third floor, I locate my room, which is next to Lulu's. I learned downstairs that she booked four in total, one for herself, one for her granddaughter, and two for my dad and me. I feel bad we've taken up so many spots when people are lined up for rooms outside, but then I realize Drummer needs a room too. I'll give him mine and stay with my dad.

I knock on Lulu's door, and she lets Matilda and me inside. Violet and Drummer are sitting on the double beds, staring at the news on television. The poodles rush over to sniff Matilda, and my bloodhound gives me a worried glance.

"Hannah!" Violet leaps off the bed, hugs me, and then drops to the floor to embrace my dog. "Matilda, I'm sorry, I'm so sorry," she says, sobbing into her red fur. When Violet turns her face up to me, I notice her makeup is off, her hair is wet, and she smells like cheap shampoo. She's changed into a horse-print T-shirt and looks about twelve years old. "I—I don't know why I yelled at you like that," she says to me. "I'm sorry, Han. Forgive me, okay, please. I was scared."

Her apology works on my fury like that pink fire retardant worked on the fire, snuffing it out. "None of us are having a very good day," I offer, and we share a weak smile.

She explains that a family picked her up right away and drove her to Bishop, which is why she's here and showered already.

Drummer leaps off the bed and holds me tight. "We probably shouldn't have split up. I was so fucking worried when I couldn't find you on the road, Han." His voice is deep and ragged in my ear. "I can't lose you."

I hug him back, smelling the hotel soap on his warm skin, feeling his lean muscles contract and his heart thrum in rhythm with mine. He says stuff like this all the time, though—when I talk about college, when I notice another boy, or when I'm mad at him: *Hannah, I can't lose you; I can't live without you.* How can he need me so badly and not want me too?

I shrug, pretending that his words don't drive me crazy. "Hey, you saved my car." And he has no idea how glad I am about that, because on the ride here I decided to return to Gap Lake as soon as possible. I need to check the site for anything we might have missed: towels, beer bottles, backpacks, Luke's missing pipe. If fire investigators find them first, we are truly fucked.

Drummer releases me and I text my dad: *I'm in Bishop at the Holiday Inn. We have a room for you.*

Good! Glad you're safe. I'm staying here to help. Give my room to someone else.

Of course he's staying; he's the sheriff. *Okay. Love you.*

Love you too.

"I could use a shower," I say, noticing that everyone else is clean. "Has anyone heard from Luke or Mo?"

"Mo called," Drummer answers. "She found her parents, and they met up with Luke and his little brother and caravanned up here. They're all fine, but their houses are gone."

Gone. I absorb that quietly. "What about Luke's mom?"

He scoffs. "She was at the casino, missed the whole thing."

"Their houses really burned down?" I had hoped Nixle was exaggerating.

"Yeah. Luke got there on the four-wheeler in time to watch his collapse."

"Oh, wow, that sucks," I murmur, a massive understatement.

After explaining how I got to Bishop—*You hitched?* Drummer asked. *Not exactly,* I answered—I take a scalding-hot shower in my room and watch the ash and dirt turn to sludge in the bottom of the tub. I scrub my skin, shampoo my hair, and let the water flow over my raw flesh, but I don't feel clean. I can't wash away the fear and guilt multiplying inside me.

8

July 9

Gap Fire: 0% contained

Fatalities: 3

4:00 p.m.

We spend the next two days at the Holiday Inn, watching news stations, receiving Nixle alerts, reading social media posts, and viewing the damage to Gap Mountain on TV. Thirty-two homes, the post office, the high school, and the laundromat are destroyed, burned to their foundations. Three citizens are confirmed dead, and seventeen are missing. Thousands of acres are scorched, and evacuation advisories are in effect for towns west of us. Firefighters from across California have arrived to help fight the blaze, now called the Gap Fire, as it lays siege to Yosemite National Park.

Archeological and forensic students from Fresno State arrive to help detectives sift through the Stony Ridge rubble for human remains. Christ Church here in Bishop has turned into a temporary homeless shelter for those who didn't get hotel rooms, and the Red Cross is setting up a disaster-claim area for wildfire victims. *Victims.* The word flashes in my brain like a neon sign. These people are *our* victims.

The question on the public's mind has already leaped to *Who started this?* A team of fire investigators arrives in Gap Mountain to answer that question, and I feel trapped in the hotel, helpless. I haven't been able to return to the lake due to roadblocks sealing off the area. I can't sleep, can't eat, and my nerves hum, pulled as tight as bowstrings. I need to go back to make sure we covered our tracks.

My dad is okay but busy. He sleeps in his office, and he's transformed the K–8 school's parking lot into a command center for all the organizations fighting the Gap Fire. They're working in conjunction with the electric company, the propane companies, the Army Corps of Engineers, city council, Cal Fire, the Red Cross, the National Guard, and county planners to ensure that the power and gas lines are safe, the roads are cleared, and the toxic dust is cleaned from public areas so residents can return to Gap Mountain. My dad texted a photo of the tents they set up at the school. With its background of charred trees and blackened earth, it looks like a war encampment.

When we're not watching the news, Luke and I call animal shelters and animal rescue agencies to ask if my horses and his cat have been found. So far, they have not.

The five of us haven't been able to speak alone until today, because Luke's little brother, Aiden, has been glued to his side. But now Aiden is napping and the monsters are in my hotel room, finally able to speak freely. Violet, Mo, and I claim the bed nearest the door, Luke stands by the window, and Drummer sprawls on the other bed with my dog's head on his lap.

"I burned down my own fucking house," Luke says, smoking a cigarette in our nonsmoking hotel room.

"I lost everything," Mo whispers.

I wrap my arm around her, and Mo sinks into me. She's been picking at her skin, and small sores have erupted on her forearms. When she talks about the things she lost—hand-sewn dresses, photos, yearbooks, awards, custom dance outfits, her childhood blanket, her baby pictures, her stuffed animals, her laptop—each item is like a punch to the gut for all of us, especially Luke. "I'm sorry," he says over and over, even though his house burned down too.

"I have to get home," Mo says. "I have to see it. I can't believe my house won't be there."

Luke also wants to go back, but my dad assures me there are barricades around the Stony Ridge neighborhood. "It's toxic," he explains. "There are power lines down and gas leaks and chemicals, and we're still searching for bodies. Stay away."

Luke crushes his cigarette out on the bottom of his shoe. "My mom will beat the living shit out of me if she finds out I did this."

Mo and I gape at each other, because Luke rarely shares details like that about his mother. It's bad at his house, we know, but we're not sure how bad. "We won't let her find out," I promise.

His eyes snap to mine, cold and sad and burning with regret.

Does he blame me for grabbing his arm, or does he blame himself for lighting the pipe? I don't know, and I'm not sure I want to know.

I release a deep breath and speak: "Time for damage control." My friends swivel to face me. Since I grew up with the law, I know the most about breaking it, and the monsters have always come to me when they think they're in trouble. "Who knows we were swimming at the Gap on July seventh?" I start. "Did any of you mention it?"

We're quiet a minute, and then Mo clears her throat. "I might have told my dad." She tugs at her long red hair. "I was packing the snacks and the muffins, and he asked where I was going. Wait." She chews her lip. "I told him we were going swimming, but maybe I didn't mention the Gap. Oh, I'm not sure."

"Okay, and maybe he won't remember the conversation anyway. Did anyone else tell?" My friends shake their heads. "Mo, if it comes up, tell your dad our plans changed. Say we canceled because it was too windy and decided to meet up at my house instead. We can all agree to that, right?"

The monsters nod and I stand, start pacing. "So this could be our alibi: Violet and I were riding horses and on our way back to meet up with all of you, we saw the smoke and galloped into town to tell the fire department. You three were waiting for us at my house. It's simple and no one can prove it's not true."

Luke grunts. "I stopped at Sam's Market first. Should I mention that?" He doesn't look up as he sketches on the hotel writing pad in violent, sweeping strokes.

"What did you buy?" Mo prods.

"Nothing, just gum." Then he slams his fist on the desk. "And I swiped a book of free matches."

"Shit," says Drummer. He peers at me. "Do they have cameras in Sam's?"

"They do, but I'm not sure they actually use them."

Drummer tucks his arms behind his head and his shirt rides up, revealing his flat, tanned stomach. "Why don't we say we were at the movies," he mutters.

"That can be checked," Mo argues.

"Whatever." He stares out the window, his jaw muscles ticking. Drummer has no stamina for discomfort, no patience for sitting around. He needs to be outside, hunting or working, and he needs physical touch—wrestling, sports, or sex. He wilts quickly without attention, and a jolt of desire rockets through me as I imagine giving it to him.

"The story we have is fine," says Mo.

Drummer re-bunches the pillows behind his back, roughing them up and disturbing Matilda, who leaps off the bed. He scowls. "Can we just wait and see if anything comes of this? Who the fuck keeps track of their whereabouts anyway?"

Mo shakes her head but gives up. If we push Drummer right now, he'll just leave. The mood shifts as we fall back into our separate agonies.

I return to practicalities. "Mo, did you clean up all the beer bottles and anything else we left behind like I asked?"

Her chapped lips fall open. "Yeah, yes. I grabbed everything I saw."

My headache turns into a dull, tight pain that collects at the front of my skull. "Everything you *saw*? So you might have left stuff behind?"

Her brows pinch and her eyes glisten. "I—I didn't know I was cleaning up a *crime scene*." Her words blast across the room, impaling each of us.

I drop my face into my palms.

Violet interjects, her lower lip quivering with stress. "What about photos and videos? None of you posted anything, did you?"

"Crap!" Mo starts madly pushing icons on her phone screen. "When we were at the Gap, I put up a selfie of me and Drummer, but it wouldn't post. When I got in range of a signal, it might have, though."

"You haven't looked?" Violet shrieks.

Mo shakes her head. "I've been following the news about the fire."

"Check!" I urge her.

"I am." She swipes and then her face freezes. "Here it is. It posted."

"Damn it, Mo!" I cry. "Which part of *we were never here* did you misunderstand?"

We rush to her side and peer at the picture on her phone. There's Mo, her eyes half closed, a beer bottle to her lips and the Gap glittering behind her. Drummer is visible in the background, jumping off a rocky plateau into the lake. His features are blurred, but the dragon tattoo he got on his eighteenth birthday is clear.

The caption Mo wrote for the picture says SUMMER DAYZ! The photo has eighty-two likes, and it posted to her account soon after the fire started on July seventh.

My scalp tightens. "Delete it."

Her fingers fly. "I am. It's done." She drops the phone in her lap and throws up her hands.

"But look how many people saw it," Violet says, groaning.

"Nice, Mo," I grumble. "Underage drinking, swimming at the Gap. They'll never catch us now."

Luke's dark eyes flash. "Don't be such a dick, Hannah. She deleted it."

I ignore him, glance at Mo. "I'm sorry. I'm—I'm scared." My mind spins into overdrive. It's tough enough covering up a crime you committed *on purpose*, but this one has too many unknown factors. "Look, we all need to check our phones and delete the photos and videos we took that day, all the texts too, and delete that stuff from the cloud. We don't want any proof of where we were if this blows up and our phones are confiscated. Be careful what you say in texts from now on. If we have to talk about this, we have to call."

"I don't feel good," Violet says. "I can't do this."

Luke releases a growl, stands up, and kicks the desk chair. It falls backward, smacking the carpet. *Here it comes*, I think, and sure enough, he charges me. "Why did you have to grab my arm, Hannah? I was being careful."

His face looms, inches from mine, but he's five feet nine inches, so when I stand up, I'm taller. I stare down at him. "Why did you have to smoke in the woods?"

He laughs through his teeth. "I do it all the fucking time."

Drummer slides to his feet and stands between us. "Sit down, man."

"Of course you take *her* side," Luke snarls. He points a shaky finger at me. "She did this! She killed those people."

Mo sucks in her breath, and I recoil as if I've been struck. "I was trying to *stop* you," I say, my voice low, since Violet's grandma is in the next room.

"I'm on probation!" he snaps.

"I'm the sheriff's *daughter!*"

Drummer shoves Luke with both hands, shocking all of us. He's not one to defend himself, let alone anyone else. "Leave Hannah alone."

Luke shoves him back, and Drummer makes a fist. Mo and Violet leap to their feet.

"Stop it!" Mo cries, her red eyebrows pulled in tight. "We can't start fighting with each other. We need to calm down and think."

Luke and Drummer drop their eyes to the floor.

"We're in this together," she adds.

I nod. "If we keep our mouths shut, this shouldn't come back on us. It's going to be okay."

Violet clears her throat. "But people have died. Maybe we *should* tell?"

Mo glances at me with questions in her eyes. Drummer and Luke stiffen and shake their heads, suddenly on the same side. "No way," says Luke.

"Fuck no," Drummer adds.

"Look, guys," I say, placing both hands softly on the bed-spread, smoothing the wrinkles. "Violet and I rode to town as fast as we could. That was the right thing to do. But telling them we *started* the fire won't help the firefighters put it out. There is absolutely nothing to gain by telling, and it will ruin our lives." I swallow and my mouth feels dry, my tongue thick. "If I thought it would help in some way, yeah, I'd say let's tell them, but it won't. Why should we risk going to prison and losing our chance at college? How would that benefit anyone?"

"But it was an accident," Violet says.

I peer at her, willing her to understand. "Starting a wildfire, even by accident, is a crime, V."

"Listen to Hannah," Luke grumbles, slanting his eyes toward me. "She knows everything."

I exhale and rub my forehead. My friends might not like hearing it, but I am the sheriff's daughter, and I need Violet to get it: we're in big fucking trouble. "It's reckless arson, V, and it can be charged as a misdemeanor *or* a felony, depending on the damage the fire causes and the decision of the district attor-ney. And you two are minors"—I point to Violet and Luke—"which means your parents will be responsible for whatever fines they charge us, which will be huge."

Mo nods. "They fined that fifteen-year-old kid thirty-six million dollars for starting the Eagle Creek fire."

Violet's hands fly to her mouth. "Grammy would kill me."

Luke chuckles grimly. "They aren't getting any cash out of my broke-ass family."

Drummer plops back onto the bed. "Hannah's right. Telling the world we did it won't help, and it's not like we're making things worse by staying silent."

I let his words sink in, and when no one argues, I ask, "We're agreed, then? No one talks?" Drummer, Luke, and Mo nod.

The four of us shift our eyes to Violet. She stares back, looking sulky in her off-the-shoulder top and long, curled eyelashes. It strikes me again that she's an outsider. She wasn't born and raised in Gap Mountain as we were. The four of us wait, watching her, and it feels like a divide is opening between us. Our first.

Finally, with a huff, she murmurs agreement. "I won't say anything."

Everyone takes a huge, steadying breath. In light of what we're facing, arguing with one another is pointless anyway. I consider the felonies and fines that have been charged in the past. There were the two laborers who accidentally started the Zaca Fire while fixing a broken water pipe, the trash-burning transient who started the Day Fire, and the electric company that caused the Camp Fire in Paradise, California—all accidents, technically, but all facing fines and criminal charges. It's imperative that we aren't caught.

"I'm driving back to Gap Lake tonight to check the area," I tell the group. "Dad said they took the main roadblock down, and I have to find that pipe and anything else we left behind."

"Won't it all be burned?" Violet asks.

I shrug. "The fire started small and traveled quickly *away* from us. Anything we left behind or dropped could still be there, with our fingerprints. Hopefully they haven't made much progress on the investigation yet, but once they do, they'll find the area of origin quickly and rope it off. Trust me, it isn't that hard. Anyone want to come with me?"

"I'll go with you," Drummer says.

I smile, glad that it's him, but my nerves remain coiled. I know how fast this can spiral out of control. The most important thing now is to remove evidence. The next is to lie low and hope this blows over.

We break apart, go to our separate rooms, and I set my phone alarm for 2:00 a.m.

9

At two o'clock my alarm goes off, and I throw vending machine snacks into a bag along with two bottles of water. As I brush my teeth, I stare into the mirror, hunting for my soul. My friends and I *killed* people, good people. I lean forward until my nose touches the glass. I look the same as I did before, but I don't *feel* the same. It's like I'm trapped in a nightmare, or an alternate reality, or in hell itself. I reach for the life I had a few days ago, but with every hour it slides further away.

Bishop has been surreal the last two days. The wildfire smoke has reached us here and smeared the sky in a dismal haze. Gap Mountain refugees amble through stores and hotel lobbies and restaurants as if they're lost or can't remember who they are. Sometimes they halt midstride and stare at nothing at all.

Anxiety claws at me all day. I don't know where my horses are—if they burned up like those deer we saw, if they fell into a canyon, or if predators got to them. Saliva fills my mouth, and I pinch my cheeks hard, glaring at myself in the mirror. "Keep it together, Hannah."

I'm determined to hide what we did, and I wonder if this makes me a terrible person. Probably. A huff escapes my lips and steams up the glass. Leaping to the wrong side of the law is easier than I ever dreamed possible.

I gather my pack, kiss Matilda, and slip out of the hotel room. Down the hall, I find Drummer's door and knock on it softly. There's no noise inside his room, no sign of him getting ready. I knock again. "Hey, we have to go." No response. Knowing Drummer, he forgot to set his alarm.

I have the extra key to his room, since it was supposed to be my dad's room, and use it to open his door. "Drummer?" I whisper into the dark.

The sheets rustle. Yep, he forgot. I flip on the bathroom light, and the weak bulb illuminates the room and the bed.

Drummer is not alone.

I squint at two bodies—their tan legs entangled, her hair a tousled mess, and his arm wrapped protectively around her small frame. I stare stupidly, unable to move or breathe. I smell sex and sweat and her shampoo. She flips over, instinctively avoiding the light, and snuggles into his chest. The sheet falls away, revealing her smooth naked back. It's Violet.

I slide out of the room before they notice me and stand in the hallway. My tall body bends in half as I suck for air. If I've been falling for Drummer since the sixth grade, then I just hit bottom with one hard smack. We promised not to do this: *monsters don't date monsters*. Tears leak from my eyes, and I rub them away. Her naked back flashes in my mind like an assault. It turns out Violet *does* have everything: endless cash, movie star looks, my dream college—and Drummer.

All I want is to return to my room and hide, but I have to get to the Gap, with or without Drummer. I start to leave, then hesitate. No, he offered to come with me, and I'm going to make him keep his promise. I text him: *I'm outside your room. You coming or not?*

After a short while, I hear movement, and then his door creaks open, just an inch. He's hiding her from me, and I bristle. I don't think he's ever hidden anything from me before. Drummer's not wearing a shirt, and he blinks as he surfaces from the world of dreams. "Sorry, I forgot."

"No kidding."

He rubs his eyes with two fists, like a little boy. "Right, just a sec."

"Hurry," I urge him.

Drummer shuts the door and then reappears—five excruciating minutes later—wearing jeans and a fresh white T-shirt he bought at Kmart yesterday. He's quickly rinsed off, put on deodorant, and brushed his teeth, washing *her* off of him. My jaw tightens, and the pain in my head returns as I rub my forehead.

"Ready," he says, adding a guilty smile, an expression of his

I know well. We walk a fine line as best friends: he needs attention and I'm happy to give it, but when he's getting it elsewhere, he practically forgets about me. Then we slip into the thick mire of his guilt and my hidden resentment as we pretend that nothing has changed. He exits his hotel room, careful to block my view of Violet, who is still sound asleep in his bed.

—

The ride to the trailhead is slow and quiet, and we reach it an hour later. I let Drummer drive, because he likes to play the role of alpha male when it suits him. "Stop," I say when he steers us off the road to drive directly to Gap Lake. "Tire tracks."

"What?"

"We don't want fresh tire tracks near the area of origin that can be traced back to the Jeep. Park here at the trailhead."

"All right, detective." He pulls the emergency brake, and we step out of the Jeep and slide on the N95 face masks we snatched from the hotel lobby. The masks are everywhere in Bishop, offered for free. Smoke from our fire has reached as far as Washington, they said on the news.

Drummer and I strike out on the trail. "I don't see how any of this can be traced back to us," he shouts through the mask.

We're the exact same height, and I easily keep pace with him. "Have you heard of pyro-forensics?" I ask.

He snorts. "Unless it's on the back of a cereal box, then no."

Drummer plays like he's stupid, but it's not true. He just can't be bothered with homework, can't sit still for it. I fill him in. "It's the science of studying wildfires and finding their causes and places of origin. A team of fire investigators will figure out where this started, if they haven't already."

He raises his brows as if he doesn't believe me.

I pull down my mask so he can hear me better. "Once they have the *area of origin*, then they'll find the *point of origin* and begin looking for clues as to what started the fire. They'll reach out through the news, question residents, write search warrants, and review CCTV of the roads leading to Gap Lake—they'll be on a mission to arrest someone." I touch his arm. "There are three people dead, Drummer, and more missing. The fire is still burning. Yosemite might evacuate. This is a big fucking deal."

"I know that." He pulls down his mask too. "But is all the damage *our* fault? I mean, we started it, yeah, but why can't the firefighters put it out? Why didn't the deputies get everyone out of Stony Ridge in time? We shouldn't get the blame for everything."

He's pouting so I let him. As long as we find Luke's pipe and anything else we left behind, his questions are moot. It's almost dawn and we break into a slow jog the rest of the way up the trail.

When we arrive at the Gap, we pause to admire the sapphire water winking in the dawn light. The mountain air brushes the surface and ruffles our hair. Drummer holds my hand, and it's like we're the first two people on Earth, back when they were blameless and happy, and I feel reassured. This lake has been swallowing secrets for fifteen hundred years; it will swallow ours.

Drummer smiles. "Let's do this, Hannah Banana."

We start at the beach and search it first, using our phones as flashlights. As the sun rises slowly behind the mountains, it casts a gray glow that makes everything look the same. After determining that the beach is clean, we trek into the woods where Luke lit the pipe. The landscape ahead of us is charred and desolate as far as we can see. Blackened naked limbs hang off the trees, and utter silence reigns. The animals and insects are gone. It's as if we landed on a lifeless planet.

"What's that?" Drummer asks, pointing toward something fluttering in the breeze.

My stomach sinks as we draw closer. I lift it out of the grass, and Drummer whispers, "Oh shit."

It's police tape.

I drop it and look around, notice another strand of tape in the distance. My gut clenches. "The investigators have already been here. We're too late."

Drummer's hands slide through his hair, and panic flits across his features. "I can't do this. I can't go to jail." He stomps in a circle. "Hannah?" His expression is pleading, and this is the exact look he gave me when he got one of his girlfriends pregnant and came to me to fix it: *Talk to her for me, find out what she's going to do. My mom will take care of the kid, but I'm not going to marry her. Hannah, help me.*

His cowardice should have turned me off, and it almost did, but his need for me overrode that. Turns out it wasn't his kid, and he got pissed and yelled at the girl for cheating. Fucking Drummer.

"How did they find this place so fast?" he cries.

I point to a tree. "There are clues that backtrack the fire to this exact spot, things like char patterns, curling leaves, bent grasses, and soot deposits. I don't understand it all, but the clues obviously led investigators here. They've already searched the area, but maybe they missed something. Come on, we have to find that pipe, but be careful, touch as little as possible."

We drop down and start searching, gently lifting fragile branches, plants, and scorched grasses. I worry about leaving footprints, in case investigators come back, but don't see how that can be avoided. Luke's fingerprint-ridden pipe is more damning than our shoe treads. Every kid in Gap Mountain owns a pair of Vans, but that pipe leads straight back to Luke. Because of his vandalism charge, his fingerprints are on file, and a match could quickly be made.

Once he's arrested, the rest of us will fall like dominoes. Our cover story is decent, but I don't think it will withstand close scrutiny. There are too many loose ends, like Luke picking up the book of matches at Sam's and the photo Mo posted. The key to controlling this is keeping the attention off of us completely.

After almost an hour of searching, we give up. "The pipe's not here. They must have found it."

Drummer squats, drops his face into his hands, and groans.

I rub his back, impatient. The predawn light spreads quicker from behind its smokescreen, lighting the forest from gray to soft gold. I don't want anyone to see us here. *Suspects often return to the scene of their crimes*, a sentence from some criminology book I read once, or maybe I heard it in a movie.

I'll find out when I get to San Diego State and start my classes, if I can just get through the next few weeks.

Drummer stands and throws a rock into the Gap. It strikes the surface with an anticlimactic splash and vanishes. I imagine it sinking, one cold foot at a time, until it reaches the bottom, where it will never be found. The tight band of tension around my forehead loosens. "Look," I say to Drummer. "Odds are, the fingerprints will have burned off the pipe, or the pipe itself will have melted. We're fine. It's all going to be okay. Let's go."

On our way back, we keep our eyes peeled for anything else we might have left behind—sandwich wrappers, sunscreen, towels—but the place has been picked clean. Drummer calms down and his mind turns to other things. "Have you ever been anybody's first time?" he asks.

For a second, I can't reference what he's talking about. "First time doing what?"

He laughs darkly and lifts his eyebrows.

Oh god. He's talking about sex. I feel instantly sick. "You know I've never—" I cut myself off. I don't want to talk about this.

"The first time is special," he says, plowing on and ignoring my discomfort.

I swallow, positive he's referring to Violet. Was last night *her* first time? Because I know it wasn't his. There is pride and tenderness in Drummer's voice, and I don't trust myself to speak. He's never called sex with any girl *special* before. I imagine the word forming a hoop around just the two of them. It edges me out, and I feel the forest spin around me like a toy top.

Drummer can't abandon me *now*, not with three dead

bodies and arson charges hanging over us. He should be lean-ing on *me*, not her. I'm the one who's trying to keep us safe. I'm the one who's going to get us out of this mess.

"Are you talking about someone in particular?" I ask with-out turning around. I think he wants to confess that he broke our pact, and if he does, I'll forgive him. It will mean she's not important.

But he doesn't confess. "No one in particular. Just thinking out loud."

My nails dig into my palms. Drummer is *lying*, and I lose my breath. He doesn't lie, not to me. My thoughts blacken like the forest behind us. He heads toward the driver's side of my Jeep.

"I'll drive," I say, forcing the words past the hard ball in my throat. I grind the gears and spin the tires as I pull out of the trailhead parking lot. I want to punch the steering wheel, drive off a cliff, scream in rage. But I don't. I drive and we don't speak. My head is pounding when we get back to the hotel.

"You okay?" Drummer asks.

"I'm tired." We separate in the hallway, and I enter my room, leash Matilda, and take her for a walk.

After a long stroll through Bishop, my rage settles. Drum-mer will tire of Violet, as he tires of all the girls. He will come back to me. All I have to do is wait.

10

Nine days after the evacuation, those of us who still have homes are allowed to move back to Gap Mountain. Three more bodies are discovered in the Stony Ridge neighborhood rubble, and an elderly Gap Mountain resident who stayed to fight the fire died in the hospital from his injuries, bringing the death toll to seven. A female firefighter was hospitalized when tornado-strength winds caused by the blaze ripped a tree out of the earth and flung it at her; she's in critical condition. Violet can't stop crying, and the rest of us are too stunned to react. We just want to go home.

As we all pile into our cars, Violet and Drummer act like nothing's going on between them, but I spent the last six nights watching his door from my hotel room peephole. She visited him around midnight each night—her makeup perfect, hair styled and glossy—and left by 4:30 a.m., makeup smeared, hair in a tangled mess. Just thinking about her blissful smile each morning makes my stomach burn.

Now in my Wrangler, I blast the hits station, and Drummer, who decided to ride with me, catches my mood. We need release, we need fun, so we sing—loudly and horribly—on the way home, sometimes making Matilda howl in the backseat. We play Would You Rather? and he tells me about every stupid YouTube prank he's watched in the last few days.

When our throats hurt from singing, he pulls me close and throws an arm around my neck, making it difficult to drive but I don't care. His blue eyes glow when he smiles. "So, you going to hit up the frat parties when you're in college?"

"You know me better than that."

"How are you going to meet dudes if you don't get wasted?"

That makes me laugh. "I think there are other ways."

"I wish I could go to college—just for the parties, though." He sucks in his lower lip and lets it pop out of his mouth, wet and full.

I imagine kissing it, and heat floods me. "You can go to a junior college and then transfer."

He grins. "Right."

"You can. You just have to want it."

Drummer shrugs. "Sounds like work."

"Dude, you work how many hours a week at the lumber yard? Thirty, sometimes forty? College is easier than humping wood."

"Humping wood?" He looks directly at me, his lips twitching. "Sounds dirty when you say it."

My pulse flutters and I want him so badly that every nerve in my body vibrates. If he kissed me right now . . .

—

Our mood shifts as we roll into Gap Mountain, which is like driving onto a movie set. Some areas are untouched, others mangled by flames. A layer of smoke hangs over the streets, and ash covers everything like an early snow. The Gap Fire is still raging, heading west, gulping thousands of acres as it moves through Yosemite National Park. The park is being evacuated; people who booked their campsites a year in advance are being sent home during peak tourist season.

Drummer turns on the radio just long enough for us to learn that before it reached Yosemite, our wildfire swept through two more communities, taking two more lives. That makes nine souls, lost forever. I quickly turn the radio back off. We also learned that the fire is 20 percent contained and the costs and losses are estimated in the tens of millions. The first funeral is tomorrow.

How can this fire be *our* fire anymore?

I drive Drummer to his house, and he kisses me goodbye. On the way home, my cell rings with an unfamiliar number, and I pull over to answer. "Hello?"

"Is this Hannah Warner?"

"Yes."

"This is Golden State Animal Rescue. You reported three horses missing on July seventh? Can you describe them?"

Oh my god! "Yes, yes! Are they all right? One's a three-year-old palomino gelding, and he should be with his mom, she's a palomino mare. And the other is an Appaloosa gelding, age fourteen. Do you have all three?"

"We do, ma'am. They've been living in the forest and have a few minor scrapes, but they're safe. The mare still had your phone number painted across her side."

I cry so hard that she stops talking and waits. When I'm calm, the woman gives me the details of where to pick them up.

"My—my trailer has two flat tires," I say. "It's why I couldn't get them out." It guts me that I wasn't prepared. My horses could have died.

"We can deliver them to you. Is your home safe now?"

"Yes. The fire passed us by." She takes my address and tells me my horses will be delivered tomorrow morning at ten o'clock. I thank her and hang up, feeling like I just won the lottery. This is a good omen. My horses are safe.

When I get home, my dad's patrol car is parked in the driveway. "Dad!" I race into the house. He's drinking a store-bought coffee in the kitchen and getting ready to leave again when I slam into his arms. "Golden State Animal Rescue found the horses!"

He sets down his coffee and strokes my hair. "Are they hurt?"

"No, not really. They're being delivered tomorrow."

He nods. "You need to buy new tires, Hannah. I'll install

them, but I told you, taking care of those horses includes maintaining their trailer."

"I know. I will." My dad looks ten years older and exhausted. "Are you getting enough sleep?" I ask.

He ignores the question, and we sit at the table for a moment. He takes my hand. "How was Bishop?"

"Boring."

His lips twitch into a smile. "Boring is safe."

"Yeah, but it's also boring." We laugh and I peer around the house, which smells like smoke. Everything inside is covered in a layer of white ash, and I wrinkle my nose.

Dad notices and says, "We have some smoke damage, and this dust is toxic. Our insurance company is sending out a crew to evaluate and clean it up. In the meantime, don't cook here." He reaches into his pocket and hands me sixty dollars. "You can eat at the Wildflower Café. We got the diner back up and running a few days ago, and they're feeding the first responders and the town. It's a good place to get news and see people." He lets out a long breath. "The whole north side of Stony Ridge is gone. Your school is gone too."

"It's not my school anymore." I lower my eyes, try to keep my tone neutral. "Any idea how the fire started?"

"Not a clue, but Cal Fire knows *where* it started."

"Oh?" I rub at a scratch on the wooden table. I know this, but I don't like hearing it confirmed. "Where?"

"By Gap Lake, in the forest near the beach. They suspect arson."

"Like deliberate arson?"

He smiles because there isn't any other type than deliberate. "It wasn't humid enough for natural combustion, and there was no lightning. I told you before, Bug, a human did this. We don't know if it was malicious, but someone brought fire into the woods, and that was not an accident."

"Maybe it was faulty power lines?"

"Not likely," he says. "The electric company shut off the power at noon. But the investigators are very good; they'll figure it out." He sighs. "Did you bring our pictures back home?"

"Yes." My thoughts drift to Mo and Luke, who lost all their family photos.

Dad leans back in his chair. "I'm sorry I couldn't join you in Bishop. You should have had an adult with you."

Translation: *You should have had your mother with you.* My dad does this—he flip-flops between guilt for arresting her and grief that we lost her. "It's fine, Dad. I had Ms. Sandoval and my friends."

"The monsters. Good." He stretches and groans, and I hear his spine pop. He turns back to me, his eyes like flint. "We will catch who's responsible for that fire. There will be a reckoning."

A reckoning? I feel the blood drain from my face. *You are looking at who is responsible, Dad.* My ears start to ring. I hadn't fully considered that by lying, I was pitting myself against my own father. I imagine confessing, right now, right here. My dad wouldn't believe me at first. Then it would sink in, and disappointment would drag his face into a frown. This would be followed by rage and then grief and then self-flagellation. He would arrest me and then hate himself for it. He might even say, *You're just like your mother.*

The moment passes when my dad raps his knuckles on the counter. "I'm off. Remember—don't eat here. If you have time today, throw out all our food. It's tainted." He squeezes me. "I love you, Bug."

"Love you too, Dad." He kisses the top of my head and strolls out to his patrol car, bending his tall frame in half to get seated.

I watch him drive away, and the good feelings I had that the fire would soon be behind me drain out my toes. But I'm also relieved that I didn't confess, because that would make the monsters the most hated teens in Gap Mountain. Still, when I think how close I came to talking, I realize how easy it would be for one of us to crack and confess . . . how awfully terribly easy.

11

Golden State Animal Rescue delivered my horses two days ago, and they are okay. The specialty house cleaners also arrived, and they attacked our cabin with an arsenal of chemicals, scrub brushes, industrial carpet cleaners, and a small army of people. The cobwebs, the porcelain stains, the dusty baseboards, Matilda's wads of loose hair, and the thick layer of dust on the blinds—it's all gone! Afterward, Dad turned up the radio and we danced—we actually danced—in the family room, laughing and spinning. The way we figure it, we won't have to clean again for a year.

The Gap Fire is 30 percent contained, but the wind has picked up, with gusts reaching sixty miles per hour—a grim situation for firefighters. The blaze is so fierce it's creating its own weather, and crews from all over the country are pouring in to help. The smoke has reached Canada. Cal Fire has kept quiet about the investigation so far.

I have nothing to do. Because of the air quality, the parks and trails are closed and it's too smoky to ride the horses. I work at the Reel Deal, a DVD rental store that does good business because Wi-Fi in the mountains is crap, but the store is currently closed due to smoke damage, so I can't earn money either.

Now it's noon and I'm sweltering on my couch, cuddling with Matilda, when a number I vaguely recognize texts me: *Hey, fire girl, how you been?*

Fire girl? Oh yeah, it's Justin, the guy who picked Matilda and me up on Route 395. I texted him once from the hotel, to thank him again for the ride, so now he has my number. *Doing good*. I write. *You?*

Gray dots, then: *Yeah, good. Can I see you?*

My stomach flips over. Is he asking me on a date?

As if sensing my confusion, he writes: *id like to take you out Hannah*

Right then, Mo sends a group text to the monsters: *Miss you guys! Let's meet at the café. Leaving now*

To Justin I write, *ok, maybe. Gtg right now*

I add him to my contact list, throw on a pair of ripped jeans and Nike sandals, and grab my Jeep keys. "Back soon," I say to Matilda. Outside, I see that a bear has flipped over our bear-proof trash can and left tracks all over the front yard. The animals are starving right now, driven down from the wilderness by the wildfire, and I make a mental note to be more careful when I come and go from my house.

When I reach the Wildflower Café, the television in the corner is tuned to a news station because Gap Mountain residents are chomping at the bit for information about the arson investigation. They want justice and compensation, and I don't even want to think about the civil suits we could face if we're caught.

"Hi, Hannah!" I turn and see Jessie Taylor waving at me from her table of friends in the corner. She's an incoming senior and someone I race against at the rodeos.

"Hey, Jessie," I say, slowing as I pass her table. "Your horses okay?"

She blows her bangs off her freckled face. "Yeah, but the high school burned down, you know, and now they're talking about holding our classes at the rec center in the fall. Sucks. I hope they fry whoever did this."

"Yeah." I laugh. "Me too." My eyes drift to a table of exhausted firefighters, and one of the younger one smiles at me. God, I'm surrounded by people who would hate me if they knew what I did. I spot Luke and Mo by the window and hurry away.

"Did you find your cat?" I ask Luke as I slide into the booth.

He rubs his face and shakes his head. "No sign of her."

"How is it, living in the Red Cross trailer?" Mo asks him.

His grin is wry. "Fucking awful. It's crowded and we have to sign in and out and show ID. I can't smoke inside the trailer or the compound, and the chain-link fence is a pain in the ass to climb over."

Jeannie, the head server at the café, interrupts: "What'll you kids have?"

We pause to order cheeseburgers, fries, and milkshakes. "I'm buying," I say, waving my dad's cash.

"Okay, Violet," Luke grumbles, because Violet usually pays for us. I change the subject, hoping to find neutral ground with him. "How's Aiden?"

Luke turns his head to stare out the window as tears wet his eyes. "He's having nightmares about the fire, so he sleeps with me on this tiny-ass bunk bed. Last night he dreamed that Mom served us our cat for dinner. Weird shit." He points across the street to a vacant lot where donations are piling up. "That's where we get all our clothes now." I notice Luke's T-shirt and jeans don't fit him, and the fabric is stained. People mean well, but Gap Mountain has become the official dumping ground for unwanted crap.

Mo suddenly stops chewing and pushes her plate away, her appetite gone. "This entire town wants to string up whoever started the fire," she whispers. Her dark-red hair is pulled back, and her cheeks are pink, making her look feverish.

Right then, someone turns up the television in the corner, and every head turns to watch the screen:

We return now to a breaking story about the Gap Fire that is burning out of control in the Sierra Nevada Mountains.

Investigators broke their silence today and announced they have located the point of origin for the fire here, in the woods near a popular recreation area called Gap Lake.

A map appears on the screen, and there is a bright red circle around the spot where Luke lit his pipe.

"Fuck me," Luke whispers.

The reporter continues:

The cause of the fire has not been determined, but due to evidence collected at the scene, investigators suspect human involvement. Containment is currently at 30 percent, but with hurricane-speed winds, hot temperatures, and low humidity continuing, there is little hope that the Gap Fire will be extinguished this week. Hundreds of structures remain threatened, and summer campers have fled Yosemite National Park, leaving the popular tourist destination desolate and quiet during this, the busiest time of the year.

The newscaster goes on to list the damage and deaths already caused by the fire, and images of our injured town flash across the screen. She tells us a live press conference will occur at 4:00 p.m. and plays a snippet from my father's interview yesterday. "We will rebuild," he says, raising his fist.

"Holy shit," Mo whispers. "Didn't you and Drummer go back to the lake? There's no evidence left, is there?"

I chew the inside of my cheek. "We were too late."

"What!"

"Shhh." I glance around the café. "Let's go to Violet's. We can talk there."

Mo texts Violet to make sure she's home, I pay using Dad's cash, and then we pile into Mo's Corolla and drive over to Lulu Sandoval's house. On the way, we pass the Stony Ridge neighborhood.

As we roll by, Luke and Mo stare out the window. All that is left of their neighborhood is driveways, foundations, a few brick fireplaces, blackened swimming pools, and burned-out cars. Their wooden homes are gone, as if Dorothy's tornado picked them up and tossed them into another world. My dad was elected sheriff to protect this town, and his daughter and her friends fucking destroyed it. God, if the truth *ever* comes out, it won't just devastate him; it'll ruin his career.

At Violet's, Lulu opens the front door and invites us inside. "You kids look rode hard and put away wet! Everything okay?"

We nod. Her house backs onto the river, and the lawn between here and there spreads past us, green and lush. The surrounding landscaping is bright with blooming iceberg roses, black-eyed Susans, hydrangeas, and peonies. Lulu's sunflower garden stands tall, the flowers like big, faceless lions' heads. The property is peaceful, inviting, and achingly impervious to the fact that our lives are falling apart or that the land beyond her firebreak is singed black.

"Are you hungry?" she asks.

"No, thank you, we just came from the café," I explain.

"Nonsense, you kids are always hungry." She loads our arms

with a jug of apple juice, a plate of doughnuts, and a bag of oranges. "Violet and Drummer are in the attic."

My spine tenses. How long has Drummer been here, I wonder?

Using the main staircase, we tromp to the third floor with the food in our arms. Lulu's three oversized black poodles follow us eagerly, leaping and whining. We find Violet sitting on the floor of the attic and Drummer pushing buttons on her TV, trying to change the input.

Violet's eyes are red-rimmed, as if she's been crying. "Did you see the news?" she asks. "They *know.*"

We flop onto the carpet around her, sitting cross-legged like when we were kids. This room was once our playroom, then our clubhouse, and now our hangout. It's grown up with us. Gone are the Disney DVDs, board games, pastel furniture, and giant stuffed animals of our childhood; they've been replaced with thick white area rugs, red chenille designer couches, and a white leather reclining chair. Dominating one wall is a mounted flat screen, complete with unlimited streaming subscriptions to video games, movies, and shows. Professional black-and-white photos of Violet and her older brother, Trey, are framed in red and punctuate the stark white walls.

"Did you hear me, Han?" Violet asks. "They know."

Everyone waits for me to answer her, but I'm adrift in memories. The gift I gave Violet when she turned ten stands on the little writing desk in the corner, the last holdout from our shared childhood. It's a rearing glass unicorn, fourteen inches tall with gold-plated hooves and a golden horn, the most expensive gift

I've ever given. I'd been trying to impress her—my rich and beautiful friend, the girl who soars into my life each summer and then flies back home for winter, like an exotic bird that can't survive the cold.

I wonder if she remembers I gave it to her. Around Violet's neck hangs a Tiffany necklace she received for her high school graduation, a platinum pendant etched with the letter *V*—a reminder to me that *all* her gifts are expensive. When everything you get is special, what's memorable?

"Hannah," she growls.

I throw up my hands. "They don't know anything. Not really."

Violet glares at me, her body braced as if I'm dragging her into a trap.

Drummer puts his arm around her, and my eyes flit around the room. Am I the only monster who notices what's going on with these two? I try meeting Mo's eye, but she's watching the news station while Luke sulks.

I release a breath and try to reassure Violet, reassure all of us: "No one can prove we were there. They can't link whatever evidence they found to us." But this isn't entirely true. If they're able to lift fingerprints off the evidence they found and run them through ALPS, the Automated Latent Print System, they might get a match to Luke.

Mo settles next to Violet and Drummer, and then Luke leans against me, his anger quelled for now. We slump into one another, and I close my eyes and breathe, inhaling the mixed fragrance of Mo's brand-new leather shoes, Violet's ninety-dollar-an-ounce perfume, Luke's cigarettes, and Drummer's deodorant. These are my best friends, my allies, and now my accomplices. I love them. I can't let this *thing* between Drummer and Violet distract me.

The newscaster finishes up a report about stock prices and then returns to the fire story: "We're going live to Gap Mountain for a live statement from local Sheriff Robert Warner."

Drummer turns up the volume and we all lean forward.

My dad appears on the screen, looking handsome. He's shaved and combed his hair, and now he stands at a podium outside the sheriff's department with a crew of officials fanning out behind him, hands clasped together. Their expressions are firm and serious, as if they can bully this disaster into submission.

My dad introduces himself and the men and women standing behind him. Camera shutters click in the foreground as he describes the ongoing process of identifying human remains collected from Stony Ridge. Afterward, he introduces Fire Battalion Chief Joanna Giles, and they switch places.

The battalion chief explains how fire investigators located the *area of origin* for the Gap Fire and then narrowed that down to the *point of origin*. I toss Drummer a look—because I told him this would happen—and he frowns, his eyes saying, *this isn't the time to gloat.* He's right, so I turn back to the TV.

Then the battalion chief adds new information that sends chills through the attic:

A team of investigators from Cal Fire has collected evidence that confirms arson of a reckless or possibly malicious nature. An individual or group of individuals is responsible.

Her eyes flash, her lips tighten.

We are actively analyzing that evidence and pursuing leads, and we'd like the public's help regarding sightings of a person or persons in the Gap Lake area on July seventh around three p.m. If anyone has information about adults or kids in this area, please call the hotline we have set up for tips.

The number appears on the screen as the battalion chief looks directly into the camera, directly at us: "We will find the individual or individuals responsible and bring them to justice."

Luke's head falls into his hands, Violet chews her knuckles, and the rest of us gape at the television as Joanna Giles gives the microphone to the next speaker.

"Arson," Mo whispers. One of the poodles jumps down and licks her hand.

Luke's face is pallid. "Do you think they found my pipe?"

I exhale. "Maybe, but I doubt they'll get prints off it. The fire will have damaged them, I think."

Luke's gaze meets mine, his eyes accusing. It strikes me again that this is my fault. I grabbed Luke's arm and I shouldn't have. I gaze back at him and mouth, *I'm sorry.*

Violet clears her throat. "If—let's just say *if*—we get caught, did all of us commit arson, or just you two?"

"V!" Mo cries. "We were all there."

"I know, I know, but I mean from a legal standpoint," she clarifies. "Who is responsible?"

I wipe my face and come up blank. "I don't know. It would depend on the evidence and how good our individual lawyers are. The state will charge us with whatever they think will stick in court, but we would plead to lesser charges, most likely. Again, depends on our lawyers and the evidence presented to the district attorney or the grand jury."

Luke kicks the leather chair, sends it spinning, and laughs bitterly. "I can't afford a good lawyer, and it was my bud, my pipe, and my matches. I'm the most fucked if we get caught. V, you'll get off scot-free. Your grammy will see to that."

"That's not fair," Mo scolds.

"Dead man walking," Luke crows and stands up fast, alarming the poodles. "Shit, I don't want to go back to that trailer." His voice warbles and I think he's about to cry. Luke, powerful Luke, is scared, and we're all quelled by it.

"You can stay here," Violet offers. "We have more bedrooms than people in this house."

My eyes snap to Violet, who is now sitting by herself at the writing desk, and for the first time I wonder if she gets lonely in this big house, alone with her grandma? Her brother used to visit with her, but he's married now and hardly comes anymore. We're her only friends in Gap Mountain. When we're busy with work or other friends, what does Violet do?

Luke shrugs off her offer. "Nah, I can't leave Aiden alone at night. I gotta go, guys. I need a walk and a smoke."

I rise, feeling defeated. "I'll see what I can find out from my dad about this evidence they have. Don't worry, okay? They can't prove it was us."

No one responds to that.

"Mo, will you drive me back to the café to get my Jeep?"

"Sure," says Mo.

Drummer and Violet share a secret smile, and frustration fills me as I realize we're leaving them alone together. Suddenly I want to stay, but Mo has her keys out and she jingles them at me. "You coming?"

"Yeah." As we drive away, I glance in the makeup mirror at the attic window tucked between two turrets. Violet stands by the glass, looking out like a princess, and Drummer lurks behind her, *very* close behind her. I'm not sure what bothers me more, that they're screwing or that they're hiding it. My stomach drops and my fingers tighten into fists.

Secrets are dangerous, especially now.

I turn up the music and flip my mirror so I can no longer see them.

12

July 19

Gap Fire: 30% contained

Fatalities: 9

Time: 7:10 p.m.

Later that night, Dad walks through the screen door and smiles in surprise. "You cooked?"

"I haven't seen you much lately, so . . . I made dinner." I glance at the slowly congealing pot of Hamburger Helper on the stove. Usually we fend for ourselves and I eat dinner in my room, but tonight I hand my dad a cold beer from the refrigerator and a plate. I'm being nice because he works so hard, but also because I want to find out what he knows. We each dish up a plate while Matilda wags her tail between us.

My dad lowers himself tiredly onto a chair. "Sorry I haven't been around much, Bug."

"It's fine, I know you're busy."

He digs into the meal as if he hasn't eaten in a year. As

the prepackaged nutrients flood his system, he begins to talk. "Some wacko called the station today," he says. "Claims the government started the Gap Fire using targeted lasers affixed to drones. He also mentioned that politicians are lizards that don't care about *humans*." He swigs his beer. "That last part might be true."

We laugh and since Matilda misses him too, she takes his mirth as an invitation to throw her front paws on his lap. "Down, girl," he says fondly.

"You looked good on TV today."

He grunts.

I decide to dive right in and ask what I need to know. "What kind of evidence did Cal Fire find by the lake?"

He shakes his head. "Mostly old garbage, but some of it is promising—a singed beer bottle that looks new, a pot pipe, and a book of matches from Sam's market. Who would light up on a Red Flag day? Probably tourists." He inhales a huge bite of beef and noodles.

I flinch and accidentally kick Matilda under the table. Cal Fire found everything! The matchbook must have flown out of Luke's hands with the pipe and the embers, and how did we miss a beer bottle? Or is it ours? Lots of people swim at the Gap, drink beer, and leave behind their trash. I take deep breaths as the room closes in around me.

My dad shoves food into his mouth, oblivious to the shrinking kitchen and the blood thumping through his daughter's veins faster than it should. He swallows and continues: "The county forensics lab is expediting the processing of the bottle.

If they can lift prints and saliva, then by next week, we may have results, but without suspects, they won't do us much good. Unless our arsonist is already in the system." He smiles.

Fingerprints? DNA? Oh god. Luke's data *is* in the system. My leg starts to bounce, and I push it still with my hand. "Wouldn't the fire or the heat have destroyed that stuff?"

He shrugs. "Fires start small, Bug. It's common to find intact evidence near the point of origin. The label on the bottle is singed, but our fire battalion chief told me she's hopeful about finding fingerprints."

"But that doesn't mean the person started the fire."

"True," he says, shrugging. "But the matchbook also looks new. We're checking the CCTV at Sam's Market and the cameras on Pine Street for clues as well. Once we have a suspect list, we can start ruling people out."

I briefly close my eyes, thinking, remembering. Luke said he grabbed the matches from Sam's the day of the fire, so they might have his image on camera. My heart starts to hammer, and I leave the table for a glass of water. Between that and the beer . . . "What kind of beer was it?" I ask, hoping for some hoppy IPA or expensive craft beer, something preferred by tourists.

"Bud Light," he answers.

Bud Light is what my friends were drinking. Luke might be right. We might be totally and completely fucked.

—

After dinner, I text Drummer: *Meet me at the park downtown.*

He doesn't answer so I pull on a hoodie—nights are cold

in the mountains—slide into my Jeep, and drive toward his house to see if he's home. My car is low on gas, so I fill up on my way.

I don't want to tell the others what I learned from my dad, not yet. They'll panic. But I have to tell someone. Where is Drummer? I text him again: *Are you asleep?*

I get nothing back. Well, if he's asleep, he wouldn't text back, would he? I drive to his house on the east side of town, cut my headlights, and park down the street. His parents go to bed early, so I sneak through the towering pines to his window and knock on the glass. "Drummer?"

His room is dark but the window is cracked open several inches. I slide the pane over and climb into his room. He's not here but his presence is powerful—his scent, his dirty clothes, his laptop, his crusty dishes. The bed is unmade, with the blankets tossed carelessly over the footboard. His clothing sprawls on the floor, as cocky as Drummer. Warmth swirls through me at being inside his lair. But where is he?

I poke around, unable to help myself. When I pull open his nightstand drawer, a pile of condoms glints at me in the moonlight and I jerk my hand back. Some of the wrappers are torn open and empty. My breathing becomes jagged, and horrible sadness envelops me. Has Violet been here?

I sit on his bed, and my mind spins with images of them together. What is it like to have Drummer's full attention, I wonder? How does Violet feel when he slides on one of those condoms and leans over her? My cheeks burn and I can't stop staring at the shiny packages.

Other than Maria, who lasted a full year, Drummer comes to me to complain about his girlfriends or make fun of them. I've felt sorry for the girls, not envious. But it's worse, much worse, to be excluded. Just then his door flies open and the light flips on. Drummer blinks at me from his doorway. "Hannah?"

I slam the nightstand drawer shut. "Yeah, it's me." I smooth his sheet. "Sorry."

He smirks. "Nah, I like coming home to a woman in my bed."

I laugh and my cheeks blaze hotter. "I was looking for you, you didn't answer my texts. Where were you?"

"Just driving," he says, and pushes his fingers through his sun-streaked hair. "What's up?"

The tears I've been holding back begin to spill.

"Hey, don't cry." He crosses the room in four strides and wraps his arms around me.

My body melts into his, and I let myself really cry for the first time since the fire, the deaths, and the destruction. "We're terrible people."

"Shhh." He strokes my hair, pulls me closer. "It was an accident."

I shrug. "We're the idiots who smoked in the woods."

"The news has you spooked, that's all this is."

"It's not just the news that scares me. My dad said they found an empty Bud Light bottle, a pipe, and a book of matches from the market."

Drummer stiffens as he processes this. "All right, okay, but everyone stops at Sam's Market for beers and shit before heading to the Gap. Like, everyone. It proves nothing."

Drummer has no idea what a gold mine of evidence it actually is. The investigators will visit all the local stores, including Sam's. They'll make a list of everyone they can identify—through receipts or license plates caught on CCTV—who bought Bud Light that day (hopefully Mo's brother paid cash). Even without fingerprints and DNA, that bottle could lead straight back to Mo's brother and then from him to us.

Also, Mo might have told her dad she was swimming at the Gap that day, and he might put two and two together. This is another possible line straight to us. Once we're added to the suspect list, we'll be swabbed for DNA and our fingerprints will be taken (assuming the lab can lift fingerprints and DNA from the evidence). If we're matched, they'll separate us and try to get us to turn on one another. They'll examine our weak alibis, and they will not hold up. "This is a disaster," I whisper.

Drummer sucks on his lower lip. "So . . . what can we do about it, Han? Nothing."

"Right," I say, my legs twitching, my eyes darting around the room. I wipe the tears off my cheeks.

Drummer draws my face to his. "I see your brain chewing on this, but I don't think you need to worry, I really don't. Look at you—I can't remember the last time you cried." He smiles. "Hannah Banana is losing her shit."

"Am not."

He elbows me. "Are too." His breath warms my cheek, his clear blue eyes peer straight through me. My gaze drops to the blond stubble on his jaw, his smirking lips. I want to touch his face, kiss him. I'm aware that the side of my breast is rubbing against his arm. Is he aware? We're on his bed and we're young and there are a shit ton of condoms in the drawer beside us. I don't understand why nothing is happening.

His voice deepens. "I can make you feel better."

"How?"

"Lie down. Watch." He tugs my legs so I fall back on his bed. Then he opens the side drawer and reaches for a fresh condom. My heart stops. I can't breathe. Drummer straddles my legs, sits back, and opens the wrapper. "Get ready to be amazed!"

Amazed? I blink at him, confused, but yeah, I'm ready.

He pulls the condom out of its wrapper, puts the rubber to his mouth, and blows, creating a huge oblong balloon with a nipple-like tip. Laughing, he holds it against his crotch. "And they say one size fits all."

I rocket upright. "Asshole!"

"What? It's funny."

I climb out of his bed and glare at him. "No, it wasn't."

He grabs me and wraps his arms around me. "I was trying to make you laugh. You know I love you."

I don't respond. He lets go and watches me, sees I'm not in the mood to play. Then, with a sigh, he switches off his light and pulls off his T-shirt. "Look, I gotta go to bed. The lumber yard is reopening tomorrow, and I have to log in the deliveries." He tucks a thumb into his belt loop and waits.

Damn it, Drummer. He knows how good he looks standing in the moonlight like that, his taut muscles glowing silver.

He made me believe we were about to have sex on purpose. He likes to keep me on the hook, and I have to admit, sometimes I fucking hate him. "Yeah, I gotta go too. The Reel Deal is also opening tomorrow."

"See, everything's going back to normal." He bumps knuckles with me—a gesture I can't stand—and empties his pockets onto his nightstand. I see not one but *two* empty condom wrappers mixed in with his keys and money. Blood rushes to my face. He was not "just driving." What a fucking liar.

"'Night, Hannah," he says, and I feel dismissed, excused, kicked out of his room.

"'Night," I rasp. I bump into his desk as I try to climb out his window. I can't see, I can hardly breathe. The moon washes red, and my pulse pounds in my brain.

"You could leave out the front door," he drawls. "My dad won't shoot you."

"No, I'm good." I struggle with his curtains, knock over his empty pencil holder, and fall out of his window onto his yellowing lawn. "I'm okay."

I hear him chuckling behind me. "Good night, Romeo, parting is such sweet sorrow."

A Shakespeare reference from Drummer? I'm impressed, but why am *I* Romeo? I answer back anyway. "*Arrivederci, Juliet.*"

When I get home, I find Mo leaning against my horses' paddock and petting Sunny in the dark. Her eyes are swollen and red, and she's wearing her N95 face mask. I park the Jeep, throw on the emergency brake, and climb out. She faces me in the brand-new clothes her family bought with their insurance money—new earrings, new Nikes, new purse—and I'm reminded again she lost *everything*. Even her underwear and socks must be new.

She slips off her mask. "I'm scared, Hannah. I can't sleep." With her hair pulled into a high bun, her long neck, and her breathing mask, Mo looks like an apocalyptic ballerina.

I glance around. "The bears have been coming close to the house. We should talk in the barn."

"No, I'm allergic to smoke *and* dust." She points at her mask.

The poor air quality doesn't affect me like it does Mo. In fact, I think I breathe better without the awful, claustrophobic face mask. "Right," I say, "but my dad's inside. Let's talk in my car." We climb into the Jeep, and I turn the key, connect my phone, and put the music on low.

"I'm afraid we're gonna get caught," Mo says. "I didn't want to worry you guys, but I did tell my dad I went to the Gap that day. He just hasn't remembered yet."

My stomach clenches. "Okay, just tell him we changed our minds if he does remember."

She shakes her head. "No, I called him from the trailhead to ask him about a warning light that came on in the Corolla. He knows I was there, Han, he's just distracted by all the insurance paperwork right now."

My body stiffens. "Okay, but don't tell the others. Not yet, because things just got worse." Reluctantly, I inform her about the Bud Light, the pipe, and the matchbook. "Where did your brother buy the beer?"

A smile flickers across her face. "He didn't. He had some stored in the garage refrigerator and gave me that."

"You're sure?" She nods and I release a huge breath. "That's good. Wow, that's really good."

Mo gazes through the windshield at the smoky night sky beyond. "Nothing about this is good, Hannah."

"You know what I mean."

Mo releases her hair and twirls the long red strands around her fingers. "I don't think you do know what I mean," she says as her fists clench in her lap. "My mom can't stop crying, Han. She lost all of her paintings and the violin her father gave her. The quilts my grandmother made for us are gone, all our photos and videos, the letters my dad wrote to her when he was in the Navy—everything is gone. She didn't get to save anything."

Mo swallows hard. "The fire came at our house so fast, my mom left without her *shoes*. Dad forgot his medication and had to go to the ER later for insulin." She turns to me, her hazel eyes as hard and cutting as diamonds. "Our street was crammed with cars, and no one would let them out of the driveway. My dad had to put the truck into four-wheel and drive across lawns. He thought the heat and flames would pop his tires. He thought they were going to die, and they had no idea where *I* was."

Tears roll down her colorless cheeks. "My mom is having nightmares, and my dad hardly speaks, and now they're drowning in insurance paperwork. They have to list every single item they lost and give it a dollar value. The adjuster already told my mom that her art—her paintings—have no value at all. She hasn't sold one in ten years, so her art is classified as a hobby. When he wrote a big fat zero next to her lost canvases yesterday, she went into her room and bawled." Mo takes a shuddering breath. "If she knew that we—that I—did this to her . . ." She trails off.

We sit in silence for a long time.

"I want to go back to that day," Mo says. "I want to take that pipe from Luke while we're still at the beach. Stop him from lighting it. Why did we let him smoke, Hannah? One of my neighbors *died*." She turns to me, sobbing.

I try to soothe her. "We didn't know."

"But we knew *better*," she argues. "My dad wants the arsonists punished. Everyone in Gap Mountain wants blood."

Blood. The word makes me shiver. "Look, Mo, why do you think criminals burn evidence—to destroy it, right? The investigators aren't going to pull any fingerprints or DNA off the stuff they found, and even if they get something, it'll most likely be too damaged to match to anyone. As long as we lie low and don't admit to anything, they have to *prove* we did it, and they can't."

Mo gapes at me. "Criminals? God, Hannah, none of what you just said makes me feel better. I have to go." She opens the passenger door, and the interior cabin light pops on.

"Are you okay to drive home?" I ask.

She nods and then shakes her head. "I don't think I'll ever

be okay again." Mo slips into her gold Corolla and disappears down my winding driveway.

I sit alone in my Jeep for a long time. I didn't tell Mo or Drummer the whole truth. I've been doing some research on-line, and approximately 60 percent of DNA can be successfully recovered after exposure to fire, depending on the temperature. The fact that the bottle, pipe, and matchbook survived the flames makes the possibility of successfully lifting DNA and fingerprints rise even higher. But to connect the forensics to an individual or individuals, they'll need suspects or a match in the ALPS database. The only one of us with fingerprints on file is Luke.

I never believed the investigation would circle back to us, but now that we've been lying, we have to keep lying. Now that we've buried the secret, we have to bury it deeper. If there's one thing the law hates more than crime, it's liars. There will be no mercy for us in court. No mercy in the public eye. Whether we get caught or confess, we will be hated and prosecuted. My need to protect the monsters shifts to protecting as many of us as possible, because there is a high probability one of us will be arrested.

Can we trust one another not to sell the others out? I don't know, but I'm afraid we're going to find out.

13

July 21

Gap Fire: 30% contained

Fatalities: 10

Time: 4:30 p.m.

"Your movie is due back on Monday," I tell the customer. I'm at the Reel Deal, and it's hopping with business since no one wants to go outside. The Air Quality Index is 155—not nearly as bad as Beijing, but crappy by our standards.

Meanwhile, the Gap Fire continues to burn through Yosemite. Newscasters call the disaster "epic" and "heartbreaking" as thousands of precious acres go up in flames. The forecast calls for the wind to die down tomorrow, and Cal Fire is hopeful they'll make progress against the blaze. Two more firefighters and a park ranger have been sent to the hospital with burns and smoke-inhalation injuries. The female firefighter hit by the tree passed away from her injuries, bringing the death toll to ten.

When news of the woman's death reached my dad last night, he slammed his fist on our table and cracked the wood. "I can't wait to arrest whoever did this!" he shouted. "The families deserve justice." While he railed, I shriveled into the sofa.

A sudden noise draws me from my thoughts as my co-worker, a tenth-grader named Amanda, bangs on the register display and starts to cry. "This stupid thing keeps freezing."

Hurrying to her side, I help her unfreeze the screen. "It's fine. Just wait a little longer between scanning DVDs. The Wi-Fi is worse than usual."

Amanda's lower lip trembles, and I know her tears have nothing to do with the display screen malfunctioning. Her grandfather burned his hands trying to save his house, and he's still in the hospital. She's worried. "Thanks," she says, and wipes her eyes.

"I'm going to stock the returns, okay?" She nods and I leave the register and head to the shelves with a stack of DVDs.

The Reel Deal looks out onto Pine Street, and as I'm replacing discs in the Romance section, a long caravan of dump trucks roll by. Many are camouflage green and belong to the Army Corps of Engineers, others to private companies. They're here to clean up Stony Ridge.

As the bulky trucks roll down the street, people drift out of the café and the stores and the sheriff's department to watch them. Children wearing N95 face masks wave at the drivers, and they wave back, a macabre parade. Our wildfire has caused tens of millions of dollars in damage already. I glance away.

Toward the end of my shift, my phone pings with a group text from Mo to the monsters: *OMG! A fire investigator and two deputies just left my house. They asked about the photo!*

I'm in the back room, marking my hours, when the text arrives, and I make a strangled squeak and drop the pen in my hand.

"You okay, Hannah?" Mr. Henley, the owner of the Reel Deal, asks.

"Yeah, I'm good. Just college stuff."

He looks perplexed but lets it go. He hires mostly teenagers and has learned to ignore us.

Luke responds to Mo's text: 💀

Drummer says: *at work. off at 5. sys*

I write: *I'm coming over*

And Mo responds: *Don't come here, my parents are home. Can we meet at the attic, V?*

Sure, she answers. *What photo?*

The photo, the photo . . . my thoughts swirl.

Mo: *the one I took at the gap*

Oh, that photo, the one she posted! One of the eighty-two people who "liked" it must have reported her. *Stop texting. Delete thread,* I write.

I rush to the break room and lean against the wall. The investigators are closing in on us. It's time to get serious. We need prepaid phones and quick. My heart rate spikes, and I can't see straight. I mumble a goodbye to Mr. Henley and barrel out of the rental shop to my Jeep. I can't get into it fast enough. I turn on the engine and the AC and breathe into my cupped palms.

Who is in that picture? I remember it in my mind's eye: Mo smiling, a beer to her lips—a Bud Light, no less! Drummer is in the background, diving into the lake, his face slightly blurred but, given modern photographic forensic techniques (and his tattoo), he's easily identifiable. It places Drummer and Mo at the area of origin on July seventh, the day the fire started. Fuck!

I call Drummer from the parking lot, and he answers on the sixth ring. "We are screwed!" I shout.

"Who is screwed? What are you talking about?"

"We are, idiot. Didn't you read Mo's text?" God, how does Drummer function when he pays no attention to details?

"Don't be a dick, Hannah."

I slide on my sunglasses. "Sorry, I'm just freaked out." I would never let the others see me like this. The monsters believe I can keep them safe, but I don't think I can.

"Calm down, Hannah."

"I'm calm!" My tone is shrill.

He clears his throat. "No, you're losing your shit."

"Mo was just *interrogated*."

"Han, if you can't keep your cool, how do you expect to become a cop someday?"

I'm speechless. Good fucking point, Drummer.

He continues. "Seriously, Han, you're . . . easily upset. You should get that fixed."

My body hums with anger. "Now who's being a dick?"

He exhales loudly, like an exasperated parent. Drummer has about as much tolerance for conflict as my colt Sunny. "I can't talk right now, I'm at work. I'll see you at V's later." Then he hangs up on me.

I gnaw the inside of my lip. Drummer is being way too mellow about this. If there was ever a time to worry, it's now. I slam my Jeep into gear and drive to Violet's.

———

Mo and I arrive at the same time, and Lulu Sandoval meets us at the door with flushed cheeks and wide eyes. "Come inside and sit down," she says, yanking us into her parlor. Violet is on the sofa with her arms crossed and refuses to look at us.

What the fuck? I mouth to Mo, who shrugs.

"Where are the boys?" Lulu asks in a clipped tone. "We need to get this fire nonsense straightened out right now."

"They're coming, Ms. Sandoval," I answer.

She directs us to sit. "Then we'll wait." I glare hard at Violet. Did she tell her grandmother what we did?

Finally, Drummer arrives. "Luke can't get away right now," he says in a helpless, angry tone that we know means Luke's mom is on the warpath. When she's in a "state," as Luke calls it, he stays home to keep her calm, protect Aiden, and manage things so no one calls CPS. In the past, the boys have been separated into different foster care homes, and Luke told us that would happen again over "someone's dead body and it won't be fucking mine."

"So, what's up?" Drummer asks as he collapses onto the

couch, dusty from filling lumber orders. His heavily calloused hands rub his dirt-smudged face, and he looks like a man who's worked hard all day, which I guess he has, and I wonder if he'll ever quit the lumberyard or if this is his life now that he's a high school graduate.

"We'll start without Luke," Lulu says. Her tiny body vibrates with anger, and the poodles whine at her feet for reassurance. "This is unacceptable," she growls, gesturing at us.

I share a look of pure terror with Mo, and my scalp tingles as if it's shrinking around my head. I think Grammy knows what we did. I think Violet told on us.

"We're sorry," Mo offers, her voice cracking.

"Sorry?" Lulu yodels. "Don't be sorry, young lady, be angry! Violet told me you got harassed over a photo. A photo!" She wrings her vein-lined hands. "Every kid in town drinks beer and swims at the Gap in the summertime. That's why Violet is *here*, for Pete's sake." Lulu paces the room. "Her friends back home won't swim if there's a bug in the pool. They drink mojitos and get their food delivered! You kids are *real*." She throws up her arms.

Mo and I exchange another glance while Violet cringes. So Grammy brings Violet here to slum with the locals. I never thought of it like that before.

Lulu plows on, oblivious that she's offended us: "Don't allow that sheriff or his cronies—sorry, Hannah—to accuse you kids of *arson*. It's indefensible. I have invested a lot of money in this town!" Her dark eyes roll, her fists shake. "Could one of you accidentally start a fire? I won't deny it, but would you *lie* about it? Never!" She sinks into a checkered chair and deflates like a party balloon.

Outside Lulu's windows, starlings chirp and hunt for seeds, wind chimes jingle, and a screen door rattles. It's a lazy lovely summer day, but we're speechless. Our guilt has rooted us to the floor and sealed our mouths.

Lulu continues: "Drummer, you're next on their list. You all need lawyers. Good lawyers."

"Why me?" Drummer asks.

"You were in that photo too," she answers, and then turns to me. "Did you know your father was after your friends, Hannah?"

The monsters creak their heads in my direction. "No!" I cry. "Absolutely not."

She nods. "I thought so. These investigators are grasping at straws because they're incompetent—sorry, Hannah—and if you three aren't careful, your names will be dragged through the mud before you're exonerated, *if* you're exonerated. I've seen witch hunts before, and they don't end well. You call me or Violet if you need help. Now I need to harvest my green beans." Lulu Sandoval storms out the back door, followed by her dogs.

"Your grandma is badass," Drummer whispers.

"She believes in us," Violet answers with a look of pride and horror.

As we process what just happened, Drummer studies Violet with such tenderness and fascination that I feel suddenly adrift and nauseated. I look away and catch our reflections in

Lulu's picture window: Violet tucked into a small chair, her glossy hair falling over one shoulder, and then me, long limbs spilling everywhere and hair unbrushed. Violet is pretty, but so what? How hard is it to be pretty? I stand. "Come on, guys, let's rescue Luke."

———

We pile into Violet's Grand Cherokee Trackhawk and drive to the Red Cross village where Luke and his mom live in their fire-victim trailer. Unlike Mo's family, Luke's didn't own their home, and they didn't buy renter's insurance, so they literally have nothing left.

As we roll past the neighborhoods, I finger the immaculate interior of Violet's SUV, noticing all the buttons and electronics and the red-trimmed leather seats, and think again about the twists of fate that make some of us rich and some of us poor. "Do you think Violet's friends back home have nice cars like this?" I whisper to Mo in the backseat.

She bites back a laugh. "Her mojito-drinking friends? Probably, or they have chauffeurs."

"Or self-driving cars."

"Or flying cars?" Mo jokes.

Violet's head tilts as if she can hear us, and we shut up.

I wonder about Violet's life back home in Santa Barbara and why she's never invited us to visit. Do we embarrass her? I doubt her regular life involves shopping at Target or eating at Applebee's. I wonder if she tells her friends what hicks we are—that my horses aren't worth more than nine hundred bucks apiece, that the highlight of our summer is the annual rodeo, or that a big night out in this town is paying full price for a movie and then skinny-dipping in the bug-infested Gap?

I can't look at her. I saved for three years to buy my Jeep, and I'll have to sell it to help pay for college. Violet got her car on her sixteenth birthday, and her trust fund will pay for her tuition, books, housing, and everything else she needs or wants. And I hate that I'm suddenly noticing our differences. I dig my nails into my palms to stop thinking about it.

Luke's trailer is at the edge of the dusty Red Cross compound, so we bypass security and roll up alongside the chain-link fence. Drummer texts Luke: *we're here.*

From inside the trailer, we hear shouting: "You are a No. Good. Piece. Of. Shit. Like your father!" Each word is punctuated with a strike and a grunt from Luke.

"Fuck," Drummer says, and his breath comes faster with each muffled blow, and his face engorges with blood. He leaps out of the car and paces.

"Don't go in there," I warn him. "Luke wouldn't want that."

Drummer spits on the ground, Mo wrings her hands, and Violet covers her mouth.

Luke's the strongest of the monsters. He could grab any one of us, twist us into a pretzel, and squeeze the life out of us and we couldn't stop him, but he doesn't fight back when his mother loses her shit. He can't risk CPS taking Aiden, and he won't move out either. He won't leave his brother alone with his mother.

His trailer door bangs open, startling a flock of sparrows

that wing out of the trees, and Luke tumbles down the steps. His mother looms behind him, wielding a broom. Her face is bright red, her hair in disarray. She whacks him like she's trying to kill a rattlesnake. "That's right, run, you little pussy!" she screeches.

Luke scrambles to his feet, climbs over the chain-link perimeter fence, and dives into Violet's car. "Go!" he cries. "Get out of here!" His voice is tight, as if he's being throttled, and tears drip from his eyes. Drummer leaps into the Trackhawk with him, and Violet spins her tires as she speeds onto the main road, leaving behind a cloud of dust.

"Drive to the bridge," says Drummer.

Violet nods and throws back her huge sunglasses, resting them on top of her shiny mane of hair. "That was—Luke, are you all right?"

He puts his arm over his eyes. His body shakes, and we hear sniffles. I don't expect him to speak, but he surprises me and does: "My mom saw the text from Mo about investigators at her house. She said if I had anything to do with that fire, she's going to kick me out."

"God!" Mo wraps her arm around him.

Violet pulls her sunglasses back down with shaking hands. "Guys, maybe we should just come clean and tell the truth."

"Jesus, Violet, did you hear what he just said?" Mo asks. "His mom will kick him out."

Her lips twist into frown. "Yes, I heard, but it's getting out of control. Does anyone else feel that way?"

"You were the first to lie," I remind her.

"Ugh, the turn!" Violet whips the steering wheel to the right and bounces over the suspension bridge that crosses the river. She parks at our usual spot near a path that leads to the water.

We find a shady area on the shore and watch the pebbled river sparkle in the afternoon light. Groups of teens have commandeered spots up and down the shore, and several kids wave at us. They're blasting music, sunbathing, and laughing. Some wear face masks due to the air quality; most don't.

Fat trout swim lazily by as Luke collects himself. I notice a welt forming across his cheekbone, and my stomach clenches at the thought of his mother striking him with the stick end of her broom. I can't help but bring it up again. "Are you okay?"

He shifts his dark eyes away. "Never better."

I take the hint to shut up about it and turn to Mo, who's chewing on a lock of her hair. "What did you tell the investigators?" I ask.

"Nothing! I told them it was an old photo, one taken earlier this summer that I just felt like posting."

I rub my face. "Good, but did they take your phone? If they did, they'll figure out that you're lying."

"Jesus, Han, no. I still have it." She throws a rock into the river. It lands with a splash, and the ripples expand toward us.

"They can't take it without a warrant anyway," Luke says.

I groan. "True, but if my dad or Cal Fire requests a warrant in relation to this fire, they'll get it. Then they'll use Mo's GPS and the geolocator on the photo to pin her at the Gap right when the fire started. You're not going to like this Mo, but you need to lose your phone."

Luke nods. "Han's right, and you should destroy it first. Just in case."

Mo's foot twitches, and her cheeks flame pink. "Wouldn't it look bad if I suddenly lost my phone?"

"It'll look worse if the forensic lab gets ahold of it."

Violet stands and paces in front of us, her sun-darkened skin glowing in the filtered light. After a beat, she whirls around. "How far are we going to take this? Destroying phones? More lies? What's next?"

"Do you want to go to prison?" Luke asks her. "Because I fucking don't."

She rolls her eyes as if he's being ridiculous, and I feel sudden sympathy for her. Lying is hard and Violet is a good person. She's generous, always pays our way when we go out. If there's one bite of dessert left, she offers it to us. When I'm overwhelmed with chores, she pitches in to help, sweating and cracking jokes beside me until the work is done.

Violet is a *happy* person, but this lie is changing her, twisting her into someone she doesn't like—but it's the price she has to pay, that we all have to pay, for what we did. For the people we killed.

I shudder the thought away. "Look, guys"—I pause until they're all facing me, my best friends—"we've already decided to save ourselves. There's no going back now. Without the phone, no one can prove when Mo took that picture or where she was when it posted. And it doesn't matter how things *look*. It matters what they can *prove*. Kids lose their phones all the time. There's no law against it. Drummer, if you took any pics or videos that day, you should delete them from the cloud and lose your phone too."

He shakes his head. "I didn't." He swipes back his hair. "Let's get our stories straight again, all right? I'll die if they put me in a cage."

And this is how we circle back to lying, to covering it up. We do it for Luke, because he's on probation and because his mom will kick him out. We do it for Drummer, because he's too soft for prison. We do it for Mo, because it will destroy her mother. We do it for me, because it will wreck my dad's career. And we do it for Violet, because she lied first.

We spend the rest of the afternoon nailing down our stories and memorizing them.

"What if one of us gets caught?" Mo asks, still spooked by the visit from the deputies and the fire investigator.

"Monsters don't rat on monsters," Luke says.

Violet smiles for the first time today, flashing her dimples. "Is that one of the silly pacts we made as kids? What were the others?" She turns her long-lashed eyes on me, her dark humor flickering. "You made us sign them in blood. God, we were weird."

Drummer nods as if he agrees.

I look away because those two broke the only pact I care

about: *monsters don't date monsters.* I feel a chasm widening between the five of us, and I don't like it, not one fucking bit.

On the walk back to Violet's car, Mo hands me her phone. "Will you destroy it? I don't want to bring it home." I nod and she continues. "Are you okay, Hannah? I mean, besides the fire, is something else going on?"

I unclench my fists and lower my voice. "I think Drummer and Violet are dating."

"Seriously!" Mo slaps her hand over her mouth. "I would not put those two together—Violet and Drummer? Sorry, but we both know he's going nowhere and she's going to Stanford, and she's so . . ."

"Rich?"

Mo sputters. "I was going to say *innocent.* I mean, Drummer has been around." She nods authoritatively. "Besides, monsters don't date monsters."

I smile, happy that Mo remembers at least one of our pacts. Her hazel eyes soften. "Are you jealous, Han?"

My smile vanishes. "What do you think?"

She pulls me into a tight hug. "I think you're beautiful and smart and strong and, no offense to Drummer, but you can do better."

I shrug. Maybe I can, but I don't want better, I want *him,* and I feel my face flush with humiliation. As long as we had the pact, I could pretend Drummer didn't date me because of it, but now that I see how easily he broke it for *her,* I have to face the truth: Drummer doesn't like me that way and probably never will. "Thanks, Mo," I say as we catch up to the others. "You're a good friend."

She cocks her hand like it's a gun and pretends to shoot. "A beer-drinking, lake-swimming friend."

I chuckle. "That's right."

Back at Violet's house, we hug and part ways, and my nerves coil in my stomach. The tension between the monsters is growing. One of us is bound to crack. Then what?

14

I drive straight to Gap Lake after dropping Mo at her house, park at the trailhead, and climb out of my Jeep. The sun has just set, and the night bugs sing, the owls hoot. A bat whooshes over my head. I carry bear spray and a flashlight as I make my way up the trail toward the Gap. The moon is dark silver, and a gentle breeze sways the treetops, as if the canopy is dancing.

It's a mile walk to the clearing that opens to the lake. I tromp noisily, so the bears know I'm here. With my height, I cut an imposing figure in the dark, and thankfully bears don't understand that humans are helpless, that we don't have their three-inch claws and sharp canines. Still, their food supply has burned up, and the bears are starving and more dangerous than usual.

As the trail widens, I reach the meadow preceding the Gap. Normally there might be a few night swimmers here, or couples making out, but the air quality and depressive mood have kept people away.

I pause in front of the lake and inhale, marveling as always at its beauty and danger. The evergreen trees that ring the dark water are flocked with snow in the wintertime and bristling with green needles during summer, beautiful. The lake spans 160 acres and drops more than two thousand feet to a dark, cold bottom. There is no shelf, no gentle slope, just a sheer slide straight down.

It's eerie to know that if you were swimming and the water suddenly vanished, you would fall to your death, or maybe to the other side of the Earth, or maybe into another world, as Violet once told us.

She likes to imagine the lake as a mirrored place where we live opposite lives. I ponder that as I observe my face reflected in the water—a mirror image—my eyes, my skin, and my hair a dusty shade of silver, devoid of color, my figure distorted, shorter, thicker. I'm the opposite of everything I am on land. It's a watery world where there is no breath to speak a lie.

A fish leaps and lands with a splash. There are creatures in this lake—giant trout and catfish and salmon and maybe ancient monsters. It's our very own California version of Loch Ness. People claim they've seen serpent heads break the surface and felt scaled flesh bump their legs under the water. Sam's Market even sells Gap Lake T-shirts that picture a huge whiskered catfish wearing sunglasses. The fish shoots toward an unaware swimmer with its big mouth agape, a whimsical spin-off of the *Jaws* movie poster. Large shapes have been recorded swimming near the surface, but scientists claim the photos and videos are hoaxes.

What I know for sure about the Gap is that it's the perfect place to lose a cell phone forever. I find a flattish stone, lay Mo's phone on it, grab another rock, and smash it to pieces. When it's good and mangled, I hurl it into the lake. *Plop. Plop.* Gone. The Gap swallows the evidence and looks as innocent as ever, its secrets sinking out of sight. I return home feeling a hundred pounds lighter.

I park beside the barn, toss the horses a late dinner, and hear my dad dragging in our bear-proof can. I pocket my keys, skip toward the noise, and call out, "Dad? Want some help?"

But it's not my dad moving the can. It's a bear.

It rears up, as shocked as I am, and chuffs. Our bear-proof garbage can is tipped on its side.

The bear is too close. If I run, it'll catch me. "Easy," I say, putting up my hand, my heart hammering. The bear drops to all fours, and its long, yellow claws scrape the gravel drive.

"Easy," I repeat, holding my ground. My eyes shift to the house. Why isn't Matilda barking? I bite my lip. I left my bear spray in the car, and I don't have my rifle or my air horn. Stupid!

From his paddock, Pistol whinnies, and the bear pivots. Sunny and Stella canter nervously around their paddocks, and the bear glances from the horses to me, agitated. It swings its neck and sniffs the air.

Sweat drips down my face as I take a slow step backward.

Just then my dad drives up and slams to a halt. He honks the horn; turns his headlights on bright. The bear snarls and bumps into the garbage can, which clatters loudly.

My dad leaps out of his cruiser and fires two shots over the bear's head.

It rears and then bounces down to all fours, stamping the earth, confused by the noise and the rolling can. Its lips curl back in a roar.

Matilda hears the gunshots and blasts out the open screen door. When she sees the bear, she breaks into furious barking and charges. My dad glides past the animals, grabs me as if I weigh nothing, and rushes me into the house.

He sets me on the floor, and I race to the kitchen window, cupping my hands on the glass to see outside. "Matilda!" I scream.

"She'll be fine," Dad says, breathing hard through his nose.

Outside, Matilda lunges and barks at the bear, her tail high and wagging. She looks five years old instead of twelve. Sunny rears and bucks in his paddock, exciting the other horses. The bear makes some tentative swipes at my dog, then whirls around and gallops away.

Matilda prances back to us with her head high and her eyes bright. "Good girl!" Dad says, and we both hug her. Then he looks at me and grimaces. "You have to be more careful, Hannah."

"I know, I'm sorry. Matilda didn't bark, so I thought it was you moving the can."

"She's going deaf, Bug." He feeds Matilda slices of cheese,

her favorite treat. "I think it's time to get a new pup. She's getting too old for this."

My dad is right: we need a younger dog. They have always been our first alarms when a bear is on the property, but this one got past Matilda's floppy, failing ears.

My dad reaches for a beer, and before I can say a word, he asks if I heard about Mo's photo. My body tenses and I try to hide it by petting Matilda. "Yeah, I heard."

He clears his throat, waiting for me to look at him. Then he says, "You need to tell me right now if you know *anything* about who started the Gap Fire."

I hold his gaze as my mind spins.

"Hannah," he prods, "you can't protect your friends from this. If they did it, we will find out."

This is my absolute last chance to come clean, and I feel as if I'm standing between two eternities: one where my soul is redeemed and one where it is condemned to hell. Confessing is the right thing to do. It has to be! In every movie and every book, the good guys tell the truth.

But besides disappointing my dad and possibly destroying his career, it will ruin mine too. My past flashes before my eyes—taking all the right courses in high school, studying late into the night, taking final exams, attending exam prep sessions, taking the SAT three times, hours of AP testing, college applications, referral letters, running varsity track for four years, and then getting those acceptance letters to schools (not Stanford, though) and leaping for joy and kissing Pistol on his big lips because he was the only creature near me at the time—and I think, *fuck it*, I'll worry about my soul later.

"I promise, Dad, I don't know who started it, but I know it couldn't have been my friends. Mo took that photo weeks ago." I add a dismissive laugh, as though he's wasting his time.

My dad rolls his cold beer across his forehead, and his flint-blue eyes squint at me, thoughts churning, then he lets out his breath. "Did you buy the new trailer tires yet?"

"No, but I will."

"Hannah Louise," he rasps, "I hope you're more responsible in college."

"Dad, I'm sorry."

"Don't be sorry, just handle your business." He takes his beer to his room to change.

———

In the morning, I wake to the smell of coffee brewing and bacon sizzling. Dad's been cooking more since the cleaning crew transformed our house into a tidy home. It's kind of shocking we never realized how dirty it was before it became layered in ash. I pull on a pair of cutoffs and approach the kitchen, yawning. Dad is at the stove, scrambling eggs and tending the bacon in the pan.

I was up all night watching Drummer and Violet on our location-sharing app. His avatar showed him at her house, right next to Violet's avatar, until 4:00 a.m., asshole. I hold on to the only hope I have: that he'll get bored with her. New girls always excite him for a few weeks, but then he starts coming back to my house to watch TV, eat my cereal, and hang out. Sometimes he uses me to hurt his girlfriends, snapping pictures of us in his hot tub and adding them to his online story, sending a clear message to whomever he's dating: *You don't own me, you can't control me, you can't put me in a cage.*

But I let Drummer be Drummer. I keep the door open and food in the cupboard, and like a friendly tomcat, he keeps coming back. Violet won't change that.

Now it's 7:15 a.m., and I feel about as lively as roadkill.

"I hope you're hungry," Dad says.

"Starving," I admit. He hands me a steaming cup of coffee, and I load it with cream and sugar until the color is blond and it tastes like dessert.

"Here's my credit card for the tires." He flips the bacon. "I'm going to miss you when you go to college, Bug. I couldn't be prouder, you know that, right?"

He's trying to make up for snapping at me about the tires last night, but I deserved it. I deserve worse, actually. What I don't deserve is his pride, not anymore. I slink up to him and circle my arms around his waist, keeping a wary eye on the grease-popping bacon. "I'll be home every holiday."

He sighs, offers a smile. "You say that now."

"I will. I've got to check on Matilda and the horses at least."

"But not me?"

For a sheriff, my dad plays the victim well. "Yes, you too, if you promise to make me breakfast every day." I nudge him playfully.

"Every day?" He nudges me back. "I'll think about it."

After breakfast, he heads to the station without a word about what he's got planned today regarding the investigation. That's okay—I have my own plans. Today I'm buying the monsters a set of untraceable prepaid phones.

I slouch off to my bedroom, kick dirty clothes out of my way, and grab the new shampoo I bought after the house cleaners threw away all the open containers. Dad got a decent-sized check from the insurance company to replace our smoke-damaged stuff, and what we didn't spend went straight into my college fund.

I start the shower and step into the spray. It's almost eighty degrees outside already and getting hotter. The winds have settled here but continue to whip the Gap Fire into an inferno at the national park. Animal rescuers have darted dozens of confused and starving wild animals and relocated them. One of the stories I read last night described an entire herd of bighorn sheep becoming trapped on a ridge. They perished of smoke inhalation before the fire reached them. A wildlife photographer with a telephoto lens took photos of the cremated sheep that made national news.

I drop my face into my hands and breathe as the water runs down the back of my neck. I adjust the knob, making it hotter and hotter until my skin is red and scalded and steam fills the bathroom. My shoulders quake, and a few tears leak from my eyes. "No!" I slap myself. "Stop it!"

I pour too much shampoo into my hand and wash my hair, condition it, then rinse the soap off my body. The bathroom fills with steam as I step out of the shower and wipe the mirror.

My face is beet red. Good people do bad things, right? I'm not unique.

After my shower, I throw on fresh cutoffs and a tank top and keep busy, cleaning up the chipped blue breakfast dishes, starting the dishwasher, feeding the horses, and shoveling manure. When my chores are done, I snap a photo of the sizing information on my flat trailer tires and then drive to Bishop with the soft top removed. Matilda sits in the passenger seat, her big red ears flying behind her, and I blast the tunes.

The road unravels ahead of us, a series of forested bends as I coast down the mountain, heading south toward Bishop. It's a beautiful stretch, normally: noble pines line the road, and ancient sequoias reach for the clouds. The first glimpse of the Mono County valley stretches ahead, and pine cones tumble in our wake. Green trees, blue skies, and mountain air—this landscape used to settle me, but not anymore.

Thousands of acres along this road burned that first day, and the pink-dyed fire retardant is still caked on the shoulders. Matilda whines at the scent of it. Maybe she remembers she almost died here.

I turn up the music and drive faster.

My errand in Bishop doesn't take long, and soon I have two new tires loaded in the backseat of my Jeep.

Next, I throw on a baseball cap and sunglasses and stop at the Rite Aid. I've brought cash, and I use it to buy five prepaid cell phones. The hit to my savings hurts, but if these phones keep the monsters out of jail, they're worth it. Back in my car, I take off the sunglasses, put them on Matilda, and snap a photo of her. "You're a star, Mattie."

She swipes the glasses off with her paw and shakes her head. Across the street is the Holiday Inn where I evacuated, and I think about Justin, the guy who gave Matilda and me a ride—he lives in Bishop. He asked me out, and I sort of brushed him off because of his age, but it's daylight and I have my dog—I'm safe.

Before I can talk myself out of it, I text him: *Hi, it's Hannah. I'm in Bishop.* The phone is quiet and Matilda yawns, showing all her teeth. I swallow, feeling suddenly stupid and young—he probably forgot about me. I start my car to go home.

Ping! A text from Justin: *shit im on the road for work. How long you here?*

Not long. I have to work at 4.

Damn. I'm off at 5. i want to see you Hannah.

I have no idea how to respond to that.

You live in gap mountain right? I could pick you up for dinner

My pulse flutters. A date at *night*—that's not what I had in mind. I thought maybe lunch or a walk with Matilda. How do I get out of this? *I have plans tonight,* I lie.

Tomorrow then?

Shit. I need to unwind this. *Can I get back to you?*

A pause and then he writes, *k.* That's it, just *k.* I feel his disappointment in that single letter and drop my phone onto the passenger seat. I glance at Matilda, who's panting. "Want to go home?"

She barks. I take that as a yes, and we drive home. Matilda sits tall in the front passenger seat, tongue lolling, eyes squinted against the wind. My skin soaks up the sun, and hope flows through me. We have secret phones, Mo explained the photo to the investigators, her phone is destroyed—we're going to be fine. We just have to stick together and keep our mouths shut.

The weak link is Violet. She can afford a lawyer, and she doesn't have to live here full-time. She can go home. Confessing wouldn't destroy her life as it would ours. I need to calm her and get her reconnected to Gap Mountain before she does something we'll all regret. I snap my fingers. That's it! Suddenly, I know what to do. It's our last summer before college. It's time the monsters had a little fun!

15

July 23

Gap Fire: 40% contained

Fatalities: 10

Time: 2:00 p.m.

When I got home from Bishop yesterday, I delivered the pre-paid phones to the monsters and invited Mo and Violet on a trail ride. "Girls only," I said, because lately I don't enjoy Violet's company if Drummer is within a hundred feet of us.

No one questioned the phones except Violet: "Burner phones? This feels criminal." I had no friendly response for that, so I said nothing. "I'm not using it," Violet said.

"Just keep it on you. We won't use them unless we have to talk about the fire."

She accepted it with a ferocious swipe of her hand and threw it into her purse.

—

Now it's 2:00 p.m. the next day, and my friends are pulling into my driveway. I drop the textbook I'm reading, slide on my boots, and run outside. "Stay," I command Matilda at the screen door. She cocks her head and whines at me.

There hasn't been another press conference about the fire investigation yet as the detectives pursue their leads and wait for crime lab results. Luke's pipe worries me the most, because his fingerprints are on file, but it's possible the heat destroyed them. The beer bottle worries me less, because it might not be ours. Most kids in Gap Mountain drink Bud Light.

Violet and Mo arrive in separate cars, dressed to ride. Violet jumps out of her Trackhawk, beaming, her dimples dark and deep. "Hannah!" she hugs me tight, as if we haven't started a wildfire and murdered ten people together. I squeeze her back. Yes, this is what we need, some normalcy.

Mo pops out of her Corolla, equally happy and relaxed. She's stopped wearing her N95 mask outside, and her cheeks are flushed with healthy color. She and Violet glance at the paddocks, and their smiles deepen. It's the horses, I realize. Riding is the best therapy, and we three desperately need therapy.

After I greet Mo, we enter the barn, chattering about college. Mo received her roommate assignment and connected with the girl already. "She seems nice," Mo says.

I got my roommate's name right before the fire and have totally forgotten about her since. Violet won't have a roommate. She put a deposit on an off-campus private apartment near Stanford. "I don't sleep well with others," she explains.

You sleep just fine with Drummer, I think, but don't say it out loud. Today is for equines, not boys. "Violet, you ride Pistol, I'll ride Sunny, and Mo, you can ride Stella."

We tack up the horses, fill our saddlebags with the sandwiches Mo brought, and mount up. "Hold the reins with one hand," I remind Violet, since she's used to riding English style.

"I know," she mutters as she fusses with Stella's mane, which is full of burrs.

God, I should have brushed the horses better. Violet's are always immaculate. "I'll go first," I say. "Sunny needs to practice leading."

As we walk onto the trail from my house, Sunny is on high alert. If a bear eats us, it'll be his fault and he knows it. He lifts his tail high and blows hard out of his nostrils, warning all bears to stay away.

Violet giggles as she watches my colt spook at every shadow. "He's such a scaredy-cat."

I shrug. "He's just young." Eventually, Sunny stops prancing because he gets tired fast, like a toddler.

"This is so great," Violet says, and I glance back to see her blissful expression. "I miss riding. We should be doing this every day—riding, swimming, watching movies, being lazy."

Mo and I agree with her. Starting the fire and driving everyone indoors because of bad air quality has ruined our summer plans.

"Where are we going, Han?" Mo asks.

"The Blue Ridge trail is nice, and it didn't burn in the fire. There's a creek where the horses can drink and a view for miles from the top."

We meander through the forest trails, and the horses relax in direct relation to the heat: the hotter it gets, the quieter they are. I inhale the scent of dry tree mulch and pine sap and feel myself unwind.

"Hey, guess who sings this?" Violet warbles a few verses of a song I've never heard before.

"I don't know. Who?" asks Mo.

"Billie Eilish. It's good, isn't it? Kind of goes with these big old trees." She gestures toward the spiraling evergreens.

We morph into more chat about college—what to bring to the dorms, what classes to take, how long we think it'll take us to graduate. We pretend that the Gap Fire never happened.

Halfway to the ridge, a pine cone falls off a tree and shatters on the ground, sounding like a small explosion. Stella rears and bolts.

Mo leans forward and grabs the horn, screaming as her horse gallops past us, but that's Stella's cue to run faster.

"Sit up!" I cry.

"I want off!" she yells back.

"Turn her in a circle," Violet calls.

Mo either can't hear or she's too panicked to listen, so I put my fingers to my mouth and whistle, like I do when I grain the horses, and it works. Stella loves grain, and she changes course and gallops to Sunny's side and skids to a halt, nickering for food.

Mo slides out of the saddle, her legs trembling violently. "Oh my god," she whispers, dropping to her knees. "I can't breathe."

"Her inhaler!" Violet shouts.

I jump off Sunny's back, dig through Stella's saddlebags, find the inhaler, and give it to Mo. She sucks on it, and slowly her breathing returns to normal. "This is why I don't ride horses," she wheezes.

Violet cocks her head. "Because you have asthma?"

"No, because they're stupid! How can something so big be afraid of a pine cone?"

Violet and I fall over laughing. Mo is fine.

Since this is not a scenic place to rest, I gather the horses' reins and hand Stella's to Mo. She crosses her arms. "I'm not getting back on."

"It's my fault," I say. "I haven't exercised the horses enough since the fire, too smoky. We can walk to the creek if you want, it's not far." So we all walk our horses to the creek, and Violet sulks because she still wants to ride. When we arrive, the horses lick the wet rocks because the creek itself is almost dry and Mo passes out the food.

"We *would* starve without you," I say as I accept my sandwich, a thick French roll stuffed with turkey, Havarti cheese, lettuce, tomato, and avocado.

"I know it." Mo offers a small, forgiving smile, and we each choose a flat rock and sit down to eat. Enormous pine trees shade us, and ferns grow at their bases and along the creek bed. There's some haze in the sky from the fire, but most of the smoke has blown into the Central Valley and beyond.

Mo swigs water from her bottle and wipes her lips. "We should see if there's an Amtrak train that runs between our colleges, so we can visit."

"We could just Uber," Violet says. It gets quiet, because Mo and I can't afford to Uber across this vast state. Violet has the decency to say no more about it. Instead she says brightly, "I brought art pens!"

We spend the next two hours doodling in Violet's sketchbook. We draw unicorns and rainbows and dragons, and then Mo draws a huge penis on Violet's page. Violet draws a marijuana leaf on Mo's, and then they both draw Krispy Kreme doughnuts on mine. I have no idea why I got doughnuts, but we laugh until our stomachs hurt.

Then Violet starts doing impressions of her favorite actors, and they are hilarious. She can reshape her face and change her voice and personality to match just about anybody. She sings well too, on key and without music. I forget how talented Violet is, because when I see her, she's on vacation and her biggest concern is the color of her toenail polish. "You're funny," I tell her.

She lifts her brows. "A compliment from Han! I'm flattered." She kisses me on the cheek, and I'm stunned. Do I not give compliments? I hadn't noticed.

"Have you ever thought about coloring your hair?" Mo asks me. "Like adding a few highlights to bring out the blond?"

Violet claps her hands, her dimples deepening. "Yes, and you should let me do your makeup!" She leans forward, examining my face, which gives me a close-up view of hers. Violet's makeup is flawlessly applied, and her hair is clean and styled, shining to the roots. I don't know how she stays so perfect seemingly without an ounce of effort. I blow-dry and style my hair for school pictures and funerals and not much else—too much work!

Violet sucks in her cheeks and tilts my chin toward her. "You aren't doing anything with what you've got, Han. Your bone structure is perfect; your eyes are huge. A few highlights in your hair, a new cut, some contouring and gloss, and mascara to bring out the green in your eyes, and you'd be really pretty."

My cheeks burn. "Would be?"

Mo butts in. "She means you're already pretty."

"Yes, but you're not trying." Violet lifts a strand of my thin, flat hair.

I bat her away, thinking about Justin in Bishop. He seems to like me the way I am. "I'm good, thanks."

After that, the conversation becomes awkward, so I give the order to move out, and we walk the horses to the top of Blue Ridge, which feels ass-backward to me, like pushing a bicycle instead of riding it. At the top, we catch our breath and take in the view that overlooks all of Gap Mountain, the valley, and Yosemite National Park.

"There it is," Violet says, and we go silent.

Our wildfire continues to burn, miles and miles away. Gray smoke rises in the distance, and the hint of orange flames flicker in the park. My eyes trace the blackened path of destruction from Gap Lake, through our town, across the narrow waist of the valley, and into Yosemite. Millions upon millions of dollars have been lost, ten human lives are gone, thousands of protected acres have been incinerated, dozens of homes are destroyed, and one flock of wild bighorn sheep has been brutally cremated. The destruction quells any joy I felt today.

"That was my house," Mo says, pointing toward the flattened Stony Ridge neighborhood, which appears as a scorched and desolate scab of land on the south side of town. The Army Corps and private contractors are hard at word, scraping foundations and piling tons of debris into long lines of dump trucks.

We're silent for fifteen minutes, maybe longer. We can't speak about what we did; we can only stare.

Suddenly, all three of our prepaid phones buzz at once, because we have a good signal up here, out of the tree line. Violet reads the text first and gasps. Then Mo reads it, and she slaps her hand over her mouth. With dread oozing through my veins, I read it last.

It's from Drummer: *the police arrested luke.*

16

I stare at my phone in disbelief. Why are the police at Luke's? He wasn't in the photo that investigators questioned Mo about. Is this about the fire or his probation? God, it has to be the fire. The fingerprint results must have come in and the police database matched them to Luke.

Next to me, Violet texts Drummer on the prepaid phone she swore she'd never use: *omg!*

Drummer adds, *they have warrants for his dna and phone. they found TWO separate dna profiles on the beer bottle. the fingerprints on the matchbook are lukes.*

Me: *what about the pipe?*

Drummer: *I don't know*

Mo: *let's meet later*

145

We pocket our phones, and Mo's hands tremble. "One of those DNA profiles could be mine."

"Or mine. I drank too," says Violet. She looks at me, her eyes like two pools of dark liquid. "You said the fire would destroy the DNA."

"It should have." I feel suddenly sick and clutch my stomach. "I'm sorry—I didn't think the lab would get anything."

"This is so messed up," says Mo, her eyes glittering with tears. "It's so unfair to Luke."

Violet leans against Pistol. "He's the one who brought the weed."

Mo frowns at her. "Hey, I saw you sucking on that pipe too, Violet."

"I just meant—"

"I know what you meant, and it's not cool. I agree with Hannah, telling on ourselves is stupid, but we all deserve what Luke is getting—*all of us*. Don't you fucking forget that."

Violet, who can't take a scolding any better than her grammy's poodles, turns her sad eyes on us. "I'm sorry. You're right."

Anxiety chews at my nerves, and I just want to go home. "Will you ride the horse back, Mo?"

"Sure." She mounts Stella with new confidence. I guess in light of Luke's troubles, my golden mare isn't so scary. Violet boards Pistol, looking absolutely miserable.

As I ride Sunny home, my heart thundering, the truth hovers over me like a toxic cloud: *this isn't over*. I could still end up in prison this fall instead of college.

Mo drives off as soon as we reach my house, and Violet stays to help me put the horses away. As we're hanging the bridles in the tack room, I feel her arms wrap around my waist. "I'm so scared, Han."

I hug her back. "I know. So am I."

"We didn't mean to do it," she says, and her warm tears wet my shirt. "None of us would ever hurt anyone. This has been awful. I can't sleep. I feel like a horrible person."

I have all the same feelings but the opposite reaction. I want to *survive* this while Violet wants to *pay* for it. "You can't make it right," I tell her. "Don't let this ruin your life."

"It already has," she whispers.

"No, V, don't say that. You're going to Stanford and getting your degree in biochemistry, and you're going to cure cancer."

She snorts.

"It's true. You're going to do amazing things, and you're going to fall in love and explore the world and ride horses and have kids. Don't throw that away."

I smooth back her dark hair. She's so small and warm and expensively fragrant, even after riding the horse. She hugs me tighter, and my stomach lurches. Drummer gets this girl, this sweet, smart beautiful girl, every night, and I can't blame him for loving her, because the thing is—I love her too.

"I really think we should tell before this gets worse," Violet says.

I watch her, confused by her need to confess when she has no problem hiding her relationship with Drummer. Violet's not a secretive person, which means it must be his idea not to tell anyone. Is it because of me? Does he think I can't handle the truth? I rub my eyes as Violet finishes her thought. "We'd feel better about ourselves if we confessed."

I shake my head. "Do you honestly think you'll feel better about yourself in *prison*, V?" I force a smile. "No flat irons, no nail polish, no cute boys?"

She lifts one shoulder. "I'm tougher than I look, Han."

Our gazes lock and hers is unflinching. I see iron pride and her grandmother's mountain grit. Violet's tough, I get it, but what she doesn't understand is that she doesn't have to be. In prison, she'll grow hard and bitter and untrusting. I mean, I'm all for criminals going to jail—but we're not criminals. We're just idiots.

"No mojitos," I add, and Violet blinks at me, looking more hurt than amused.

When we're finished, she slips into her Trackhawk and pops on her sunglasses. "This isn't your decision alone, Hannah. I can do what I want." Then she drives away.

I watch her go, my fists clenched. It occurs to me again that Gap Mountain isn't Violet's home. She's an outsider, and if the others find out how close she is to talking, I'm not sure what they'll do.

—

Later that evening, while I'm watching TV, Matilda leaps onto the sofa and licks my face. None of the monsters could get together tonight to talk about Luke, and honestly, there's not much to say. He's caught in the investigators' net. Now we just wait.

Matilda pants in my face, and her bad breath is comforting, familiar and safe. I drape my arms over her warm, furred body, and she flops on top of me with a happy grunt. As the sun sets, soft golden light stripes the room, spotlighting particles of dust as they dance in the air. My dad's old clock ticks on the wall in the kitchen. Our cabin creaks and breathes with the mountain, feeling peaceful and safe. It's hard to believe that our worlds are exploding silently, like old stars.

I'm mulling this over when my dad enters the house and spots Matilda and me lounging in the family room. Halting, he stares, as if he's not sure how to approach me.

"Hi, Dad," I say casually.

His anger flares. "Don't pretend you don't know what happened today." He nods at my phone. "You kids triangulate information faster than the CIA. I served search warrants on your friend Luke."

"I heard you arrested him?"

"Not yet. I questioned him, took his phone and DNA, and let him go." We watch each other like two poker players. I wonder what cards he's holding, and he wonders the same about me.

Dad breaks first. "I've asked this before and I'll ask it one more time: Do you know anything about the fire you haven't told me?" He shifts his belt. "This is off the record, for now. Tell me everything and maybe I can help whoever else is involved. I don't want to put your friends in prison, Hannah, but the evidence against Luke is growing, and there's not much I can do for him now."

"Is the case against him that strong?"

My dad flexes from foot to foot; his belt squeaks and his firearm glints in the evening sunset. He needs to shave, and he looks haggard. "His prints match those on the matchbook. Through his cell, we should be able to trace his movements. If we can prove beyond a reasonable doubt that he was at Gap Lake on July seventh around three p.m., then I'll arrest him and charge him with arson."

Holy shit. "Dad, it's *Luke.* You can't do that to him."

His cheeks puff and then deflate in a long, slow breath. "Ten people are dead, Bug. One casualty was a firefighter with a husband and two young daughters. Dozens of homes are destroyed, businesses lost, vacations canceled, and national parklands burned to ash. You know what that means?"

I sigh. "Felony charges."

"That's right." He reaches down to pet Matilda. "The law is the law, Hannah."

Yes, I've heard that before, but what my dad doesn't know is that Luke keeps his geolocator turned off. Forensic scientists won't be able to track him through his phone, and the matchbook could have been dropped on any summer day. It's good news for Luke.

My dad studies me, his expression guarded. "We found a second set of DNA and fingerprints on the beer bottle that don't match his. We're looking for another suspect." He rubs his eyes, appearing old and tired. "I think you know more than you're saying, Hannah, and I think you're involved. Is that second set going to belong to you or one of your other friends?"

I throw up my hands. "You know I don't like drinking, Dad, and you know *why.*"

His face crumbles. It's a cheap shot, bringing up Mom. It's not his fault she got drunk and killed someone, but it feels good to be honest about something. His body slumps, but his tone is edged in steel. "You're keeping something from me, Bug. I feel it."

Coldness washes over me even as my heart rate ratchets higher. To calm myself, I imagine the Gap, glittering and fathomless, a magical place that swallows secrets.

My heart rate settles, my breathing becomes flat and even, and I speak as directly and naturally as possible. "I'm just scared, Dad. We're all freaking out about Luke. I didn't see him that day until later, so I mean, it's possible he started the fire, but I don't believe it. We swim at the Gap all the time, and you know my friends drink, and you know Luke smokes pot. He's not old enough to buy a lighter, so he grabs matches from Sam's practically every day. He could have dropped that matchbook any time this summer."

"Did you rehearse that speech, Hannah?"

I decide to stop talking. Lying to strangers is easy, but lying to people you know, especially trained investigators like my dad—not so easy. I scroll through the Netflix shows to hide my expression.

He trudges off to the kitchen, annoyed. "Did you get the damn tires?"

My answer bursts from my mouth. "Yes, I got the damn tires!"

Dad reappears and points at me, his voice tight. "Go to your room."

My mouth falls open. I'm eighteen fucking years old.

"Did you hear me?" His voice is so calm it's scary.

My heart flutters. "I heard you."

"If you're involved, Hannah, you better tell me. We're getting more forensic results soon."

God, I want to tell my dad *everything*, throw the burden of what we did onto him, but he can't protect me *and* do his job. He will have to choose, and I know my dad—he'll choose his job. He'll arrest and process me, just as he did to my mom twelve years ago, and I can't put him through that again. I would lose the little bit of father I have left. "If I was involved, I'd tell you."

Another lie.

17

Four days later, I finish my shift at the Reel Deal and step outside, shielding my eyes from the bright sun that I haven't seen much of since July seventh. The wind has finally cleared away the last of the smoke. Some residents still wear N95 masks, but most of us have ditched them. The Gap Fire continues to burn miles away, but Gap Mountain proper is safe, and life is shifting into a new normal.

Dump trucks continue their steady parade as they clear debris from Stony Ridge. The dead have been buried, the insurance claims filed, and the lost possessions and vehicles replaced with new ones. Every business that wasn't damaged has reopened, and the citizens are no longer walking around with shell-shocked expressions and tearful eyes. We are rebuilding. We are strong, but we are exhausted.

Luke was questioned, searched, and released. Now we wait while they dig into his cell phone history and the CCTV footage. We're also waiting on results of the second set of DNA and his fingerprints. If the prints don't match anyone in the ALPS system, then Cal Fire or the sheriff's department will have grounds to subpoena Mo. She remains a "person of interest" due to posting and deleting the lake photo on July seventh.

The first blurb about the recent developments appears on the television's ticker, running below the main news stories: TWO LOCAL TEENAGERS ARE SUSPECTED OF IGNITING THE GAP FIRE, WHICH KILLED TEN AND DESTROYED DOZENS OF HOMES. So far, Mo and Luke's names are being withheld from the media, but everyone in Gap Mountain knows they've been questioned. Reporters arrive, smelling a story.

Luke's in hiding and we're worried about him. He texts us via his prepaid phone, but he won't come out of his Red Cross trailer. Drummer's driven by twice and hasn't seen Luke's little brother either. The curtains are drawn day and night, and as the heat wave continues, we imagine Luke and Aiden being baked alive inside their aluminum house.

My stomach rumbles and I don't bother to use the crosswalk but jaywalk instead to the Wildflower Café across the street. The head server, Jeannie, frowns at the sight of me. It's a small town and everyone knows I'm best friends with Luke and Mo, and since Luke is the kid with the criminal record, he's everyone's favorite suspect: *That boy is violent. He's on meth. He started the fire on purpose.* Mostly lies.

I grab a seat at the counter, and a boy from school takes my order. "Hey, Hannah, what'll you have?"

"Hi, Omar. Can I get a tuna melt with fries and a root beer?"

He writes that down and then lowers his voice: "How's Luke?"

"Okay, I guess. I haven't seen him. Have you?"

He clucks out of the side of his mouth. "Dude, I've barely seen my boy this summer. We hung at the river a couple times in June but nothing since that stupid-ass fire tore through."

I change the subject. "Which college are you going to?"

Omar grins. "Fresno State, computer science."

I smile back. "That's cool. Mo's going there for nursing."

"No shit? She'll be running that place before she's done."

Jeannie gives Omar "the eye" for talking too loud. He lowers his voice: "I don't believe Luke did it. That guy can't get a break. I mean, his own house burned down."

"And his cat is missing," I add.

"Is your dad going to arrest him?" My expression sours and Omar backs off. "Forget it, you probably can't talk about it. Let me get this order in." He bustles away, pretending disinterest, but the entire town is waiting to see what my dad is going to do with Luke. I'm waiting too.

Morale is at an all-time low in Gap Mountain. The annual tricounty rodeo and 4-H fair was canceled due to the air quality. I wasn't barrel racing or selling animals this year, but I know how disappointed other kids must be. Losing the rodeo and fair is a huge blow after working hard all spring and summer raising and training animals.

When Omar brings my food, I scarf it down and then get out of the café as quick as I can. The townsfolk are on edge, they want answers, and there's nowhere to hide, but I don't want to go home, and I don't want to see the monsters (except Drummer), or my barrel-racing friends, whom I usually only see at competitions or trainings anyway. I don't feel like riding or doing chores. I just want this over. They say it's impossible to commit a perfect crime; well, it's more impossible to cover up an unplanned one.

Inside my car now, I text Drummer: *want to hang out?*

Working, he texts back.

I wonder if *working* is code for *screwing Violet* or if he's actually at the lumberyard? In a moment of self-flagellation, I open the location-sharing app to see where Drummer is, and my stomach floats, as if I'm waiting for AP test results. Immediately, I see his and Violet's avatars at their separate homes, and relief floods me.

But it's a trick.

The app simply hasn't refreshed yet. As soon as it does, his avatar travels at lightning speed to her house, and I see them standing together on the two-dimensional outline of Lulu's house, in the attic.

Liar!

My foot taps the floor, and my heart thumps in time to it.

It's summer and it's hot and my dad is hunting my friends, and my best friend is lying to me. I text Mo: *what are you doing?*

Mo: *house hunting with my parents. They decided not to rebuild.*

Me: *can you talk?*

She's slow to respond: *I'm busy, Han. I'll call as soon as I can.*

I stare out the window of my Jeep, sweltering in this parking lot, wondering who else I can hang out with. My thoughts reach like tentacles—Violet? Nope, she's screwing the love of my life. Luke? No, he has his own problems. My dad? Hell no! Drummer? Fuck him.

I'm alone—as I have been most of my life—and I'm trying to keep my friends safe, but no one cares. They're all busy. I need—I want—someone to promise *me* I'll be all right. I want someone to take care of Hannah. Someone to tell me I'm beautiful, lovable, and perfect just the way I am.

Tears flow down my cheeks, and I slam my fist into the steering wheel. Is this what mothers are for—for when you have no one else? I laugh bitterly. I don't even have a mother.

I know one thing: I can't be alone.

Then an idea hits me: Justin from Bishop—*he* likes me. He wants to see me. Fuck the monsters. I have other options.

I wait until my pulse slows, and then I text him: *Hi, it's Hannah. I'm free tonight if you still want to hang out. lmk*

Little dots appear on my screen. He's reading my text *right now*, and my pulse speeds. I instantly regret writing it. What if he says no?

Then he texts back: *tonite is good*

I stare at my phone in disbelief. *Ok. Where?*

Justin: *Want to see a movie? We could meet at the Pine Street Theater. Should we get dinner first?*

Is this a date, a real date? It feels like one, but I can't imagine keeping up a conversation through an entire dinner with someone I don't know. *Just a movie is fine*, I text.

Justin: *it's a date*

Me: *ok*

Holy fuck—I'm going on a date with a man.

I drive home, my mind spinning. What if Justin and I fall in love? What if he wants to be my boyfriend? Maybe he'll move to San Diego with me and we'll live together while I go to school.

I enter the house and blindly trip over a chair, laughing at myself. I don't even know Justin. He could own a house, a business; he could have a cat, or a kid! I didn't ask his last name. My dad will kill me if he finds out what I'm doing.

I imagine telling Drummer and Violet I have a date and decide to go all out. I'm going to curl my hair, put on makeup, and wear my shortest, tightest skirt. Maybe Justin is a leg guy? I have legs for days. I might even post a picture of us so everybody can see.

Justin likes me, I'm sure of it. I twirl into the shower.

18

July 27

Gap Fire: 55% contained

Fatalities: 10

Time: 7:30 p.m.

I'm standing outside the Pine Street Theater, and my emotions have shot back to earth. Justin is not going to show up. Why would he? I'm just a kid straight out of high school. I've never had a real boyfriend or a real job. What are we going to talk about if he does show? I'm an adult, technically, but I don't feel like one. I lean against the brick wall and try to appear casual.

Justin strolls up a few minutes later. He looks different than he did on the highway. He's freshly shaved and he's wearing a broken-in denim jacket, a baby blue T-shirt, jeans, and cowboy boots. "Hey," he says, his eyes sweeping down my body. He's cuter than I remember.

"Hey." I feel my skin flush from my neck up.

He kisses my cheek, and the clean scent of shampoo and aftershave fills my nostrils. His lips are soft and warm. "You look beautiful. Come on, let's go inside." He takes my hand and leads me to the ticket booth.

My heart skitters and heat floods my groin. I've had two boyfriends—one in ninth grade, but he was so shy he rarely touched me—and one in tenth grade, a boy I dated to make Drummer jealous. His name was Marcus Hoover. He was mean and always had food stuck in his braces, and he dumped me when I made a face about kissing him. But this—this feels different.

Justin buys two tickets and then asks what I want from the snack bar. He pays for everything without waiting to see if I'll offer to split it. When I order a small bag of popcorn, he asks if I want a larger size and candy too. I stick with the small but I do accept the candy, and he buys Hot Tamales and sodas for both of us.

We pose in front of the movie poster, and I take a selfie of us with my phone. In it, Justin gazes at me while I smile at the camera. I wonder what Drummer will think when he sees it.

Inside the theater, Justin follows me as I choose the seats. We settle in and he whispers to me before the movie starts, "I felt bad that I lost track of you after I dropped you off that day. You were all alone except for your dog. I should have walked you to the front desk."

"It's okay, I had friends waiting for me."

His eyes roam slowly across my face, and his arm slides around me and massages my shoulder, sending another flush of heat between my legs. "Is your family all right? Did you lose anything in the fire?" he asks.

Did I lose anything in the fire? Great question. Just my sanity, maybe my best friends, and perhaps my future in law enforcement. "No, my family and house are fine," I answer.

"Pretty awful, what happened to your town."

"Yeah." His free hand takes mine and draws it to his lips for a quick kiss that makes my nerves twirl. "What do you do for work?" I ask. It's ridiculous that I'm holding hands with a guy and only know his first name. Everything inside of me screams: *Stupid girl!*

"I drive for the quarry," he answers. "It's a union job. Good benefits and vacation time."

Benefits, vacation time? Justin is definitely a real adult, and I squirm a bit.

"How about you? What do you do?" he asks.

I feel young, too young, and the lie slips out quickly. "I'm a junior at San Diego State, just home for the summer."

"Oh?" He raises his thick brows, looking surprised. Is he surprised that I go to SDSU or that I'm a junior? I can't tell, so I chew on my soda straw.

After the movie, Justin walks me to his car, a black Altima, in the parking lot. Last time I saw him, he was driving a truck, and I wonder if he owns two vehicles or if he borrowed this one. I glance at the license plate. I should text the number to Mo in case anything happens to me. God, what the hell am I doing?

"I know a great place to see the stars," Justin says. He entwines his fingers with mine. "Want to see it?"

Oh, wow! My heart stalls and my breathing grows shallow. I know better than to go anywhere with this stranger, but I hear my answer as if I'm somebody else: "Sure."

Justin smiles and I slide into his car. He pulls smoothly out of the lot, the radio on low. The Altima is an automatic, and he holds my hand as we drive. He takes me to Lookout Point, a place I've been to with my friends, but the partying crowd hasn't arrived yet and the lot is empty. He pulls into a spot overlooking the valley. The moon has risen over the mountain, full and swollen, washing the understory in silver light.

"You can see where the fire traveled," Justin says, pointing at the scorched dark areas below.

My voice pitches uncomfortably high: "I don't want to talk about the fire."

"What do you want to talk about?" His eyes trail toward my lips, and the atmosphere in the car shifts, becoming heavy and buzzing—like a sky full of lightning.

"I don't know," I whisper.

"I have an idea." He leans across the car, cups my face, and kisses me softly. "Do you like that?"

The truth is, I do. I close my eyes in answer, and he kisses me again, more urgently. I sink into the leather seat as his upper body covers mine. He kisses my lips, cheeks, eyes, then moves down to my neck. My heart flutters and his breathing grows deeper, faster. My head bumps the glass window.

"Let's go to the backseat," he suggests.

Again my voice comes, unbidden: "Okay." We crawl to the back, where his head grazes the ceiling and he laughs at himself.

I sit upright on the seat, and we kiss some more. When his hands find my breasts, a moan escapes his throat and he pushes me flat on my back. My heart begins to slam. My entire body tenses, and Justin pauses. "Do you want to keep going?" he asks.

I can't answer. I don't know what I want, but I'm curious and I'm here, so I nod.

Justin grins and tugs off his T-shirt. His bare skin is smooth and muscled, and I forget myself and touch him. He shivers; his smile broadens. He's more deliberate now. He takes off my top and expertly unsnaps and removes my bra. He groans at the sight of me, and suddenly his mouth is all over my naked chest. My body vibrates, and this feels good, very good.

"Hannah," Justin whispers, "you're so fucking gorgeous." He presses his hardness between my legs, and his lips cover mine. His tongue plunges into my mouth, making me gasp. His hands slide down, and he pushes up my skirt and then unbuttons his jeans. "Hannah," he murmurs, but I feel like he's lost in his own world.

Suddenly, a condom appears in his hand, and I stare at it in shock. Unlike Drummer, Justin isn't playing around. He rubs his palm down my thigh, then back up, and rests it between my legs. My thoughts spin away from me.

"You okay?" he asks. I'm on my back and his thumb is hooked in my underwear, ready to pull them off. His breath is hot on my cheeks, and his body is heavy. There is a trail of dark hair on his stomach that leads down.

I nod and he hesitates. "You sure?"

To shut him up, I pull him down and press my tongue into

his hot mouth, and that is all the reassurance he needs. A deep shudder rolls through his body. There's inevitability in his excitement, like a roller coaster at its apex, just before it drops—there is no stopping Justin now. I mean, if I screamed, I could probably stop him, but I don't want to. Someone has to be my first time, why not him? It will never be Drummer.

Justin rips the condom wrapper open with his teeth and sits back to roll the condom on. His torso scrunches, constrained by the low headroom in the car. Every muscle in his body flexes, and the sight of his erection shocks me as if a bucket of ice water has been dumped on my head. This is real. This is happening. I close my eyes and brace.

He enters me and the pain is blinding at first, then surprisingly pleasant, then hot and slippery, and then it's over. Justin flops on top of me, utterly spent.

I breathe in the silence. My mind empties.

Justin slowly comes back to life, and one hand plays with my hair while the other moves to wipe me dry with his T-shirt. He's about to throw his shirt on the floor when he sees the blood. "Hannah?" His brows knit together. "Was this your first time?"

I close my eyes, feeling suddenly embarrassed.

He sits up and I feel him staring at me. "Hannah, shit, I'm sorry it was so fast. You should have told me. I would have got us a room, taken more time. Fuck, I'm really sorry."

I bristle at the implication I made a mistake. It's my first time; how am I supposed to know what I should have done?

And maybe he should have gotten a room *anyway*. I curl on the seat so he doesn't see my tears.

"Hey, no, it's my fault," Justin amends, pulling me into his arms. "I—I felt some resistance. I should have stopped and talked to you."

His sudden regret makes me feel worse, and my body grows stiffer.

Justin senses I don't want to talk about it. He gets dressed (all but the soiled T-shirt) and helps me find my clothes. We climb back into the front seats. "I'd like to see you again, make it up to you," he says with a slow smile warming his face. "You're beautiful, Hannah. I had a great time."

"Me too," I say, but the words jam in my throat. There is no going backward, no do-over for our first time, and we both know it.

The drive back to the theater is quiet. Justin walks me to my car and tries again. "I like you, Hannah, and not just because of what we did. I think you're pretty, and I want to know you better." He forces a hug that I don't return. Justin feels more like a stranger now than he did before we had sex. I smile to urge him on his way and then slip into my car. There, I let out my breath and delete the selfie we took with my phone.

When I get home, I'm glad my dad isn't here. He's either working late or he's at the tavern talking with townsfolk and having a beer. He likes keeping his finger on the pulse of the community, especially when it's suffering.

In case there's a bear prowling the yard, I honk the horn and rattle my keys. A couple of raccoons slip into the shadows, but no bears.

Matilda greets me at the porch door. She's upset and barks at me, reacting to the blood in my underwear. I stroke her head. "It's okay. I'm okay." She licks my face, and her big brown eyes tell me everything I wanted so desperately to know—that I'm beautiful, lovable, and perfect just the way I am.

I sink onto my porch, hug her tight, and sob into her fur.

When I'm finished crying, I draw a scalding-hot bath, swallow a dose of ibuprofen, open a pint of Java Chip ice cream, and eat it while soaking in the tub. I'm not a virgin anymore. It's weird. I don't feel different, just sore.

Right as I finish my ice cream, the screen door bangs open downstairs and my dad stomps into the house. Shit, shit! Did one of his friends see me with a strange guy and call him? I unplug the drain, towel off, and rush downstairs in the rumpled clothes I wore on the date. "I can expl—"

But what I see stops me cold. It's not my dad; it's Violet. Her tan skin is ashen, her sable brown eyes are wide, and her pupils have contracted to tiny points. My gut sinks. "What happened?"

Her voice is strangled: "It's Mo. She's in jail."

19

July 27

Gap Fire: 55% contained

Fatalities: 10

Time: 11:30 p.m.

"Mo's in jail!" My hand flies to my mouth. "No! Why?"

"You're the sheriff's daughter, you tell me," she snaps. "All I know is that your dad arrested her and she has a bail hearing tomorrow. A bail hearing, god!" Her gaze zips over my short skirt and smeared makeup, but she doesn't ask. "It gets worse— the boys are at the bowling alley, stoned out of their minds. Drummer said Luke was crying in the bathroom. Everyone is falling apart, Han."

"Do the boys know about Mo?"

She glares at me. "Why do think Luke is crying? Come on, we have to get them out of there!"

"Okay, I'll drive."

"I brought my car, Hannah."

"You don't know the shortcuts."

Violet shakes her mane of hair. "Oh my god, you guys act like I haven't spent every summer here since I was seven. I know Gap Mountain as well as you do. I'm driving."

She stares me down until I cave. "Fine, let me grab shoes and a jacket."

As I find my things, she opens cupboards and pours herself a glass of water in the kitchen. "Uh, Hannah," she calls. "There's a bear in your yard."

My brain ping-pongs between Mo, the boys, and the bear, leaving me dizzy. I toss on my jacket, slide on the heels I wore for Justin, and glance out the window over Violet's shoulder. Sure enough, a huge animal is lumbering across our lawn, but that damn hungry bear is the least of my worries. "I'm ready."

As we exit the house, I grab my air horn and blow it on the porch, waking old Matilda and scaring off the bear. Then we climb into Violet's Trackhawk, and she expertly steers the over-sized vehicle down the country roads, taking every shortcut I would have chosen.

The bowling alley is across the street from the burned-down post office. Violet parks the Trackhawk and jumps out. With her rolled sweats, cropped T-shirt, wild bun, and keys dangling from a lanyard, I have a vision of her in ten years, chauffeuring raven-haired, pink-cheeked toddlers to private school, organizing parent brunches, attending charity events with her handsome husband, and making it all look effortless. She'll stop coming to Gap Mountain, just as her brother did after he got married, and this world—my world—will fade. I'll probably never see Violet again after college. A sick mixture of sadness and anger floods my stomach.

Violet halts and her Tiffany necklace glints in the moonlight. "You coming or what?"

"Yeah, I'm coming."

She grips my arm and we cross the parking lot together. She rants about the boys. "When I called Drummer, he said he and Luke crushed three or four beers *before* they got here, and then they smoked weed."

"Idiots. We should be lying low right now." I pull open the door of the bowling alley and hear loud singing and shouting coming from the lobby. There are our boys, leaning over a dirty table littered with French fries and chicken nuggets. Luke's hair is uncombed, and he's singing the "Star Spangled Banner" loud enough to earn stares while Drummer bends over a chair, laughing, his light hair flopping into his eyes.

The manager stands by, red-faced, clearly trying to get them to leave.

Violet and I hustle to the table. She grabs Drummer's hand, and I approach Luke. "We'll take care of them," Violet tells the manager. Her dimples disarm him, and he backs up, mumbling something unintelligible.

We usher the boys out, and the manager shakes his fist at them: "I don't want to see you two again unless you're sober." He tries to slam the glass front door behind us, but it's on a pneumatic hinge and closes slowly as he shoves on it.

In the parking lot, Luke stumbles to his old Chevy Malibu, leans across the hood, and lights a cigarette. "Our lives are over," he says. "Fucking over." He breaks into a squeaky rendition of "Good Riddance" by Green Day while Violet tries to talk to him.

Drummer ignores them both and stares at me, his body swaying. "What are *you* dressed up for?" His bloodshot eyes take in my tight skirt, skimpy top, and tangled, curled hair. His eyebrows crinkle in confusion.

"I was out," I answer.

He sucks in his lower lip and eyeballs my body so hard I start to squirm. "On a date?" he asks.

I look away.

Drummer grabs my arm, pulls me closer. Our eyes meet and his jaw muscles clench, his nostrils flare. Justin's scent is all over my clothes, and I wonder if Drummer can smell him. He lifts his chin like a child. "Mo's in trouble and you're out meeting dudes?"

My mind reels. "Fuck you!"

"No, fuck you!" he shoots back. Violet glances over and then turns back to Luke, who's crying again.

I drop my voice to a low growl. "I'm tired, Drummer. I want to go home, but I'm here. I dropped everything for you assholes." Tears flood my eyes.

He comes to his senses and releases his tight grip on me. "Sorry. I'm just worried about Mo." He takes a closer look at my smeared makeup and messy hair. "Are you okay, Han? Did somebody fuck with you?"

I suppress my budding hysteria. Yes, somebody fucked with

me. Or maybe I fucked with him. I'm not sure, so I close my eyes and swallow past the hard lump in my throat. "I'm fine, I'm worried about Mo too."

Drummer tucks me tight against his body, and his voice rumbles from his chest. "She's going to be fine, Han. We all are."

God, how can he say that? I feel queasy. "We really messed up, starting that fire."

"I know." His smile is quick and half-hearted. He pushes back his gold-tinged hair, and his eyes seem to change colors in the light like polished crystals. He's wild and beautiful, and I can't imagine him, or any of us, living in a tiny cell with a narrow, barred window and, worse, sharing that cell with a real criminal. My heart beats harder, my breathing quickens. Everything, *everyone*, is falling apart.

He takes my hand. "Calm down, Hannah."

My guts unravel. My chest grows tight.

He rubs my back. "Breathe with me."

I focus on his heartbeat, his slow, steady breaths. In the distance, Violet is trying to calm Luke the way Drummer is trying to calm me.

"I won't let anything happen to you," he says. It's a ridiculous promise, but I let myself believe it. He wants to protect me as much as I want to protect him, and I soften against his chest. He tucks his palms around my cheeks and brings my face to his. "Do you trust me?"

"Yes." We're so close I can feel his breath on my eyelashes. This intimacy is nothing new, but everything has changed. I'm losing him—if not to prison, then to Violet, and if not to Violet, then to college.

I've never tried to kiss him before, not for real, but I'm running out of time. My heart climbs out of its pit. "Drummer?" His name is a breath, a prayer. Ignoring his confused expression, I lean forward and kiss him, grazing his inner lips with my tongue.

He pulls away so fast I fall out of his arms. "Han, what are you doing?"

He wipes his mouth dry, and heat glides to my cheeks. God! I repulse him! "I'm sorry." I press my lips together and stare at my hands. My heart vanishes back into its cave.

Drummer fidgets, glances at Violet, who's still checking on Luke by his car. "We're going to be okay," he says to me. "You feel better now?"

I nod but I want to scream with shame. What is it about me that's so unlovable?

Violet returns and interrupts, a hard edge to her husky voice. "Luke needs a ride home."

She scowls at Drummer, then me, and I wonder if she saw me try to kiss him. I straighten up and lift my chin. "We probably shouldn't hang out together until this investigation blows over."

"Huh?" asks Luke.

"I said, we should lie low and stay away from each other."

Luke hiccups. "Right, so we don't start another fucking fire."

"Shut up," Violet snaps, glancing around, but the parking lot is quiet. There's no one around to hear.

"We'll drive you home," I say to Luke, trying to wrangle him into Violet's car.

He lunges past me and wraps Drummer in a viselike hold. "Let's go back inside," he slurs, laughing.

Drummer tries to fight him off, but he's no match for Luke. They wrestle and Luke gets heated and starts to choke Drummer for real.

"Stop it, would you?" Violet cries. "We're supposed to be talking about Mo. She's in jail!" The boys stop and we stare at one another in the parking lot that's surrounded by whispering trees and littered with pine needles. "Mo's mom said your dad yelled at her and then took her away," Violet says to me.

I let out my breath. "Well, he's under a lot of pressure to find out who did this, you know." The Gap Fire is the deadliest and costliest crime of his career. As far as my dad's concerned, the gloves are off. I chew my lip. "So why did he arrest her anyway?"

Luke answers: "Her dad remembered she went swimming at the lake on the seventh and mentioned it at the bar, thinking Mo might be a good witness. He had no idea she'd already lied to the police about where she was. It got back to your dad, and he arrested her for giving a false report."

"Shit," I mutter. "Now he can get her DNA and fingerprints and maybe match her to the beer bottle."

"I can't believe this," Violet says, tapping her foot. "It's gone too far." Her eyes flip to mine. "If we come forward, will your dad go easier on us?"

I laugh out loud. "It's not up to him, V. If we fess up, we can plead to a lesser charge, but that doesn't mean the district attorney will let us go. It means we'll spend two years in prison instead of six, that's all."

"Can't your dad give us community service hours or something?" Drummer asks.

I shake my head. My friends don't understand. "Look, the sheriff has no control over our sentencing, and the fact that I'm his daughter won't help me. If anything, it will hurt me. Of all of us, I'm the one who should have known better."

Violet crosses her arms over her flat, exposed stomach. "Well, I'd rather go to prison for two years than six."

"I'd rather not go *at all*."

Luke exhales smoke like a dragon. "They have my pipe and my matches," he murmurs. "When the lab is done with them, I'm going to jail, aren't I?" His dark eyes meet mine. His unruly hair flops over one eye. "But I can't—I can't leave Aiden." A sob rips from his chest, startling all of us.

"Shhh, it's okay." I peer over Luke's shoulder and meet Drummer's gaze. He looks as shocked as I feel.

"I can't," Luke repeats. He rushes to his car, vomits all over the back tire. Violet shakes her head and glares at me, as if this is my fault.

"Let's go home," I say to Luke.

He wipes his mouth and points at us. "All of you stay the fuck away from me." Before we can stop him, he leaps into his Chevy and peels out of the lot. Smoke wafts from his spinning tires.

"Jesus!" Violet cries.

"Go after him!" says Drummer. We dive into her car, and she follows Luke with me in the front seat and Drummer in the back. Luke veers onto a side road and accelerates into the mountains. Violet stomps on her gas pedal.

"No, slow down," I cry, my muscles tensing. But Violet doesn't listen. She steps harder on the gas and tries to keep up with Luke. Her big car leans and drifts around the tight mountain turns.

Ahead, Luke's Malibu is swift, cutting corners and flying around blind curves as we climb higher toward the peaks. Tears blur my vision. "Please, Violet, not so fast," I murmur. I don't mind speed when I'm the driver. I hate it when I'm not.

Drummer's hand snakes up from the backseat and gently touches my shoulder. He understands why I'm scared.

I was six when my mother crashed our car. It was dark and I rode illegally in the front seat. As the road looped ahead, I laughed and my stomach twirled. I thought my mom was playing a game, veering from lane to lane with the music blasting. I threw up my hands. "Go, Mommy!"

She'd taken me with her to the bar that night because my dad was at work. I'd colored pictures and drunk Shirley Temples while she tossed back shots and argued with whoever would listen. She called it our "special date," our secret.

No one noticed when we left out the back door, because that was also the way to the restroom. Soon after I said *Go, Mommy*, she sideswiped an oncoming car, and my broken crayons slid off my lap. The other driver slammed headfirst into a tree, and

I heard the long, lonely beep of a horn as we drove away. Mom stared at me, her blond hair tangled, mascara running down her face, and said, *Don't tell Daddy.*

I glimpse my reflection in Violet's side mirror, and it makes my heart kick into high gear and my chest squeeze tight. With my streaked makeup and unkempt hair, I look just like her. Just like Mom.

Violet's tires squeal around a turn, and I think I'm going to puke.

"Hannah?" Drummer says, prodding me. "Violet, pull over. She's not okay."

"What? No!" Violet drives faster.

"Slow the fuck down!" he screams at her.

She slows but continues to follow Luke's vanishing red tail-lights.

Drummer shakes me hard. "Hannah, it's okay. You're safe."

I sputter and draw a breath. Violet finally slows and glances at me. "I'm not going *that* fast."

I shake my head, wishing they would both disappear. "Where's Luke?" I ask.

Suddenly, Violet screams and slams on her brakes, throwing us forward. "Look!"

Ahead, I spot rising dust and dimming lights. For the second time in my life, the long, lonely sound of a car horn pierces the mountain air.

Luke drove his Malibu off a cliff.

20

After Luke's crash, Drummer called 911 from the road, and medics airlifted Luke to a county hospital in Fresno. A week later, the hospital released him. Luke had a moderate TBI, traumatic brain injury, but that didn't stop my dad from charging him for driving while under the influence. "I had to, Han. The law is the law," he said, just like when he arrested Mom.

Mo's free on bail. Her parents dipped into her college fund to pay her bond and hire an attorney. Luke has a court-appointed lawyer. He calls her the Pit Bull and can't stop talking about her. For the first time in his life, Luke has an adult on his side. His mom isn't as sympathetic. When she learned that Luke totaled his car, she kicked him out, so he's staying at Mo's for now.

Reporters camp out at the police station, harassing my dad, and Mo and Luke when they can find them.

Since Luke's accident, I've lost my appetite and I feel zero joy for anything, even my dog and my horses. I stand in the middle of rooms, frozen. I can't remember how to work the register at the Reel Deal. I have nightmares about my mother and see broken crayons when I close my eyes. I remember my mother's screams when my dad's partner took her away: *I'm your wife!*

On top of all that, I've had sex for the first time and still haven't told anyone. My friends have their own problems right now, and anyway, the sex feels surreal, like it happened to someone else. Justin has texted me twice, but I haven't responded.

The Gap Fire, which continues to terrorize Yosemite National Park, no longer feels like *our* fire. If no one can stop it or control it, how can five teens be held responsible for it? It's not like it's doing our bidding. No, the fault lies with fossil fuels and melting ice caps and a quickly heating planet!

This lie that started so small is now blazing through our lives like the wildfire that roared through our town. Each piece of evidence is going to lead to a new piece of evidence, and there are too many factors we never considered or thought to consider. In wildfire terms, our lie is zero percent contained. Luke and Mo are suspects now. Who's next?

———

The day after Luke gets out of the hospital, the monsters meet in Violet's attic. Lulu lets me inside, and she looks every bit her age today. "Luke's going to be all right. He's a fighter," she says as she hands me a pitcher of lemonade and a platter of cookies. "You can take the back staircase, Hannah, it's closer." She points to the narrow staircase behind the kitchen. "Keep your voice low, and don't say anything that might upset Luke."

Is she serious? Everything we have to talk about could upset Luke, but I agree and tiptoe to the attic. "Hi," I say as I shoulder open the small door and enter the attic from the backside. All the monsters are present. "I brought snacks."

Violet huffs. "Grammy can't stop feeding us." The shades in the attic have been pulled down and the lights dimmed.

I sigh. We're together for the first time since Luke drove off the cliff, and it's the only thing that feels right.

"I'll take some of those," Drummer says, grabbing a fistful of cookies. I stiffen because I'm still embarrassed about that awful kiss I gave him. I should have known better. I'm his best friend. I might have fallen for him, but he's still floating free. Drummer smiles and I let out my breath. So we're going to pretend it never happened—maybe that's for the best.

Mo sits cross-legged on the sofa, looking small and frail in her skinny jeans and halter top. "How are you?" I ask her.

She waves her hand. "Better than I was." Her texts after she was released from jail went like this:

no fucking privacy!

I'll never be clean again.

if the inmates don't kill you, the food will!

We're all glad she's back.

Last, I see Luke. He slouches against the wall, his dark eyes burning holes in the rug. The hair on his head has been shaved off, and there's a fresh incision on his scalp from some hospital procedure. He looks like he's either sick or has just joined the military. In spite of his already pale skin, I can tell he's lost color. His lips flicker into a smile. "Hi, Han," he croaks.

"Hi." I sit cross-legged next to him. "How's your brother doing?"

Luke's voice is bitter and charged with grief. "How the fuck should I know? Mom doesn't answer the phone, says she'll call the police if she sees me." He rubs the stubble across his head.

"So you're staying at Mo's?"

"Yeah, and Violet's grandma is helping me with the hospital and legal stuff."

Luke's Chevy crashed into a tree after sliding forty feet off the embankment, and his head struck his side window. He's lucky the airbags deployed and his brain injury is moderate, but via a text from Drummer, I know Luke's suffering severe mood swings.

Because he was stoned, his blood alcohol was over the limit, and he's underage, my dad impounded his car as part of the DUI investigation. Did Luke crash due to drunkenness or distracted driving, or did he swerve off the road on purpose? We don't know and he's not saying.

There's a long silence as the monsters avoid looking at one another. Our summer hasn't turned out the way we hoped, and I don't know how to fix it. I wipe my face, feeling miserable. "I'm sorry," I offer to the group. My lips tremble and stress courses through me, making me shiver. "I'm sorry for everything." And I am—for the arrests, for the accident, for Luke getting kicked out, and for grabbing his arm that day.

"We're sorry too," Drummer says, sliding down next to me.

Mo gathers our attention: "So I heard from my lawyer this morning. The fingerprints and saliva on that beer bottle are *not* mine. I'm cleared of that, at least."

Luke slaps his hands over his face and groans.

"They still have me for lying about my alibi," she amends, adding a sad wink that assures Luke *you're not alone.* "But now they're looking for another suspect."

"God, will this *ever* end?" Violet moans.

"Will this affect your college admission?" I ask Mo.

Tears glitter in her hazel eyes. "The judge gave me permission to attend, but I have to commute for now, because my parents canceled my campus housing. They can't afford it with my legal expenses. Besides that, my lawyer warned me that if I'm convicted of giving a false police report, my acceptance might be rescinded."

"But that's a two-hour drive each way!" Drummer says.

She shrugs. "I rearranged my schedule so I only go Mondays, Wednesdays, and Fridays."

I dig my fingernails into my palms as my chest tightens. "That's not fair."

We stare at our shoelaces, helpless. Mo peers at me. "Did you know we could get in this much trouble for lying?" Her tone is not critical, but I feel my cheeks go hot all the same. I glance at Violet, because I was not the first to lie.

Violet sucks on her lower lip and then exhales. "It's not her fault, Mo. When Hannah and I rode into town, I could have told Sheriff Warner the truth when he asked me what I'd seen, but I didn't. The fire department was on their way, and I thought they would put the fire out, plus, I was high, remember? I didn't—I had no idea . . ."

Her eyes go round and soft, and she scrunches herself into the smallest size she can. I don't know if she does it on purpose, but she softens everyone in the room, including me. I wish I could draw sympathy the way she does, but there is nothing helpless or cute about my tall, wiry body. Still, I'm glad she took the heat for telling the first lie.

Luke moans and rubs his head. "I don't want to talk about this." Mo snuggles up to him, and he hooks his arm around her.

"Let's watch a movie," Drummer suggests. He selects a horror flick—something that will entertain us and make us forget.

Halfway through the movie, Drummer tosses a piece of candy at me, making me smile. Luke takes off his socks, and we all complain about his smelly feet. Then Mo runs downstairs to carry up more snacks from Lulu's kitchen, and Violet lays her head on my shoulder.

As the jump scares increase, we merge into a ball, a mass of limbs and hair and skin, just like when we were kids. I have an elbow in my side, a head on my lap, and breath in my ear, and I don't want this moment to ever end.

We are the monsters because none of us wanted to play the

human in that community center rendition of *Where the Wild Things Are* when we were kids. Now we are facing capture and separation, and we are terrified.

—

The final blow comes to our group after the movie. Mo and I are playing checkers, the boys are watching YouTube, and Violet is changing the music when we hear cars drive up the circular driveway and skid to a halt.

Luke rushes to the third-story window and peers out. "No fucking way!" He covers his head, and his chest begins to heave. "I can't do this again." He throws a punch at the wall and leaves a gaping hole.

Violet backs into the desk and almost knocks over the glass unicorn I gave her when she was ten.

Mo leaps to her toes. "What's happening?"

"Police," Luke answers, and his expression shatters into a thousand pieces.

My scalp goes cold. Downstairs, we hear Lulu throw open her twelve-foot-tall front door. "What in the hell do you want now?" she shouts.

I recognize my dad's voice, and then Lulu Sandoval emits a slew of curses and threats, but they don't stop what is coming. My dad and his two deputies plod up the stairs, holsters creaking, boots thumping, and radios hissing.

My heart hammers. *Oh god, oh god!* I want to hide, but I race to Drummer's side instead.

"What is this?" he asks me.

I don't know, I mouth.

My dad's large frame fills the door, and the five of us gather together, arms linked. We face him as if we're facing a firing squad.

"You're all here," he says, his eyes burning into mine. "All the monsters."

Violet inches away from the desk and clutches Drummer so tightly her knuckles turn white.

I imagine we five look as guilty as hell.

Dad's hand automatically rests on his handcuffs, and I see that he's not fucking around. "Lucas O'Malley," he starts, "new evidence has placed you at Gap Lake on July seventh when the wildfire started, and I'm arresting you for malicious arson, giving a false police report, and obstructing an arson investigation."

Malicious? My eyelids spring wider.

"You have the right to remain silent. Anything you say can and will be used against you in a court of law. You have the right to an attorney. If you cannot afford an attorney, one will be provided for you."

My mind spins as memories of my dad arresting my mother flood me, and now he's after another one of my best friends.

"What are you doing?" Violet cries and reaches for my dad's arm.

I yank her away before she can touch him. My dad and his deputies don't like being grabbed on a good day, and today is not a good day. We can't react—not yet. We have to let my dad play his hand.

"Luke, do you understand the rights I have read to you?" he asks.

Luke gazes at him, tries to focus and can't. Right then, Lulu rushes in behind the deputies, her hair loose and her face blazing red. "This boy is sick," she spurts. "He's still under medical treatment for a TBI. He does not—he cannot—fully understand what you're saying to him." She thrusts out a handful of hospital papers.

My dad takes the papers and scans them, lets out a frustrated sigh. "It's been a week. I was not aware he's still under treatment." He tries to hand the papers back.

"Those are copies," Lulu snaps, refusing them. "Luke's attorney will be in touch to straighten this out, Sheriff. If you don't have solid evidence against him, you can expect a lawsuit for harassment." She points at the stairs. "Now you may leave, and you should be ashamed of these dramatics." She gestures at the deputies.

My dad sets his jaw and stands taller. "Ms. Sandoval, Luke lied to my deputies, and ten people are *dead*." His voice ricochets like a bullet, striking each of us. "His mental state does not change my evidence or the fact that crimes have been committed."

Lulu quivers angrily as she drags her eyes up to meet my father's, but her tone softens. "This young man is not fit to travel, and he has a doctor's appointment first thing in the morning. It's in the papers there." She points. "He's fragile and I will ask his attorney to contact you tomorrow, *after* his appointment."

My dad could force the issue and take Luke into medical custody right now, but Luke's in no shape for questioning anyway. And if his condition were to go downhill, well, my dad won't want that lawsuit on his head. He nods in resigned agreement. "Luke, I'll see you tomorrow." Then he turns toward Violet and me but won't meet my eye. "Girls, I want your official statements on record about what you saw the day the fire started. Come down anytime tomorrow and my deputies will take care of it. Good night."

Blood rushes to my head. Oh god, this isn't good.

After he leaves, Lulu asks us to go home. "I think there's been enough excitement around here for today."

We glance at one another, reluctant to part. The shit has hit the proverbial fan and we're scared, all of us. But Lulu insists. "Break it up, kids. You all need to go home."

Reluctantly, we follow her downstairs. "Here," she says, "I made dinner, but you can take it home." Lulu opens a slow cooker and scoops out large helpings of beef stew into individual containers, hands one to each of us, and shoos us out the front door. Violet walks outside with us.

In the driveway, we huddle together. "What's this new evidence?" Luke asks me. He strikes a match, and his hands tremble so hard he can barely bring the flame to the cigarette.

"I don't know," I answer, feeling as if I let him down. "No one tells me anything anymore."

Violet throws up her arms. "Because look at the world of shit you've led us into!"

"Led you into! I'm trying to lead you *out*!"

She taps her foot. "I'm done, Hannah. I've had enough."

The monsters shift, moving closer to me, and we face Violet together. "What do you mean, you're *done?*" I ask.

She peers at us with her big brown, guilt-ridden eyes. "I started this; I'll end it."

"Violet!" Lulu's head pops out the door. "Come inside now."

Violet crosses her arms, looking like an expensive doll in her short skirt, Gucci combat boots, gauzy scarf, and shining Tiffany necklace. "It's over," she says, and then she stares straight at Drummer. "All of this is over." She stalks back to her house.

Drummer calls after her, a desperate pleading pitch to his voice. "Violet, don't do this! It's not over. Please!" She ignores him.

"She's losing it," I say. "Violet can't handle the pressure." Drummer shakes his head, denying it.

"Hannah's right," says Mo, and Luke flicks his ashes onto the driveway, his hands still trembling.

"It's not okay for Violet to decide things on her own." I look at the monsters. "Right?"

Slowly, they nod.

Drummer pulls on his hair. "Let's come back tonight, after Grammy's had her wine. Violet's not thinking straight. Nothing is *over.*" The rest of us agree, and we drive to our homes, waiting for dark.

———

At 8:25 p.m., Violet sends a group text to our regular phones: *tomorrow I'm telling the police everything.*

I drop the manure rake I'm holding. My heart stalls.

Luke: *WTF! You cant*

Mo: *what do you mean by everything?*

No answer from Violet. No gray dots, nothing. I dial her phone and the call goes straight to voicemail. I dial Drummer, my hands shaking. He doesn't answer either.

I pull up the location-sharing app. Shit. He's already there, in the attic! He went to her house without us. Fucking Drummer. He can't handle Violet on his own, not about this.

I rush out of the barn to my car and text Luke and Mo on our prepaid cells: *meet at the attic. Now.*

Luke: *10-4*

Mo: *I'll try*

I crawl into my Jeep and feel my regular phone slide out of my pocket and shatter on the ground. Shit! I can't think, can't breathe.

I slam the Wrangler into gear and spin the tires, throwing rocks into the shrubs as I fishtail onto the main road. My boxy Jeep leans precariously around the bends, but I don't care. I just drive.

We have to fix this together; we have to change her mind. And if Violet's so hell-bent on telling the truth, she *and* Drummer can start by confessing to *me*, and I don't mean about the fucking fire!

part two

The Missing

21

My throat aches and I feel like I'm floating. Where am I? Something beeps and I recognize the sound but nothing else. The bed is stiff, the air cool. I open my eyes, not surprised to see a hospital room. I'm shocked, don't get me wrong. I have no idea how I got here, but I'm not surprised. The regular beeping noise was a dead giveaway.

Hey, I'm not dead, that's good, but there must be something wrong with me. I try to speak; my mouth feels full of paste. I sit up and tingles rush across my body. That's pain, but it's dull. Drugs, yeah, I think I'm on some good fucking drugs.

My head swivels to check out my body. I'm wearing a hospital gown and fuzzy socks from home. My left arm and shoulder are bandaged and numb. My scalp itches something awful. I flail around for a button or something that will call a nurse. I grab the TV remote by accident, and the television mounted on the wall flickers on. It's a news station, but the sound is muted. I survey my bed for another button.

Right then a nurse enters, hips swishing. "You're awake," she says brightly.

Her relaxed greeting surprises me, because I feel as if I teleported here. Wasn't I just at my barn?

I try to speak but moan instead.

"Relax, honey," she says as she places a cuff around my upper right arm. "How is your pain from one to ten, ten being the worst? You can hold up your fingers."

I stare stupidly at her.

"Are you having pain right now?"

I shrug. I can't feel much but a distant throbbing, as if my pain is on the other side of a wall. I smile at her and she smiles back. "Let me know when you start feeling it, all right?"

I nod obediently.

She takes my blood pressure and temperature and checks my bandages. "You have a catheter in, but we'll take it out if you can stay awake. For now, if you have to pee, just let it flow." She smiles as if peeing through a tube is a glorious thing.

"Wh-what happened?" I croak.

Her smile droops. "Your father is in the waiting room. I'll fetch him," she says. "And I've paged the doctor. She'll be here soon."

My dad enters moments later in full gear—gun, handcuffs, radio—and my heart thumps. His uniform never used to scare me, not even when I was a little girl, but everything has changed. *Arson. Murder. Dad arresting Luke in the attic.* I turn away from the memories.

His eyes are raw and puffy. "How you feeling, Bug?"

I push out a few words. "Okay. Was I in a car accident?" I ransack my brain. The last thing I remember is getting into my Jeep. I was scared about something, really scared, and angry too. I probably shouldn't have driven.

His Adam's apple bobs as he swallows. "No. It was a bear attack."

"A bear? Are you joking?" I laugh and it hurts. "Owww!"

My dad holds my hand. "You don't remember?" I shake my head. "The doctor warned me you might not remember everything right away. Animal attacks are traumatic." He glances at my head. "And you might have a concussion."

"Like Luke?"

"Not that serious."

I glance at my bandages. "A bear, really? Where?"

My dad's eyes water. "At our house around midnight. We think she got you when you opened your car door. She dragged you out and . . . and mauled you, then she climbed into your Jeep and completely destroyed it. Looks like you had food in it."

I groan. "The beef stew." My head starts to ache. "Violet's grandma gave it to me to bring home. But that's all I remember. What time is it?"

He glances at his watch. "It's eight-fifteen at night. This happened three days ago, Han."

"Three days?" I study my bandages, suddenly fearful. The

attack must have been terrible if I've been unconscious for three days! I grab my covers and throw them off.

"Easy, Hannah," Dad says.

I count two legs and two arms with ten fingers. I gently pry up the bandage on my lower arm. There are deep claw marks and some scratches. Half-moon indents on my forearm seem out of place yet familiar, like human fingernail marks, and a wave of dizziness assaults me. I replace the bandage and fall backward. "I'm okay, right?"

He squeezes my hand. "You'll heal. You have bite wounds, whiplash, and some torn muscles in your shoulder. You'll never play softball." We both laugh at this inside joke. The last year I tried out for softball, I ducked each time the ball flew my way. "Nothing is broken," he adds, and then squeezes my hand tighter, his eyes brimming, his voice thinning. "The worst damage is to your head and face."

Face? I reach up and feel my head. It's bandaged and sore.

"The bear got her jaws around your skull when she dragged you."

I see that my dad is relying on years of training to tell me this without breaking down, and I listen in utter fascination. "So I was in her mouth?"

He nods and suddenly I feel the blood drain from my face. Shivers of horror roll through me. "I have to see."

"You're all covered up, there's nothing to see," he assures me. "They had to shave off parts of your hair for the stitches."

I grip the bed as nausea rolls through me. "Oh, god." I touch my face; feel a bandage over my cheek and one on my forehead. Frankenstein comes to mind. "Am I scarred?"

He blinks and tears roll down his unshaven cheeks. "You'll be just fine, Bug. A plastic surgeon handled the facial lacerations."

"Stop," I cry, gasping. "No more."

"I'm sorry."

"I need water."

He wipes his eyes and collects a cup of ice chips for me.

I crunch on ice and lean back against my pillow. I need to think about something happy. "What did Matilda do?" I imagine brave old Matilda, ferociously barking and chasing off the bear.

Dad lowers his eyelashes. "She was brave," he answers. "She protected you."

Something in his voice warns me there's more to it. "Dad? Is she all right?"

Now his tears flow in rivulets, and he collapses into his hands. "I'm sorry, Han. I didn't want to tell you this today."

My injured scalp prickles, and goose bumps erupt across my arms. "Is she dead?"

He nods. "It was quick."

A shriek pierces the air—mine. My throat closes and I sob so hard the physical pain from my injuries rears up and suddenly everything hurts. I grab my pillow and bawl into it. "No, not Matilda. Not my dog!"

My dad holds me, cries with me.

Pins and needles shoot throughout my battered body, and the pain is blinding. The nurse rushes back into the room, her face ashen. "Is she remembering?"

"No, I told her about our dog." His voice cracks and the nurse flashes him a stern look.

She bustles to a machine, presses a button, and her frown turns sympathetic. "I've upped her morphine. Your daughter needs to rest, Sheriff Warner."

He nods and stands to leave, but I grab his hand. "What happened to the bear?"

Dad grimaces. "Bug, all that matters now is whether or not she had rabies."

I squeeze his fingers; force him to look at me. "Tell me, Dad, where is she? She killed my dog. She almost killed *me*."

He releases a shallow breath. "I shot her."

I fall back on my pillow, feeling sad and relieved, and whisper, "Good."

Dad clears his throat. "Animal control took the body, and they're testing her for rabies. Look, I'll be close if you need anything, Bug." He steps out the door of my private room.

The nurse takes my blood pressure again and glances at my wounds. "How is your pain?"

I gaze at her, my mouth slack. There is no number for my pain. The morphine hits and she must see it in my eyes because she says, "Is that better?"

I wipe my tears and shrug. The edges of the physical pain soften, and my muscles uncoil.

"Try to rest, Hannah. Press this button if you need anything, okay? The on-call doctor will be in to check on you soon, and here's a warm meal if you're hungry." She slides a dinner tray from her cart to mine.

She leaves the room, and Matilda fills my brain. I remember her as a puppy, trotting toward me with her big ears flopping, her red hair shining. I see her soft brown eyes gazing up at me from her favorite spot on the kitchen floor. I hear her tail thumping when she's too lazy to stand up and greet me.

I can't believe she's gone. I can't believe she saved me from a bear! When I needed her most, she was with me, attacking an animal four times her size and strength. I cry quietly.

A doctor arrives. She asks me a bunch of questions about my name, the date, the president's name, and the last thing I remember, which is driving away from my house. "Do you know where you went, or how you got back home?"

I shake my head.

After a few more questions, the doctor seems pleased. "You're young and healing fast," she says kindly. "I expect your memory will return in time. Don't try to rush it."

Do I want to remember being inside the jaws of a bear? Do I want to remember Matilda's final moments? I don't think so.

The doctor leaves after encouraging me to sleep. I'm warm and floating now, and the painkiller elicits a sense of well-being. This helps me think about Matilda without crying. I haul up truckloads of memories: Dad and I teaching her to hunt, the time she had to wear a cone on her head and she kept bumping into furniture, her snores in my ears at night, how she ran from me when I turned on the hose for her bath, how she always lay down with a dramatic flop.

I doze off and then wake and chew more ice chips. A new nurse comes in, checks my machines, murmurs a few words, and leaves. I turn up the volume on the television and start changing channels, settling on a local news program. I'm relieved to hear that the Gap Fire is 100 percent contained. *It's over.*

I'm about to change the station when Violet's picture fills the screen, bringing an instant smile to my face. "Violet," I whisper.

It's her senior photo, and she looks gorgeous. Her dark hair cascades in shining waves around her dimpled smile. Her deep brown eyes sport pinpoints of light, her teeth are a perfect pearl white. She leans against a bridge that spans behind her like a path to her future, leading over glittering water to a field of blooming mustard flowers. The evening sunlight illuminates her natural walnut highlights and bronzed cheeks.

My thoughts sharpen as an odd sensation of love and terror fills me. Why is Violet on TV?

The newscaster explains:

Seventeen-year-old Santa Barbara resident Violet Sandoval remains missing tonight. Police have no new leads in this startling case. The accomplished teenager disappeared from her grandmother's home in Gap Mountain, California, on August second. If you have any information about her whereabouts, please call the number listed below.

A montage of recent photos ends the clip: Violet dressed for her homecoming dance, Violet and Lulu posing outside the Victorian home, Violet with one of her horses, and a candid shot of Violet sticking out her tongue.

Missing? I shake my head, and the hospital room suddenly tilts. I throw up my hand as if to catch myself and accidentally overturn my dinner tray. It smashes to the floor.

I try to stand up, but too many tubes are holding me down. Why is Violet missing?

Sounds scream through my brain: squealing tires, angry voices, and a growling bear. I see blood dripping on white carpet. I glimpse a hunched figure in a window. I remember Violet's last text: *tomorrow I'm telling the police everything.*

Clutching my injured head, I rock side to side as sickness envelops me. Violet can't be missing. I see her face; it's furious and twisted. I remember in a flash that I was on my way to her house to talk to her with the monsters, and that I was scared. Did I make it? Did any of us? Who do the angry voices belong to? Whose blood is dripping on the carpet, and who is lurking in the window?

I try to stand again and crash to the floor.

22

August 5

Days Violet has been missing: 3

Time: 10:01 p.m.

When I open my eyes, I'm back in my hospital bed and it's full dark outside the window. My dad dozes on a padded chair that unfolds into a short bed. "Dad," I call out to him.

His eyelids flip wide, and he jerks upright. "Hey," he says, rushing to my side. "You fell out of bed. Are you all right?"

I shake my head. "I saw the news."

His face pales. "Oh."

Tears rush to my eyes. "Why didn't you tell me Violet is missing? What happened?"

My dad rubs the bridge of his nose and inhales slowly. "The doctor wants you to stay calm and rest, Hannah. You gave us a scare when you fell out of bed. Don't worry about Violet, I'm looking for her."

"Where?"

He offers a wan smile. "We've put out an Amber Alert and we're processing tips. I've set up a special task force, and my station received an agency assist to help my deputies handle routine calls while we're dealing with this."

"Dealing with what?"

"It's a high-profile case, Bug." He sighs and then continues. "The National Center for Missing and Exploited Children is here. They're working with Lulu and Violet's parents to organize search parties, make flyers, and get the word out on social media and to the news anchors. The family has offered a hundred-thousand-dollar reward for information. I've also notified TSA, in case Violet leaves or is taken somewhere by plane. Homeland Security and Border Patrol are also aware, and the FBI is helping. Everyone is looking for Violet."

In that jumble of agencies he rattled off, all I heard was *FBI*. "The FBI is here, in Gap Mountain? Is it really that serious? It's Violet, Dad, she's probably at the mall."

He frowns. "It is that serious, Hannah. She's not at the mall."

"You know what I mean. It's Gap Mountain! Nothing like this happens here."

"And now it has."

God, I can't believe this is real. "But why the FBI and TSA and stuff?"

He turns down his radio. "There's some concern she was kidnapped." He peers at me. "Did you know Violet has a personal trust fund worth six million dollars and that she'll receive another six million on her twenty-first birthday?"

I feel my cheeks color, because I did not know the dollar amount or that she had more money coming when she turned twenty-one. Another secret she kept from me. "No."

"That money doesn't include what she'll get after Lulu passes," he adds.

A panicky feeling fills me. I never considered Violet in these terms before, as an object of value that might be stolen. "When did she disappear?" The news mentioned it, but I already forgot.

"August second, the night you were attacked by the bear." He stands and leans over me, feeling my forehead like he did when I was a kid. "Are you in pain?"

I ignore that. "Maybe she went home to Santa Barbara?"

He grimaces. "I don't think we should talk about this right now."

"Why? She's one of my best friends."

"Because you're recovering, that's why."

"Dad, if you don't tell me what's going on, the news will."

We both glance at the television mounted to the wall. He grunts and sits on the edge of my bed. "All right, this is where we're at. It doesn't appear Violet ran away, she didn't pack any clothing or take her ID, purse, or car, but a significant amount of cash is missing from her purse, so we haven't ruled that out completely. Her last known location is the attic at her grandmother's house. She went up to watch a movie, and Ms. Sandoval passed out on the couch. A few hours later, Lulu woke and went to say goodnight. Violet was gone."

"Wait, wait, wait." A bolt of pain shoots through my forehead as I remember hearing raised voices and seeing blood on white carpet. Violet's attic has white carpet. "You think some-body took her from the *third floor?*"

"Or she snuck out of the home, but I'm not going to specu-late on that. We're still gathering information and looking at the evidence."

I rub my head and try to remember that night. The mon-sters and I were on our way to talk to Violet about her text. Did I make it? Are these fingernail scratches on my arm *hers?*

"I got you something," Dad says, changing the subject. He retrieves a small box tucked on the chair and hands it to me. "A new phone," he explains. "I found yours smashed outside our house. Looks like you dropped it. Must have run over it too. It was beyond repair, so I got you this."

I open the box and pull out a phone that is much fancier than the one I ran over. "Thanks. That was nice."

He moves to leave, then pauses, considering me. "I wasn't going to do this, but if I ask you a few specific questions about Violet, would that be okay? It might help."

My heart rate speeds up. "Yes, yes, I want to help."

He grabs his pad and a pen. "Can you think of anywhere Violet might go if she wanted to hide?"

"I don't know, maybe one of her grandmother's vacation rentals?"

"We've searched the family's real estate holdings. Any-where else?"

"Maybe a friend's house?"

He shakes his head. Of course he would have checked those leads first. "Did Violet take drugs or drink in excess?" he asks.

"In excess, no, not really."

"Was Violet dating anyone?"

Drummer's face flashes in my mind. He was there. I remember seeing his avatar standing beside Violet's in the attic. "No," I answer quickly, and tingles erupt across my scalp.

My dad consults his pad. "Luke might have been suicidal when he drove his Chevy off the embankment. Was Violet in a similar frame of mind? Was she upset about anything?"

My head begins to throb. She was upset about *everything*. "Yeah, she was upset about her friends getting arrested, but I don't believe she'd hurt herself."

I chew the inside of my lip, wondering if that's true. I wouldn't have thought Luke would drive drunk and high and veer off the road either, but he did. And guilt was eating Violet alive. "I mean, she might have done something out of character, like Luke did."

"We're considering that option." He exhales and puts his pad away. "If you remember anything that might help, call me." He nods toward my new phone.

"I will."

I curl into a ball and let the morphine drag me into a deep sleep.

———

The following day, a parade of nurses and doctors come and go, and they remove my catheter, run tests, and check my vitals. I download my contacts from the cloud into my new phone and text Drummer: *Come visit me.*

Drummer: *I tried before and they said no*

Me: *It's okay. Come now*

A half hour later, Drummer enters with a knock and a handful of balloons. His face contorts at the sight of me. "Hannah, oh fuck, are you all right?"

I gently touch my bandages. My dog is dead, my friend is missing, and I was almost eaten by a bear. I'm not fucking okay. "I'm doped up," I say in answer.

He lowers himself onto the bed beside me. "I wish I was." He takes my hand, and he looks so good—his hair shining, his tan skin darker than ever, his shirt tight, his blue eyes drinking me in. I open my mouth to, I don't know—to kiss him, to profess my love, to swallow him whole—but the meds are kicking hard, so I say nothing.

He lowers his voice, strokes my fingers. "Did you hear about Violet?"

"Yeah, and I don't think she ran away. She'd never ditch her grandma like that." *Or you.*

He lifts his shirt to wipe his eyes, showing his taut, bronzed stomach. Fucking Drummer. He makes it difficult to focus.

"Detectives were all over Violet's house, pulling out bags of evidence," he says, dragging me back into reality. "They think something bad happened to her." His voice warbles, and I realize Drummer is *crying.* Before I can ask if I or the other monsters made it there that night, he says, "I'm in trouble, Han."

I sit up. "What are you talking about?"

"I was the last one to see her," he answers. "I parked down the drive and snuck in through the back door."

"The one Grammy never locks?"

"Yeah. I should have waited for you like we said, but I thought I'd have better luck on my own."

"Why did you park down the drive?"

He inhales a long, regretful breath. "Because we're dating. It started right after the fire." He turns his eyes to me like a bad dog would. "I'm sorry I didn't tell you."

"I fucking knew it," I mutter.

He blinks and his eyelashes spike with tears. "We kept it from everyone, including Grammy. It just became a habit to park out of sight and sneak into the house."

"A habit? Jesus, Drummer, we don't lie to each other." My jaw muscles clench, and that sends shooting pains through my skull. I feel no satisfaction he's finally admitted to the relationship.

"At first, I didn't expect it to last," he explains. "And then it got serious and I—I wasn't sure how to tell you guys."

Because you're a coward, I think but don't say it.

"Plus, there's the stupid pact we made when we were kids."

"It's not stupid."

He squeezes my hand. "Yeah, I know. Don't tell your dad I was there, please? Violet and I had a fight, a bad fight—but I didn't do it."

Angry voices. Blood on white carpet. "Do what?" I ask him.

His voice pitches higher. "I don't know, whatever happened to her!"

My heart thumps—loud but slow. This can't be real. That bear either killed me or I'm dreaming.

Tears roll from his eyes and streak his tan cheeks. "They

lifted fingerprints from all over the house, and they're writing search warrants like party invitations. My prints are fucking everywhere. And there's that text she sent to the four of us: *tomorrow I'm telling the police everything.* If the FBI finds out about that, we're all fucked."

I glance at my closed door and lower my voice to a hiss. "How do they not *already* know?"

"She must have both her phones on her, because they're missing too," he answers. "I made Violet delete that last text—but what if it's still in the cloud? Damn it, Hannah, you were right about her. She can't handle the pressure."

Now he sees what I saw. "Look, you're not a suspect, right? And even if you were, you're her friend and it's natural your fingerprints and hairs and stuff would be at the house and in the attic. Don't worry."

Drummer goes silent mid-sob. His voice is flat when he speaks again. "I didn't hurt her, Han. Don't believe what they say."

"Don't believe what *who* says?"

"Them, the FBI. If she turns up dead or something, I didn't kill her." He stands up, tears leaking down his face, lips twisted. "Forget it. I gotta go."

"Drummer!" I reach for him and drop my phone. The new screen cracks. Fucking great. When I look up, he's gone.

I call his cell immediately, and it goes straight to his cheery voicemail: "It's Drummer, say what you gotta say, this ain't me anyway!"

I hang up and think about his words: *I didn't kill her.* No one said Violet's dead, and I can't imagine Drummer hurting *anyone.* He's a master at defusing, not fighting—he kisses girls out of their bad moods and jokes with his enemies until they're friends. *We had a fight,* he said. But hell, *I've* fought with Drummer, and it's always one-sided—me fighting, him poking fun or apologizing or admitting guilt, even if he did nothing wrong. Drummer wants to go back to having fun as quickly as possible; that's his modus operandi, not murder.

But he also said, *I'll die if they put me in a cage.* It's the one thing Drummer can't tolerate—constriction—and Violet threatened his freedom. Even a mouse will fight to protect itself. What will a man do?

23

August 7

Days Violet has been missing: 5

Time: 11:00 a.m.

The hospital releases me in the morning. My discharge papers include a referral to a psychologist who will treat me for post-traumatic stress disorder and traumatic dissociative amnesia.

I see my face for the first time. The bear's tooth sliced open my cheek, up along the bone, across my left eye, and up my eyebrow. The center of the brow is missing and my eye is swollen, but the eyeball itself is undamaged. There are tooth punctures and abrasions on my forehead and hairline, and another long gash leads down my temple. A few patches of my scalp are shaved, and neat stitches have sewn my skin back together. Yep, I'm Frankenstein, but I don't cry; I simply stare. Instead of feeling ruined, I feel revealed. I'm starting to look like the awful person I've become.

The plastic surgeon stops by before I check out. He advises me to wear my bandages to reduce scarring. And he tells me I might need another surgery later, after my left eye heals. He says he'll make me look "as normal as possible." Thanks, Doc, that's real comforting. I'm issued a sling for my arm and powerful painkillers and then discharged with a follow-up appointment in a few days.

Dad picks me up and drives me home, the radio tuned to country. "So what's happening with Violet?" I ask, feeling twitchy.

"Still processing leads and evidence, Bug. Nothing new."

We pull into our driveway, and there's an empty spot where my Wrangler should be. "Where's the Jeep?"

"At the repair shop, but the insurance adjuster says it's totaled. The interior is ripped apart. The metal frame is bent, and there's fur, saliva, and beef stew spread all over it."

A memory of the snarling animal, her ripping claws, and the shaking car flashes sharply in my mind. Grief rolls through me for my beloved Jeep. "Can I see it?"

Surprise flickers in my dad's eyes. "You want to?"

"It might help me remember."

He nods. "I'll talk to the shop, but not today. When you're feeling better."

I open his car door with my good arm and ease out. "I was going to sell that car to help pay for college."

"The insurance company will reimburse us," he assures me.

I face the porch, ready to greet Matilda, and remember all

over again that she's gone. The loss hits me fresh, and I can't move my feet.

"Come on," Dad says, guiding me gently into the house. "The neighbors sent food over for you. There's soup in the fridge, a casserole or two, some fruit, desserts, wraps, all kinds of stuff."

Six families live on our street, none closer than a mile. "That was nice of them."

"I have to get to work." He rolls on the balls of his feet, thinking hard, and opens his mouth as if he's going to say something, or question me again.

I pretend not to notice and yawn widely. "I need a nap. My brain feels fuzzy."

He takes the hint and leaves with a soft goodbye. Before driving away, he gives me the keys to his off-duty F250 pickup, should I need to go anywhere, and he unlocks the hunting rifle in case another bear shows up. To everyone's relief (mostly mine), the bear's rabies test was negative.

The house feels empty without Matilda in it. Dad has cleared away her food and water bowls, her bed, and her toys. We'd talked about getting another puppy while she was still alive, but I can't imagine that now.

I stare at my new phone and the small crack on the screen. My old data, photos, and contacts have been restored, making this phone a shinier reincarnation of my last. I swipe through the saved photo albums, which are filled with images of my best friends—the monsters—my horses, and Matilda.

Violet smiles in almost every one of her pictures, her dimples deep, her eyes shining. She has a knack for posing, and every shot is perfect, her head cocked, her body angled. She's been cute and beloved and cherished since the moment she popped out of the womb. I wonder what that's like? My mom put whisky in my baby bottle to make me stop crying.

I send a group text to my friends and include Violet, just in case she's out there somewhere, reading them: *I'm out of the hospital.*

Mo texts me privately: *don't include Violet, what if a murderer or kidnapper has her?*

Jesus, Mo, that's dark. I send a new group message to the four of us, minus Violet: *I'm home. Is there anything new about Violet?*

A long silence and then a simple answer from Luke: *no*

Mo: *I'm sorry about Matilda*

Me: *can you guys come over? I don't want to be alone*

Mo: *I can come over*

Luke: *me too.*

Drummer: *I'm at work*

Luke and Mo show up an hour later, and we sprawl in my family room with sodas and chips. My dad finished arresting Luke on the malicious arson charges while I was in the hospital, and Luke's out on bail for now. Lulu Sandoval paid his bond.

"Makeup will fix that eyebrow," Mo says matter-of-factly.

I recount for them what I remember about the bear attack—mainly, that she dragged me by my head.

"The wrestling team could use talent like that," Luke jokes.

"Thanks, asshole."

Luke's speech remains slow, his expression flat, but he has more color in his face since the last time I saw him. He shrugs and avoids looking at me; in fact, he hasn't looked at me once since he came over. I touch my bandaged face. Is it because I'm gross or because my dad arrested him?

"Not all the news is bad," Luke says. "I found my cat."

Mo claps her hands. "Where? How?"

"She's been living in some guy's barn, and he finally caught her and brought her to an animal rescue. Her paw pads are burned, but she's okay."

We release a collective breath, as if finding the cat means everything is going to be okay, which obviously it's not. "Are you still staying with Mo?" I ask.

He stretches his legs, stares at his hands. "Nah, my mom took me back because Aiden wouldn't stop crying for me." A fond glow lights his face at Aiden's name, and then he lowers his voice. "What has your dad told you about Violet? Does he have any leads?"

I drain my soda and enjoy the sugar that floods my system. "I don't think so. Everything he told me was also on the news."

Luke finally looks at me, his forehead crinkled with thought. "Is it true you really don't remember anything about that night or the bear attack?"

Blood on white carpet, angry voices, a hunched figure in the window—I have memories but I don't actually *remember*. "It's true."

He clears his throat, his eyes shifting between Mo and me.

"So, uh, you don't know if you went to Violet's after getting her fucked-up text? You told us to meet you there."

My stomach rockets to my throat. I peer at him, mentally circling like a wolf, and tug on my long sleeves to hide the fingernail scratches. Does he know something I don't? I decide to hold my cards close. "No, I mean, I don't remember. Did you go?"

Luke flushes. "I didn't make it." But his nostrils flare, and that's Luke's "tell"—has been since he was seven. It means he's lying or hiding something.

I untie and retie my Converse shoes, thinking. "Maybe she freaked out. Maybe she drove off the road or something like you did, Luke."

He scowls at me. "I didn't drive off the road because I *freaked out*. It was an accident."

My mouth pops open then closed. I know better than to prod Luke when he's pissed.

He stands, paces slowly. "I was angry 'cause it's *my* fault you got arrested, Mo"—he peers hard at her—"I brought that shit into the woods. But I didn't mean to crash. I just lost control." His laugh is humorless and cold. "Wrecked my mom's car too." He drags his fingers across his shaved head.

Mo appears at his side, tries to soothe him. "It's not your fault," she whispers. "We were all there, and I didn't get arrested for the fire, I got arrested for lying."

He pinches the bridge of his crooked nose. "You were protecting me," he rasps. "You lied to protect me."

"All of us," she corrects.

He continues, shaking his head. "Did you know, Hannah, that after your dad impounded my car for the DUI, his department used its GPS to track my movements on July seventh?"

"No!"

Luke continues: "That piece-of-shit Chevy placed me at the Gap Lake parking lot at three p.m.—that was his 'new evidence'—but my lawyer says tracking my car on an unrelated offense is illegal. She's trying to get it thrown out. I might go free, but Violet's text makes us *all* look guilty: *tomorrow I'm telling the police everything*," he says, imitating her higher-pitched voice. "Why couldn't she keep her mouth shut?"

"She's missing, Luke. Don't be a dick," Mo scolds.

Luke bends in half and moans like a wounded animal. "I'm confused," he cries. "Violet should be here, with us, drinking fucking Coke. She should have just stayed quiet and lived her perfect life. I—I miss her." His tears drop and splatter my floor.

"Luke, it's okay, we all miss her," Mo says, reaching for him.

"We're all guilty," I murmur.

Luke gapes at me, panic flitting across his features, and Mo sputters, "Guilty of starting the fire, yeah, but not of hurting Violet."

I crush my empty soda can. "Right, but her text gives each of us a motive."

"Not you," Luke rasps as he sits back down. "The police have no idea *you* were at the Gap."

My throat tightens. "I'm not talking about what the police know. I'm just saying the timing is odd. She threatened us and now she's missing."

Our eyes shift to one another, and Mo shivers. "You're scaring me, Han. None of us would do anything to Violet. That's fucking ridiculous."

I shake my head, also confused. Voices, blood, and a figure in the attic window—I saw and heard these things. I must have been there, and I wasn't alone. At least one of the angry voices was male. And while I couldn't see the person in the window very well, he looked as tall as me. The other angry voice was female. I peer at Mo. "Did you go to Violet's house? You said you'd try."

Her eyes widen. "No, my parents wouldn't let me leave. We watched a movie with my brother."

I look from her to Luke. "Weren't you two together? You were living at Mo's."

"He left after dinner," Mo says, biting her lip as if she'd rather not have told me this.

Luke recoils from her. "What are you getting at, Mo?"

She blinks. "Nothing, just wondering where you went. You didn't answer when I called, and you didn't call me back. It's not like you."

Luke leaps to his feet and looms over us, his expression raw. "You think *I* hurt Violet?" he asks, spit flying from his mouth.

"No!" Mo cries, holding out her hand as if to ward him off. "What's wrong with you?"

"I'm fucking tired," he says, his eyes cutting to mine. "You said you'd take care of this, Hannah." He flexes over me like a marble statue—beautiful, strong, and pale—frozen in a moment of livid fury. Is he guilty or scared or both? I'm not sure.

He scoops up his jacket. "Hanging out was a stupid idea. Fuck you both. Don't call me." He kicks a kitchen chair on his way out, and then we hear his bicycle chain squeaking as he rides away as fast as he can.

Mo starts to cry.

"It's the head injury," I tell her. "Luke didn't mean it."

She shakes her head. "It's not that. It's us, our group. Nothing will ever be the same again."

It's true and I put my arm around her. "No matter what, this was going to be our last summer together," I say. "You realize that, don't you? College will change us. We'll meet new people and get married and get jobs. We'll move away."

Mo sniffles as I follow my thoughts to their inevitable end. Our loyalties will shift with time. Maybe they already have shifted. The days of being the monsters are almost over, and it's too bad we have to go down like this—in flames.

24

August 7

Days Violet has been missing: 5

Time: 3:00 p.m.

After Mo leaves, I do my chores, using my good arm. I fly-spray the horses, shovel manure, sweep the stalls, and think about Violet. Her case has snatched national headlines due to her grandmother's wealth, because our town is currently famous for the Gap Fire, and because Violet is a gorgeous teenager headed to Stanford University. The terror I felt when she threatened to tell on us has drifted away like the smoke from the wildfire. Now I simply miss her.

When I'm finished, I head inside, down a bottle of Gatorade, and notice the dust building up on the baseboards and tables. Damn house is already getting dirty. This makes me wonder how Lulu is going to get the blood out of that white carpet. Right then my phone rings, startling me.

It's Justin, from Bishop.

I stare at his name on the screen, my heart fluttering. Do I answer? Oh fuck, why not? After the bear attack and the news about Violet, our evening together doesn't feel so . . . monumental. "Hello?"

"Hey," he says, "I just saw your name in the paper."

My throat closes and my brain stumbles. "What paper?" *Shit, am I in the news?* I grab the remote control and turn on the TV, wait to see if my face gets plastered on the screen. "What did I do?"

He laughs. "Damn, girl, are you wanted or something? I read you got bit by a bear."

"Oh, right." I lean one hand on the counter to catch my breath. "Yeah, I'm fine, just banged up."

He absorbs that, then drops his voice an octave. "Anything I can do to make you feel better?"

I remember his lips kissing my chest, his hands all over me, his eyes drilling into mine. "I look terrible," I say, glancing at my scarred face in the mirror.

"I don't care."

He doesn't care? What the hell does that mean? "I'm not really up for it, Justin. I'm sore."

He's quiet a moment. "I could give you a hot bath, and you could take a painkiller. I want to see you, Hannah. I like you. A lot."

My spine tightens because I'm not sure if I believe him. Does he want me, or more sex? It's confusing. "Can I call you when I feel better?"

He releases a deep sigh. "Sure, if that's what you want. Hey, I was wondering, do you like to ride horses?"

Do I like to ride horses? We really don't know each other at all. "Yes."

"I got two ropers if you want to go on a trail ride sometime."

A real cowboy, I should have known it. My shoulders loosen, because I've been around enough rodeo boys to understand the drill. He's circling me, keeping his reins tight until he's sure he's got me where he wants me. Then he'll swoop. The key is to keep moving until I'm sure I want to be caught. "I'll call you."

"'Kay," he says.

I hang up and reach to turn off the news when Violet's sunny image fills the screen, followed by a press conference that is happening live outside the new command center my father set up at the church. Dad is at the podium, looking grim. FBI agents, county officials, his deputies, and a representative from the National Center for Missing and Exploited Children stand behind him.

I sink to the floor and watch.

Camera shutters click away as my dad begins speaking:

We now suspect foul play in the disappearance of Violet Sandoval. Evidence we collected from her grandmother's home on August second has been analyzed and expedited at the Department of Justice crime lab in Fresno, California.

He pauses before continuing:

Broken fingernails and blood droplets have been identified as matching Violet Sandoval's DNA. A window on the third level of the family's home shows signs of forced entry, and cash was stolen from her purse. The fingerprints lifted from the window are being run through the Automated Latent Print System to be matched to possible known perpetrators.

My dad swallows and glances down at the podium.

Finally, and most upsetting, detectives discovered deposits of fresh semen in the Sandoval attic. The sample was hours old at the time of collection, and we are not ruling out sexual assault.

There's a flurried reaction from the press.

My hand flies to my mouth. Broken fingernails? Blood? Semen? What happened in that attic? I grab my sleeve and pull it down, hiding the deep half-moon indents on my arms. I need to remember.

My dad plows on as the reporters quiet:

We are investigating the possibility that Violet was removed from her home by force, possibly by more than one suspect. We're asking for the community's help in solving this case.

He goes on to request that people report any odd behavior they might have witnessed the evening that Violet disappeared or in the preceding days—noises coming from a car trunk, anyone purchasing rope or knives or zip ties, suspicious vehicles in the area, signs of fresh campsites in the woods near the Sandoval home. He takes a few questions.

Sheriff Warner, has there been a ransom demand?

He shakes his head.

There has been no communication or request for money.

She has a follow-up question.

Has kidnapping been ruled out in this case?

Nothing has been ruled out.

A male reporter asks:

Has the semen been matched to a known offender?

The sample is being cross-checked against CODIS, the Combined DNA Index System created and maintained by the FBI, and against voluntary genealogy databases. This may help us develop a suspect list through family trees. At this time, we have not identified a specific suspect related to the DNA.

Do the genealogy databases you're referring to belong to companies like Ancestry.com or Family Search?

Yes, sir.

A female reporter blurts out:

Is it legal to access that DNA, Sheriff Warner?

Yes, ma'am.

Another question from someone in the back:

Sheriff Warner, do you believe that Violet Sandoval is alive?

I will not speculate on her condition. That's all for now. We need to get back to finding her.

He walks away, followed by his task force, and the number for the FBI tip line flashes on the screen.

Bumps erupt across my arms, and I feel as if I've been punched in the gut, but I'm also really proud of my dad.

My phone rings again. This time it's Mo. "Did you watch the press conference?"

"Yeah, I can't believe it."

"Maybe Violet's disappearance doesn't have anything to do with the fire or us," Mo says. "Maybe she was kidnapped!"

"But the timing is suspicious, Mo. Do you really believe strange men randomly kidnapped her on the same night she threatened to tell on us?"

She gulps. "Well, we didn't do it! Jesus, Han."

Drummer's face appears in my head. *I didn't kill her,* he said at the hospital, but no one knows for sure she's dead. "Of course we didn't," I murmur.

"There are search parties meeting every day. Do you want to join one when you feel better?"

My scalp prickles. "Sure, I guess so."

"They'll find Violet, Han, they have to. She can't be gone. I gotta go. Get some rest, okay? You sound tired."

"Bye, Mo." I glance at the scratches on my arm that look like fingernail marks and then quickly cover them again. The detectives found broken fingernails in her attic, which means somebody's skin is beneath Violet's nails. I was there, I'm sure of it, and my stomach lightens as a new thought dawns: *Maybe I tried to help Violet, and if I saw who took her, maybe I'm in danger too.*

25

August 10

Days Violet has been missing: 8

Time: 1:45 p.m.

Each day that passes without finding Violet feels surreal. We expect her to turn up at any moment. I'm prepared to feel relieved and then throttle her for worrying us, but with each day it becomes more difficult to imagine a plausible explanation for her absence. I rest and take my pain meds every four hours. Matilda's death and Violet's disappearance have ripped me to shreds.

Violet's parents, who've been in touch from their private yachting trip from San Francisco to Australia, finally arrive in Gap Mountain, to the flash of many cameras. They stay with Lulu Sandoval at the house and make very public pleas for the safe return of their daughter.

I call Drummer and Luke repeatedly on the prepaid phones,

but neither will answer. One of us is missing, and no one wants to talk. It's like everyone is hiding out, or hiding something. I'm scared for the monsters.

When I sleep, I have nightmares about a bear popping my head like a balloon. I see red blood dripping onto white carpet. The half-moon outside my window becomes Violet's fingernail, digging into my skin (*burrowing* into my skin). I want to know if I was in the attic. I want to know who the angry voices belong to. Did I hear Drummer and Violet arguing? Was Luke there? Semen and missing cash is upsetting information to absorb.

Oddly enough, life continues. My dad helps me care for the horses each day, talks to the doctors, and handles correspondence with San Diego State about my paltry financial aid award. The fire investigation stalls while Luke's lawyer dukes it out with the district attorney over my dad's using the Chevy's GPS data as evidence in Luke's arson case.

Meanwhile, Violet's case ramps up. Hundreds of leads have been called in about her, sending officers on wild goose chases across California and around the country.

A witness reports seeing two strange men at a gas station just outside town the day Violet disappeared. They drove a dusty blue van, and after filling their tank, they filled two extra gas cans. An APB is out on the make and model of the van. Grainy images of the men, printed from the station's CCTV, circulate in the news.

There still has been no demand for ransom money.

When the skeleton of a woman is found three miles from Gap Mountain, the reporters swarm, but when the county coroner states that the body belongs to a woman in her fifties or sixties, the fevered mood quickly cools. My father believes it's the remains of a demented resident who wandered from her home five years ago. The body's DNA is sent to a crime lab for positive identification, but there is no possibility that it's Violet.

It frightens me that my town is so eager to accept a body in place of my friend. People would say: *Her suffering is over. She was so bright, so beautiful. It's a shame.* It would be sad, a tragedy, but Violet would be *accounted* for. I guess being dead is better than being *nowhere*.

My dad comes home only to shave, sleep a few hours, and go back to work. It seems like he's busier now than when he was dealing with the wildfire. Everything I learn about Violet's case, I learn on television. The nation is eagerly anticipating the CODIS results on the semen sample and the ALPS report on fingerprints lifted in the attic, because this evidence might produce the case's first viable suspect or suspects. As of now, there are none.

My manager at the Reel Deal has given me time off to heal, but aside from home, there's really nowhere to go. Mo tells me reporters are staked out in front of the Sandoval home and the sheriff's office, and they are often seen buying takeout meals from the Wildflower Café, just waiting for news.

Reporters describe Violet as *single*, but I know that she is not single.

I text Drummer's prepaid phone, hoping for a response: *Does anyone know that you and Violet were dating?*

Gray dots appear, meaning he read the text, but he doesn't answer; he calls instead. "Why are you asking me this? Did something happen?"

"No."

Drummer exhales. "Is your dad there? Is he listening to us?"

"Of course not! I'm trying to help you. Why haven't you returned my calls?"

His voice breaks. "Because my girlfriend's missing, because I'm fucking scared." He hiccups and I imagine he's as fragile as an egg right now. "I loved her, Hannah."

My spine tightens. "Loved?"

"No, I mean, love, I *love* her. Fuck." He sucks for air. "I would never hurt her, not on purpose, you have to believe me."

"I do, I believe you." But my mind trips over his qualification— I would never hurt her, *not on purpose.*

He goes quiet.

"Drummer?"

His voice rattles like he's chewing gravel. "I don't know, Han, nothing has gone right since the fire, you know, nothing except falling for Violet. I've been so spun on her, I wasn't really paying attention to anything else. I'm so totally fucked. . . ."

"Why, Drummer? What are you not telling me?"

He spins the conversation. "Was Violet seeing another guy?"

"Not that I know of. Do you think she was?"

"No, hell no, but if she wasn't, that sample"—his voice creaks on the word—"it might be mine."

I've been pacing and now I fall onto my couch. "Are you talking about the *semen?*"

"God, don't say it like that," he mutters. "Violet and I, we did it in her attic that night. I might have, you know, left something behind."

"I thought you had a fight?"

"Yeah, we did. Sex and a fight." He laughs weakly.

I rub my forehead; the headache of the last few days returns with a roar. "I thought you used condoms."

"I do, but uh . . . she went on the pill. Shit, you don't want to hear about this."

"I've had sex," I blurt out.

He inhales deeply. "When? With *who?*"

There's no going back now, so I bluster on: "With the guy who drove me to Bishop the day of the fire."

"Like, on the way to the hotel?" he asks, confused.

"Don't be an idiot. We went on a date two weeks ago. Remember the night at the bowling alley, when I was dressed up?"

"Yeah." He groans. "So you slept with him on the first date?"

"Fuck you." I melt into tears. "It was special." It was not special, not at all, and I cry harder.

He swallows several times, as if something is stuck in his throat. His voice is soft when he speaks again. "I'm sorry. I'm just surprised you didn't tell me."

"You didn't tell me about Violet."

There's a long pause. "You're right. We shouldn't keep secrets."

It's too fucking late for that, I think.

Drummer switches the conversation back to himself. "If the lab matches that sample to me . . ."

"Hey, relax," I say. "You don't have DNA on file. They can't randomly match a semen sample to you. You have to either be in the database or be a suspect with a cheek swab. You're safe, Drummer. Except . . ."

His breath catches and I imagine him blinking furiously. "Except what?"

I close my eyes, chase my memories, but they scamper away like rabbits. There's a new one, a quick flash of Drummer yanking on Violet's arm. There's also the blood on the carpet and the person in the window, but the images are like mirages that vanish when I get too close. "Except you should tell my dad you and V were together. If he finds out on his own, it won't look good."

"No, Han, no way."

"It will explain the . . . sample you left behind," I add. I imagine he and Violet having sex in the attic—our attic, the place we all hang out. I see them cuddling and kissing and . . . and it's like being walloped with an oar. Suddenly the floor rolls beneath me and blood whooshes between my ears. "Why won't you tell him?" I whisper.

Drummer is dead silent for a full minute. Then he hangs up on me.

26

August 10

Days Violet has been missing: 8

Time: 2:20 p.m.

I shove the prepaid phone under my mattress and pace my bed-room floor. How can Drummer be so thoughtless? He left his DNA at a crime scene and believes he can ignore it, just as he ignored his pregnant girlfriend two years ago, just as he ignored his cancer-ridden dog until it was too late, and just as he ig-nored Violet's threats. Now I have to clean up his mess, good old Hannah Banana.

He said he's at work; good. I swallow a painkiller, reach for my Jeep keys, and then remember that the bear mauled it. I blow out a breath and grab the keys to my dad's pickup instead. His vehicle is better, actually—less flashy—for what I'm about to do.

When I arrive in Drummer's neighborhood, I park in the shade of an old sycamore on a street behind his house. I cut through the woods, approach his side window, and slide the single-pane glass open. Glancing around, I don't see anyone watching. Most folks are at work or hiding from the blistering sunshine in their homes at this time of day, which is good for me.

I crawl into his bedroom and inhale the scent of his cheap body wash as tingles rush through me. How does he affect me like this when he's not even here? I glance longingly at his unmade bed, at the indent of his body in the mattress. It's his childhood bed, and I remember Drummer when he was small—towheaded with big teeth. We played every single day in the summertime, but it wasn't always fun. He threw the football too hard, he slaughtered me at video games, and if he couldn't find me right away when we played hide-and-seek, he gave up and went home, leaving me waiting and alone.

But one day when we were twelve, he didn't want to play games anymore; he wanted to "hang out." He threw his arm around me and invited me to watch a movie. His voice was deeper, and I thought maybe he was sick, but he didn't look sick. He looked thicker and darker and taller and cuter. He smelled good. We watched a movie in the dark, and he touched me all over. I couldn't breathe, couldn't think. Afterward, he whispered in my ear, "Don't tell anyone we did that."

I agreed because it was our special secret. But it never happened again, and we never talked about it. It was as if it had never happened *at all*.

My heart swells, painful and throbbing. I'm still twelve, still waiting to watch a movie *in the dark*, still wanting Drummer's full attention on me.

God, Hannah, you're here for a reason, and it's not to reminisce.

I force myself to get moving. He says he didn't hurt Violet, *not on purpose*, but what does that mean? I think it means he did hurt her. God, I thought their relationship would end in disaster, but I never imagined this. Violet shouldn't have threatened him. Monsters don't rat on monsters, monsters don't date monsters—we made these pacts to keep us together, and now we're falling apart.

After sliding open his closet door, I squat and sift through his crap—hunting boots, dirty laundry, old homework assignments, gum wrappers, bullet shells, fishing gear—not sure what I'm looking for. When my fingers touch one of his concert T-shirts, my stomach lurches. There's dark blood splattered on the hem.

A vision slams me from the night Violet went missing: Drummer grabbing her arm in the attic and yelling, *Take that back!* He's wearing this shirt, and I'm watching them through a keyhole in the attic door. Dizziness overwhelms my equilibrium, and I crumple over. Oh god, I was definitely there, but I was hiding. I'm a *witness*!

I close my eyes, visualize the attic, and try to follow the voices, the argument, the attack. Images rise—Violet's tears, Drummer's clenched teeth, and the dull smack of flesh—but the pictures in my head expand and pop like balloons. Did

Drummer see me? I don't think so. I clutch the T-shirt and smell Violet's perfume. "Drummer, what did you do?"

Right then, the front door of his house creaks open and footsteps *click-clack* across the tile floor. Someone plunks grocery bags onto the kitchen counter. His mom or dad is home!

I finish my quick and silent search of his room. The rest of the outfit Drummer wore that night is fresh in my memory, and in seconds I've retrieved his black Levi's, his old-school checkered Vans, and the bloody concert T-shirt.

I check the surrounding clothing for droplets of blood or long dark hairs. I rifle through his pockets and drawers for Violet's missing cash and scan all his scraps of paper, looking for any written record of his plans that night. I've learned a fair amount from living with my father, and Drummer ought to be grateful. I bag up the "evidence" in an old shopping bag and return everything else to the way it was.

I step onto his desk chair, crawl out his open window, and race to my dad's F250. Turning the engine over, I cringe at the dull roar and then pull away from the curb, my hands shaking. The bag of clothes sits on the seat beside me, pulsing in the afternoon light like Pandora's box. That bloody outfit holds secrets. It knows what happened to Violet and—maybe—so do I.

Tomorrow I'm calling the psychologist. I can't help Violet or protect Drummer until I know exactly what happened. As I roll out of his neighborhood, one thought ticks louder than all the others: *burn the fucking clothes.*

27

Mo texts me just as I turn onto Pine Street in downtown Gap Mountain: *can you come over?*

I glance at the bag of Drummer's clothes and tuck it beneath the seat. *Sure. On my way.*

Her father answers the door when I arrive at their single-story rental. "Hi, Hannah. She's in her room," he says, returning to the kitchen. The low voices of Mo's mother and brother reach me through the clattering of pots and the sizzle of meat cooking as I pass the kitchen. They look like Old Navy mannequins in their brand-new outfits, another reminder that they lost everything they own in the wildfire.

I pad down the hallway. "Mo?" I call outside her closed door.

"Come in." She lounges on her bed, phone in hand, also wearing a fresh ensemble—pink sweats, a tank top, white Jordans, and a black scrunchie around her wrist. Her face is freshly washed and free of makeup, and she's chewing on a Red Vine. When I was in the hospital, my dad told me she quit her job at the general store.

Everyone in Gap Mountain knows that my dad arrested her for lying to police about where she was when the wildfire started, and customers have been rude. I sit beside her. "What's wrong?"

Her fingers swipe her phone screen as she shakes her head. "I got my court date, and it lands right in the middle of classes during first semester. I don't know how this is going to work." She blinks back tears. "College was supposed to be fun."

I climb farther onto her bed and lie beside her. "I'm sorry, Mo."

She hands me a piece of licorice. "I might have to withdraw anyway."

"What do you mean? Why?"

"My college fund is going to my lawyer, and I'm not even sure he's worth it." She slides her scrunchie from wrist to wrist. "Luke's lawyer, the Pit Bull, is way more passionate. She calls him every day, works overtime, and fights hard for him, and he doesn't have to pay her a dime. Mine files a lot of paperwork, directs our calls to his paralegal, and charges four hundred dollars an hour."

"He's probably very smart," I assure her.

She lifts one shoulder. "The lawyer Lulu recommended costs nine hundred dollars an hour."

"That doesn't mean they're better."

"I think it does," Mo argues. "How is this justice?"

Guilt rears inside me. "I'm sorry."

She lifts her hand. "Don't be. My lawyer doesn't believe I'll serve any time, because I have a clean record, good grades, and great character witnesses. Besides, my charges aren't as serious as Luke's. It's college I'm worried about. I don't know how I'm going to pay for tuition and housing and books."

"You can work your way through, or apply for loans."

She rolls her eyes. "Whatever. At least I'm not going to prison. The prosecutor is pressuring Luke hard. If he doesn't confess with all the details, they'll pursue the malicious arson charges and ask for a nine-year sentence, plus a twenty-million-dollar fine. Can you fucking believe it?"

Shit, I had no idea. "What's he going to do?"

"I don't know. If he confesses, they'll lower the charges and the sentence, but from what I hear, he's going to plead not guilty and take his chances. He says he believes in the Pit Bull."

I laugh. "Sounds like she believes in him too."

"Yeah. No one's ever fought for him before." Mo blinks and two perfect tears skid down her cheeks. "Luke brought the pipe and the matches, but he doesn't deserve nine years in prison."

"I know," I say, but I doubt the families of the dead would agree.

"Did you see the national paper this morning?"

I shake my head. "Another article about Violet?"

"Nope, it's about Luke and me." Mo riffles through the newspapers stacked at the end of her bed and hands me today's.

The headline says SUSPECTED GAP MOUNTAIN ARSONISTS OUT ON BAIL.

"I can't believe they're calling you arsonists!" I cry. "The media has already convicted you."

"Yep."

I scan the article, which paints Luke as an angry seventeen-year-old from a bad home (okay, that's true) and Mo as a promising teen who made a terrible mistake (also true). Before we started the wildfire and ruined summer, Luke talked about taking an EMT course and applying at the fire department (irony of ironies!), and Mo's family had enough money saved for her to become a nurse without taking out student loans. I'm suddenly overcome by gratitude that my friends are taking the hit for what we did.

Mo and I hang out until her dad calls us for dinner and invites me to stay.

"Thank you," I say past the hard lump in my throat. My dad arrested their daughter and they're *feeding* me. God.

After dinner, we sit around the table and speculate about Violet. "There's nothing worse than a mother losing her child," says Mo's mom. "Nothing in the world."

Without thinking, I add, "Except maybe a child losing her mother."

Everyone at the table sucks in their breath, including Mo's older brother, and my face grows hot. "I'm sorry," I murmur.

"No, honey, I'm sorry!" Mo's mom jumps up and hugs me tight, and her warmth envelops me.

Are all mothers this squishy and loving, I wonder? Luke's mom isn't. And mine didn't take care of me. But if I couldn't have a mother like Mo's, I'm good with not having one at all. I bet Luke would agree with me on that.

When I get home, it's dark and my dad's not there. I grab the bag full of "evidence" I collected from Drummer's and decide to add the clothing I wore that night to the pile. If I was a witness, I don't want to end up a suspect too.

After retrieving the clothes from my room, I pad outside and toss both our outfits into a metal feeding trough, douse them in lighter fluid, and set them on fire.

28

The next day, I wake up feeling restless, pad into the kitchen, and brew a cup of coffee in our new Keurig. After the caffeine hits my system, I call the psychologist, and she schedules an appointment for me tomorrow. She says that since my memory loss was brought on by acute trauma, she believes we should "act fast."

After that, I clean the horse stalls and dump the ashes from the clothing fire into the trash. I've called Drummer three times since searching his room last night, but he hasn't answered. Idiot. I still can't believe he was going to leave that bloody shirt in the back of his closet for the special agents to find.

My dad claims that the FBI agents are assisting his department, but really, they're running the show. I haven't seen the agents yet, but I heard they drive a black SUV and wear suits, just like on TV. A thrill runs through me at the thought, and I wonder if I could work for the FBI instead of becoming a peace officer like my dad. Then I wouldn't have to worry about policing the community where I live and arresting my friends, or my neighbors, or my future kids' friends.

But first things first: I need to figure out what happened to Violet. I text Mo: *feeling good today. let's join one of those search parties.*

Mo: *You sure you're up to it?*

Me: *I'm fine. Will you drive?*

She agrees so I text my dad and he sends me information about a search party meeting at the Gap Lake trailhead at 11:00 a.m.

My stomach lurches at the mention of the lake. If Violet's body is in the Gap, she'll never be found. The huge fish at the bottom will chew off her flesh. The cold water will keep her body from rising. Time will grind her bones to sand.

Mo pulls up in her Corolla twenty minutes later with the music on and the air conditioner blasting. "Hop in, fool!"

A grin spreads across my face at the sight of Mo wearing big sunglasses, chewing gum, and twirling her dark red hair around one finger, and I forget for one blissful second that it's not a normal summer day.

The drive to Gap Lake's trailhead cools the mood as we retrace our fateful steps from the day we started the fire. Folks are gathered in the parking lot when we arrive—high school kids, parents, grandparents, and volunteers from the Find Violet organization that Lulu established. They're wearing orange vests and drinking coffee as they wait to be sorted into groups.

The volunteers peer at Mo and me, curious. Most of them know we're Violet's best friends—along with the boys, but the boys aren't here. I feel their absence the way people feel their missing limbs.

"I can't believe we're looking for a *body*," Mo whispers as she pulls her hair into a bun. Her freckled skin has already turned pink in the heat. "Violet can't be . . . dead."

"I know; this is so fucked up. But if Violet's not dead, where *is* she?"

"I can't think about that, Han."

An official wearing a Find Violet T-shirt directs Mo and me to a folding table. It's set up with sign-in sheets and water bottles with labels that display Violet's senior photo. Mo and I write our names and record our driver's license numbers. Writing hers in a large, loopy script, she asks, "Why do they want our IDs?"

I answer in a whisper, "Sometimes a suspect will return to the scene of a crime. Detectives will check out everyone who volunteers today."

She blows back her long bangs. "Seriously? They're going to check *me* out."

"Yep."

"How? Like, they'll question me?"

I finish writing down my ID number, and we move out of the way so others can do the same. "Probably not. They'll compare us to their suspect's profile and make a list of who they want to talk to first." *Angry voices, a hunched figure in the window, blood on white carpet, Drummer shouting, Take that back!*—the memories flash through my mind, and the forest shrinks. "Don't worry," I add, "we don't fit the profile."

Mo lifts an eyebrow. "Let me guess, white male, twenty-five to thirty years old, lives with his mother?"

That draws a laugh. "Not quite."

"But close?"

"Maybe. He's male for sure."

Mo rolls her eyes. "Obviously."

Volunteers pass out orange vests, whistles, and plastic booties to cover our shoes so we don't leave tread marks, and then a short man with a megaphone organizes us into teams of eight people. The lead person in each group holds a map with a color-coded grid.

Our leader is Jeannie, the head server at the Wildflower Café. After introducing herself to our group, she holds up two spray bottles. "Bug spray? Sunscreen? Anyone?"

A few people take her up on the offer and spray their exposed skin.

It's not until this moment that I realize I'm not dressed to find a body. I'm wearing cutoffs and a thin white tank top. The mosquitoes are going to suck me dry, and my new Vans are going to get trashed. I'm dressed for summer, not for crawling around in the woods, searching for one of my best friends with a bunch of overcaffeinated volunteers.

Unlike me, Jeannie *is* dressed to find a body. She's wearing hiking boots, a wide-brimmed shade hat, and a backpack, and she's slathered in greasy sunscreen and bug spray. She takes quick charge of our directionless group. "Gather up," she calls out.

"It's GI Jane," Mo whispers, and a young man from the auto-parts store snickers.

Seven of us merge around Jeannie as she shows us the map and points out our grid. "When we get there, we'll spread out. Go slow, mark anything unusual—a shoe print, a candy wrapper, broken branches, and of course the obvious stuff like clothing or blood." She hands out fluorescent orange tape to use for marking.

Sweat dribbles down my forehead as I take the tape.

Jeannie rattles her backpack. "I've got a first-aid kit and granola bars, so come see me if you need anything. Use these sticks to prod long grasses and thick brush, but be aware of rattlesnakes." Jeannie grabs seven walking sticks leaning on the parking lot fencing behind her and hands them out one by one. My body is still sore from being tossed around by a bear, and I use my stick like a cane. I probably shouldn't have come, but I can't turn back now.

As we hike up the familiar trail, I remember all the years we came before—Violet, Luke, Mo, Drummer, and me—with our parents when we were young and had to wear life vests, on our own in middle school when we snuck here without telling our families, and then as teenagers when we drove here with coolers full of beer.

After Violet turned thirteen, she tried to swim all the way across the Gap without a life vest. Luke freaked out and insisted on following her in his inner tube. Good thing too, because she got tired halfway across and started to panic. He rescued her and they floated in the center of the lake, legs entwined, while the sun glittered on the water.

The depth of the Gap fascinated Violet, especially after the Army Corps discovered that it was deeper than Lake Tahoe and our town made national headlines. *Maybe it leads to another world*, she speculated. *Maybe the Gap is a mirror and copies of us live on the other side, leading opposite lives. In that world, you four visit me in Santa Barbara and I'm not the outsider.*

You're not an outsider, Mo countered.

Violet's gaze shifted sadly back to the water.

I didn't get it then, but Violet was right. Gap Mountain might be a part of her, but she's not a part of Gap Mountain. Her memory brings a smile, though, as I lift a heavy branch and glance under it. Leave it to Violet to imagine something exciting, perhaps wonderful, in that ancient watery pit.

I, on the other hand, imagine freezing, killing darkness, a lair for leviathans and sea monsters. The truth is, while the surface of the Gap soothes me—its utter calm in the face of jutting tectonic plates and a warming earth—its floor terrifies me, because I know what hides there. It's a graveyard for secrets and lost objects and skeletons. It's where I tossed Mo's phone. It's where you put things you want to disappear.

Could Drummer have dragged Violet here after their fight? Did I try to stop him? Are the fingernail marks on my arm hers or *his*? My head aches as I imagine Violet sinking down, down, into the murk, her body coming gently to a halt in the dark silt, her eyes open, staring up toward the surface, realizing too late that the other world she imagined is not an alternate reality but death.

Mo touches my arm. "Hannah? Are you okay?"

We've reached the lake and I stare at it, frozen.

"Hannah?" She shakes me gently. "You're scaring me."

"I don't feel good," I admit to her.

"Let's go back."

I shake my head. "We're here. We have to help."

Jeannie notices I'm not moving and frowns. I force a smile, take my stick, and spread out as the others have, nodding to her that I'm okay. My arm is bandaged and in a sling, and the wounds on my cheek and forehead are covered in gauze. I doubt I inspire confidence, but when Jeannie sees me searching, she returns to what she was doing.

Mo and I are about ten feet apart, poking gently at shrubs. "Violet wouldn't come here on her own," Mo whispers across the distance. Since the fire, none of us have wanted to return to Gap Lake.

We glance past the "beach" to the burned area in the woods where we started the fire. The area of origin is no longer staked off or guarded. The arson investigators got everything they needed: photographs of the area, shoe impressions (if there were any), the singed beer bottle, the matchbook, and Luke's pipe. We're still waiting for fingerprint and saliva reports on the damaged pipe. While my mind has shifted to Violet, I can't forget that the fire investigation isn't over.

Mo pauses to redo her bun and wipe her forehead. "They should bring in search dogs."

At the mention of dogs, I think of Matilda. My bloodhound had a fabulous nose. If she were alive, I would have brought her to help find Violet. "I bet my dad will call them in from Kern County, if he hasn't already." The idea of dogs sniffing the woods for Violet's body makes me quiver.

Our time slot is two hours, and after an hour and a half, I'm exhausted, dizzy, and dry-mouthed. I pause to drink water, but really, it's just an excuse to rest.

Mo tromps over to me. "Let's call it a day."

"No, I can finish."

"But you shouldn't. GI Jane is busy, see, so let's go." Jeannie is on all fours, tugging at something. Her skin is red in spite of the sunscreen, and the back of her shirt is wet with sweat, as all of ours are.

"Fine, let's go." Mo and I swing around and start walking back. Neither of us believe Violet is here, not *our* Violet. Our Violet is at a four-star hotel, soaking in bath bombs, oblivious to the scare she's caused. At any moment, she'll plug in her phone, read that she's been reported missing, and send a group text: *can't a girl get some me time without you all alerting the national guard?*

We will laugh and then harass her about "that time she went missing" for the rest of her life.

The sharp blow of a whistle pierces my thoughts, the shrill notes skipping across the lake. Birds flap out of the trees in a whir of wingbeats. "Holy hell, what's that?" Mo covers her ears.

We turn to see Jeannie blowing on her whistle as if she's Kate Winslet from that *Titanic* movie.

The volunteers abandon their grids and come running. Ice creeps up my spine. We were told to blow the whistle only if we find evidence or encounter a bear. Jeannie rises to her feet on the steep shore of the Gap with a triumphant expression pasted on her face. There's no bear in sight.

We crowd in as close as we can but instinctively leave a semicircle of open space around her. "What did you find?" the lead organizer asks.

Jeannie points at the ground. "A scarf, a woman's scarf!" She's marked the area with fluorescent orange tape.

My eyes drop to the silk fabric that is half covered by a bush, and I instantly recognize the trendy pattern. It's a Louis Vuitton, and the first time I saw Violet wrap it around her head, I told her she looked like a pirate. Later, I searched for the scarf online and saw that it retails for about six hundred dollars.

No teen in Gap Mountain wears scarves like that except for Violet Sandoval, and everybody knows it. Besides that, the scarf is listed in the description of what she was last seen wearing: white camisole, tweed miniskirt, Gucci combat boots, Tiffany pendant necklace engraved with the letter *V*, and a gauzy Louis Vuitton scarf. There's a dark red stain on the silk fabric that could be blood, and a hush falls over us. Mo covers her mouth.

"That's hers," I say, and every single pair of eyes turns to me. "That's Violet's scarf." And then my stomach lurches and I vomit, splattering bile into the weeds.

29

August 13

Days Violet has been missing: 11

Time: 12:45 p.m.

Detectives immediately sent the stained Louis Vuitton scarf to the Department of Justice crime lab at Fresno State. My father's task force would neither confirm nor deny that it belongs to Violet.

Media attention exploded all over again. Because of the bloody scarf, Violet was presumed dead—drowned or dumped in the lake—and voyeuristic tourists descended on Gap Mountain. We're the proud home of the state's deepest lake, the starting point of the devastating Gap Fire, and now the dumping ground for a missing teenage heiress.

Cadaver dogs arrived last night, just in case Violet is not in the lake, and the area has been taped off and closed to the public. There are no more volunteer search parties.

A roving reporter snapped a photo of Gap Lake at sunset, and the pretty picture, ominous in this context, went viral. Newscasters display it along with Violet's senior picture every time they talk about her case. I hate the reporter's photo, which depicts blood-red sunlight striping the center of the lake, but I can't stop staring at it. Is Violet in that deep, deep pool?

Yesterday, I met with the psychologist in Bishop. We didn't get far on our first visit. We "built trust" and "got to know each other," all the bullshit that precedes getting actual help. She said she's going to use hypnosis, and that makes me nervous. What if I blurt out something incriminating, like *I think Drummer killed Violet?* I want to know what happened, but I don't want *her* to know. Our sessions might be confidential, but I'm not sure they'll stay that way if I reveal information about a murder.

While I was in Bishop, I thought about Justin. He texted me last night to ask how I'm feeling. When I told him I'm healing, he said, *good.* That's it. There was no pressure. He didn't ask for a date. He's still circling.

—

Now, as Gap Mountain holds its breath for news about Violet, I text the monsters: *let's go to the bridge.*

Each monster pings back, and we agree to meet at 2:30 p.m.

I text my dad: *heading to the bridge to meet my friends*

Which friends? Dad requires me to check in, now that there might be a killer or a kidnapper loose in the mountains.

Drummer, Mo, and Luke, I text back. Who else, I wonder? Since the fire, I don't hang out with anyone else.

The monsters and I arrive at the same time, and we skid down the steep path to the shore. Kids from town sprawl in groups up and down the beach on each side of the river. Music and laughter and the hiss of beer cans opening fill the air.

We grab an empty spot near the water. It's rocky and too shady but private. The other teens watch us, and a few girls smile at Drummer, but they stay away. Luke and Mo are arson suspects, I look like Frankenstein, and we're the missing girl's best friends. Only Omar from the Wildflower Café acknowledges us with a wave. I spot Amanda from work, wearing the tiniest bikini I've ever seen, but she avoids my gaze.

Luke pulls off his T-shirt and glares at the other kids. "Fuck these assholes," he growls. A sudden image of Luke and me hunting for crawdads when we were kids fills my mind. We used to hang out here all the time, laughing, playing, climbing trees, and swimming. So much has changed, I think.

"They're just curious," Mo says. She passes out sandwiches that we stare at half-heartedly. Drummer refreshes his phone screen every few seconds and reads comments and news to us about Violet via the hashtag #FindViolet.

"Anything new?" I ask. We haven't spoken since he hung up on me.

"Nothing new," he says without looking up.

Luke paces the water's edge, his expression somber, his eyes stony. He skips a smooth rock across the river. "At least no one's talking about the fucking fire."

Mo snorts.

Drummer lifts his eyes from his screen. "Why can't anyone find Violet?" he asks.

I cock my head, studying him. Drummer's a terrible actor, which means he really doesn't know where she is, but how can that be? Whose blood was on his clothes, if not Violet's? But if Drummer didn't hurt her and take her somewhere, then who did?

Mo tries to lighten the mood. "Remember the time Violet took the poodles to the movies and told the manager they were comfort dogs?"

"Don't do that," Drummer snaps. "No memories of Violet. She's missing, not *gone*."

Mo bursts into tears, and we all stare at Drummer wordlessly.

He swipes his phone over and over, refreshing the feed that relays news faster than the television. "This—this isn't real." He crumples and drops his head into his hands. Luke stalks helplessly, and Mo and I watch the boys, unsure what to do.

By some unspoken connection, the four of us come back together, drawn like magnets, and sit with our heads touching. We used to create truth circles like this when we were kids. We held hands, touched heads, and closed our eyes. Whatever we said or confessed or admitted had to be true, and no one was allowed to react. This is how we first learned that Luke's mom uses drugs.

Slowly, our hands link together. Mo speaks first: "I've been thinking a lot about what Hannah said. The timing of Violet's disappearance is suspicious. It makes us all suspects."

We collectively flinch but no one lashes out, no one turns away. We were once joined by our love; now we're joined by our secrets, and we have to face them.

"But we all love Violet," Mo continues. "So it had to be strangers or stalkers or robbers, right?"

"Robbers?" Drummer snorts. "Some cash was stolen, yeah, but they left behind all the valuable shit."

"They stole *Violet!*" Mo cries.

He sucks in his breath, and the circle tightens.

"Was anyone stalking her?" Luke asks me. "Any weirdos following her accounts?"

I shrug. "No, they're all private. Her parents drilled that into her skull since she was a kid."

"They must want more money," Mo says. "They took her for ransom."

"But no one has asked for money," Luke counters. He clears his throat. "How about you, Hannah? Get your memory back yet?"

"No." Something about his tone is unfriendly.

Luke nods, as if he's gotten the answer he wanted. "It's kind of convenient you can't remember." His dark eyes meet mine.

I don't speak because I remember some things, some very bad things.

"Stop it," Mo snaps. "If we're going to hash this out, we all need to be honest. It's time to fess up, Drummer. You and Violet are dating, aren't you?"

Tension whips through the circle, and Drummer pulls back, breaking it. He glares at me, and I shake my head, because I never told Mo about his confession. She and I only speculated together.

Drummer backs out of the truth circle, his eyes wide. "I didn't kill her."

Mo's lips part. "Whoa, I didn't say you did."

Luke unfurls. His eyes widen, his jaw clenches. "You're dating Violet and you didn't fucking tell us?"

Drummer's face scrunches. "We didn't want anyone to know."

Luke's breathing quickens; his cheeks color. He sweeps his finger around in a circle. "We aren't *anyone*. She's been missing almost two weeks—how could you hide this?"

Drummer's beautiful face twists; his blue eyes gleam with tears. "I'm sorry."

Luke glares at him. With his shaved head and chiseled, furious features, he looks like a stranger. "You were there, weren't you? You took Violet."

"No! God, no!" Drummer glances at me, terrified, and then decides to tell the truth. "I mean, yes, I was there, but when I left, she ... she ..." He can't finish.

Mo clutches herself. "God, Drummer!"

Luke pinches the skin between his eyes. "Were you ... you know, *with* her?"

We understand what he's getting at: Could the semen sample belong to Drummer?

I already know the answer to this, and I watch as my best

friend struggles to speak. Luke grabs Drummer and shakes him, rattling his teeth. But I know Drummer. If he won't fight back when he's innocent, he certainly won't fight back when he's guilty. "Yeah, I was *with* her," he admits.

My stomach sinks.

"And you didn't tell the police!" Mo cries.

Drummer throws up his hands, tries to back away. "I told you, I didn't kill Violet."

"What *did* you do to her?"

Tears leak down Drummer's face. He wipes his nose and fumbles for words. "Nothing. We had a fight. That's all."

Luke shoves him. "They found blood in her attic. Did you hurt her?" He's trying to keep his voice low so the kids on the shore, who are staring harder at us now, don't overhear.

"Maybe a little," Drummer cries.

"Oh my god," Mo says, gasping.

Luke dives at Drummer, lifts him off the ground, and slams him onto his back. "You fucking bastard! She's our friend and you let us believe some sickos raped her and killed her when all along it was *you*." He punches Drummer in the face.

"Stop!" Mo screams.

Kids collect around us, holding up their phones.

I jump onto Luke's back, and he throws me off. I land in the shallow river, and my head slams against a rock and searing pain roars through my skull. Mo sprints to my side and helps me up. We splash to the embankment. I banged my ear too, and it's numb and ringing.

"I didn't— I don't know what happened to her after I left."

Drummer curls up and covers his head as Luke pummels him. His blood splatters across Luke's shirt and face.

"Stop, Luke! You'll kill him!" Mo turns to me. "What do we do?" She digs into her bag for her inhaler and takes two deep puffs.

But Luke loses steam when he realizes Drummer won't fight back. He drags Drummer's torso off the ground. "You're a lying sack of shit." He throws him several feet down the shoreline.

Mo wheezes next to me, and I come to my senses.

"Let's get out of here," Luke snaps at us.

We're all distracted when a police cruiser speeds into the parking lot. "What now?" Mo murmurs.

Two of my dad's deputies, Vargas and Chen, emerge and march toward us. Drummer is on the shore with blood pouring from his nose, his shoulders hunched.

"We got a call about a fight," Deputy Chen says, nodding toward Drummer's bloody face.

"He fell," Luke lies.

Our teenage audience quickly retreats, and Vargas sighs. Chen shakes her head at me. "Is everything okay here, Hannah?"

Before I can answer, Luke points hard at Drummer.

Don't do it, my mind screams.

"He's Violet's boyfriend," Luke says thickly.

Chen tenses and shifts her gaze to Drummer. "You're dating Violet Sandoval?"

Luke can't shut up. "He was there the night she disappeared. He said he hurt her. He just admitted it."

Mo shakes her head; her lips part and tremble. My feet sink

deeper into the river mud, and I can't believe this is happening. Our protective circle is punctured. We are no longer five best friends.

Chen sways from foot to foot and prods Drummer: "Is this true?"

Drummer squeezes his eyes shut, and his pulse thumps in his throat.

Vargas and Chen exchange looks, and then Chen says, "We're going to need more information. Come to the station with us. Let's go." Chen's known Drummer since he was a kid and expects obedience as she turns toward the parked cruiser.

Beneath his wrinkled shirt, Drummer's chest rises and falls, too fast. His eyes glaze over, and his muscles flex. Then he makes an animal sound and bolts.

"Drummer, no!" I scream.

Chen shouts for help and takes off after him. Deputy Vargas leaps to join her, but Drummer is fast, really fast. And he's terrified. He races downstream and crosses to the other side, leaping over brush and boulders, and then he veers into the woods.

He has a head start, and I know the deputies won't catch him, not right away—*I'll die if they put me in a cage.* Oh Drummer, I think, exhaling, you might outrun Vargas and Chen, but you won't outrun the law.

30

August 13

Days Violet has been missing: 11

Time: 3:00 p.m.

Mo and I face Luke. "Why the hell did you do that?" she asks.

"Because he fucking lied to us," he says, spitting on the ground.

Monsters don't rat on monsters is one of our pacts, but so is *monsters don't lie to monsters.* Our friendship has been slaughtered by secrets, lies, and fire. I start crying, because I'm worried that Drummer's going to get shot in the woods. Luke stalks away, his hands balled into fists.

I wipe my forehead, and my fingers come away bloody from where I hit my head on the rock. The sight of the red fluid makes me stagger. "I gotta go."

"Can I drive you?" Mo asks.

"No, I'm fine."

"You're not fine, Hannah." I ignore her and climb the path to my dad's truck. Mo's voice follows me: "Call if you hear anything about Drummer!"

"I will."

My phone rings soon after I arrive home. It's my dad, sounding harried. "Have you seen Drummer? Is he there?"

"No, he's not here."

He lowers his voice. "When I asked you if Violet was seeing anyone, you said she wasn't."

My chest tightens. "Drummer lied to me, Dad. I didn't know." That's mostly true.

"He lied to us too, Bug, and now we have grounds to swab his DNA. If he matches the sample we collected, he could be her assailant. Lock the doors. Don't let him in."

I lurch out of my dad's reclining chair. "That's insane, Dad. Just because they were dating doesn't mean he killed her." *Not on purpose*, I add in my head.

He expels a long breath on the other end of the phone. "We're still investigating but you should prepare yourself."

"You're reaching—what's the motive?" I shut my mouth as soon as I say it, because I know the motive. Violet planned to tell on us.

"Drummer was in Mo's photo at Gap Lake, and she lied to us about being at the Gap on the seventh, which makes Drummer another suspect in the arson case," he answers. "The FBI agents believe the two cases are related somehow, which explains why there's been no ransom demand."

Fuck me. The agents are drawing the lines, following the

leads, connecting the dots. But do they know about Violet's final, damning text? I don't think so, not yet.

"Look," he says, sounding tired. "I called because the special agents want to speak to Drummer, to rule him out. Do you know where he is?"

Rule him out? We both know that's bullshit. An investigator's hope is never to rule anyone *out*. No, the FBI wants to nail the POS who harmed Violet, and they have their sights on Drummer. Nothing I say will change that.

My heart rate spikes. "N-no, I don't, but he would *never* hurt Violet." I see Drummer sobbing in my mind's eye, his admission that he drew blood, that he hurt her *a little*, but I can't reveal anything until I understand how I'm involved. If I witnessed a murder or an assault, *I* could be in danger, and if I did nothing to stop Drummer, I could be considered an accomplice. Now more than ever, I need to know what happened in that attic.

"I have to go," Dad says. "Call me if you hear from him." He hangs up.

———

I hop into my dad's F250 and spend hours driving around Gap Mountain, looking for Drummer the way people look for their lost dogs. When I return home, I pop open a Coke and guzzle it on the front porch, thinking. I believe that Drummer is telling the truth about not knowing what happened to Violet after he attacked her. It's just like him to make a mistake and then run away. And it's just like me to rush in and protect him.

"Oh no!" My stomach lurches and twists. I lunge forward and vomit soda onto the front lawn. What if I saw Drummer kill her and then *I* moved her body? "Please, no," I whisper to myself. "No, no, no."

Hands trembling, I glance over at the empty spot in the driveway where my Jeep is usually parked. Hypnotherapy could take a while to work, and I need answers now. I wipe my lips, grab my phone, and dial my dad. "I'm ready to see my Jeep," I blurt out.

"Hannah, I'm busy."

I shake my head. "The psychologist recommended that I look at it. She said it might help me get my memory back. Please. Where is it?"

He agrees but insists on going with me. Twenty minutes later, he walks through the kitchen door. "I don't have a lot of time."

"That's okay."

"Here," he says, handing me a small cedar box. "The vet dropped this at the station this morning. It's Matilda's ashes."

I rock back on my heels, and we both start crying. "Thanks," I whisper. "Where should we put her?"

"Fireplace mantel, I guess."

Past dogs were buried on the property, but Matilda died saving my life, so I guess she's staying in the house. "Okay." I open the box and view what's left of my beloved dog: a plastic bag full of gray ash. I close the lid, kiss the box, and set it gently on the wooden mantel. Then I slip on my shoes, grab my purse, and we climb into my dad's truck.

An excited young man meets us at the body shop and leads us to my car. He can't hide his stares, noting my sling and bandages and scarred face, and I feel my cheeks color. I look like a freak. At least this guy knows what happened to me, but the kids at college will have no idea.

"Bear got you good," he says. "What did you have in that backseat, a fresh kill?"

"What?" I ask sharply.

He recoils, glances furtively at my father walking ahead of us, and lowers his voice: "Last time I saw damage like that was when these out-of-towners bagged up a fresh-killed deer and loaded the carcass into the back of their Suburban. The blood and meat were a black bear's dinner bell." He clucks his tongue, like *What are you going to do?*

"I had leftover beef stew in the backseat," I say.

He eyeballs me, because we both know that leaving leftovers in a car is as dumb as—if not dumber than—leaving a bloody deer carcass. "You're lucky to be alive," he adds in a conciliatory tone. "That animal wrecked your car, like totally." He makes an exploding noise and then points ahead of me. "There it is."

I halt, catch my breath. The first things I notice are four deep claw marks cutting through the Firecracker-red paint.

Dad pauses and turns to me. "Hannah, you all right?"

"I'm fine." I slink forward, as if the bear is still trapped inside my Jeep. The black soft top is torn and bent around the roll bar. A wave of nausea grips me, but I soldier on and peek inside.

"Oh!" The interior fabric and foam are ripped to shreds. The passenger seat is off-kilter, the headrests are cleaved off, and the backseat is clawed to ribbons. Dirt and streaks of dried saliva mar the cloth. Tufts of black fur cover everything. There are teeth marks in the steering wheel.

My breathing quickens as I remember the growling, the force of being knocked over and dragged, and the bear's chuffing rage. "Why didn't it just take the food and go?" I whisper. The bear attacked my interior as if it were an enemy.

Dad rubs his chin. "Animal Control believes that the container of leftovers broke open and spilled under the backseat. As the bear dug for the scraps, the car door must have shut, trapping her inside. Most of this damage is her trying to get *out*, not in. Eventually the door popped open, and she got free. We aren't sure if you were attacked before or after that. The autopsy showed that the bear was starving."

"Autopsy?" the young man says, clearly impressed, and we both glare at him like *You're still here?* He takes the hint and leaves us to examine the Jeep alone.

"That guy was right. I'm lucky to be alive."

"You were smart to climb into the bear can," Dad says. "You saved yourself."

"I'm kind of glad I don't remember."

He sucks in a breath and puts his arm around me as we gaze at the Wrangler. "Why don't you poke around and make sure all your stuff is out before they tow it?" he suggests. "I'll talk to the people inside, let them know they can haul it to the scrap heap tomorrow."

"Okay." He leaves and I walk to the passenger side to pry open the glove box. Inside are my sunglasses, my registration, a few tampons, and old papers. I grab the sunglasses and leave the rest. Checking under the front seats, I find spare change and straw wrappers. When I get to the back, I balk as I remember sliding the leftovers onto the backseat.

Leaning deeper into the car, I try to remember more. Beef stew juices stain the carpeting, and a few red droplets sprinkle the backseat. Is it bear blood? My pulse quickens and my chest tightens uncomfortably. Something shiny glints at me from under the back bench. I force the passenger seat forward so I can lean farther inside, my hand reaching, reaching . . .

My fingers land on a small object that is hard and cool to the touch. I stretch farther, and my long arm helps me grasp it and pull it out. When I see what it is, I stifle a scream and let go. It sprawls on the asphalt, sparkling in the evening sunshine.

I glance around for my dad, but he's inside the shop, not paying attention.

No one is watching me. No one notices what I found in my car. I bend over, grab it, and study it more closely. Yes, it's what I think it is, and white light washes across my eyes, blinding me for a moment. I pocket the sleek metal and breathe slowly.

It's Violet's Tiffany necklace, the link chain and circular pendant with the letter *V* engraved on it. This necklace is listed as one of the items she was last seen wearing. It's her favorite piece of jewelry, and she never takes it off.

How did it get inside my Jeep?

31

Two days later, I remain in a manic state about the necklace, because it confirms my burgeoning theory: that I witnessed Violet's murder and then moved her body to protect Drummer from being caught. I am either a really good friend or a really fucked-up friend, and the fact that I'm not sure which I am is confusing as hell. I wonder if the blood on my backseat is Violet's too? God! I rub my eyes, exhausted. I should turn the necklace in, I know it, but I can't—not until I'm sure what Drummer did to her.

Dad is working late again tonight, so I sit on the sofa with Violet's platinum necklace wrapped around my fingers. Tears sting my eyes as I stroke the letter *V* and think of pretty words that begin with *V*, like *valiant, vivacious,* and *victorious,* and awful words like *vindictive, violent,* and *vanished.* I keep it in my top drawer, but I need a better place to hide it.

Glancing around the family room, my eyes land on Matilda's box of ashes. No one would ever look for it in there, and since I love them both, I open the cedar box and lower the necklace inside, mingling my dog and one of my best friends. They will keep each other company. I feel cold as I do this, and horrified. Burying this necklace is like burying Violet—I know it's wrong, I know I'm hiding evidence—but I do it and shut the box and then run back to the sofa. My heart gallops as if I've just sprinted a mile.

It's done. I can always take it out later.

I make a cup of steaming coffee and sit down to watch the television, because there's supposed to be breaking news on Violet's case. I wonder if they found Drummer. He's been missing for *two days!*

A female newscaster opens the show with the new developments:

California's Automated Latent Print System, known to law enforcement as ALPS, identified the fingerprints taken from Violet Sandoval's attic window earlier today.

I lean forward, lick my lips. This is it—they're going to name Drummer.

The prints were matched positively to Lucas O'Malley, a close friend of the missing girl. The special task force led by *Sheriff Robert Warner made a statement late this afternoon.*

My heart stutters—*Luke?*

The screen cuts to a clip of my dad, talking about the evidence. I turn up the volume.

We questioned and released Lucas O'Malley today as a person of interest in Violet Sandoval's case, and we executed search warrants at his place of residence. I can confirm a second suspect, Nathaniel Drummer, who remains at large this evening. We believe the seminal fluid collected in the attic will positively match to one of these men. If you have knowledge of Nathaniel's whereabouts, please call the number provided.

Drummer's handsome image flashes on the screen along with the number.

After my dad's announcement, the newscasters interview a lawyer, who explains why there's been no official arrest in Violet's case. "It's simple," she explains. "There's no body. No victim. No way to prove that a murder was committed."

I turn down the television volume, clutch my head, and rock back and forth. Luke doesn't fit into my theory at all. What am I not remembering about that night? Drummer admits he was there and that he hurt Violet bad enough to draw blood, and I know she ended up in my car. But maybe he didn't kill her. Maybe Luke did. If he did, then how am I involved? I can't explain any of this.

I call Luke's landline, and his younger brother answers: "Hello?"

Their television mumbles in the background, and somewhere outside their trailer, a toddler screams and cries. "Hey, Aiden, is Luke home? It's Hannah."

"Hi, Hannah!" I let Aiden ride in the police cruiser with me during Gap Mountain's Fourth of July parade this summer, and I've been his favorite person ever since. "Hold on. *Luke, phone!*"

Luke's voice crackles in the background: "What the fuck, Aiden, don't tell anyone I'm here."

"But it's Hannah."

Luke exhales and then his angry voice is on the line: "Are you calling because you remember?"

"Remember what?"

"Fuck me," he whispers.

"Remember what, Luke? Why did you break into the attic? Did they arrest you?"

"Not yet. Look, I'm going to say this one time: when you remember what you saw, don't fucking tell. You got that? Tell no one."

"What did I see?" I'm so frustrated I want to scream.

"When you remember, you'll understand."

"Luke, please, I'm really confused. I might not ever get my memory back. Why won't you tell me?"

Luke gets quiet and his entire tone shifts. "This line might be tapped."

His words catch me off guard. "What do you mean, tapped?"

"I mean that the fucking FBI might have a warrant to listen

to my calls. They're building a case, Han. I gotta go. Don't call me again. Like ever." He slams down the landline.

Ever? I slide my phone into my pocket, my heart banging. God, was Luke there too, with Drummer? I imagine the boys confronting Violet, her stubbornness, and Luke's temper. Holy crap! What did they do to her?

I phone Drummer but he's still "at large" and the call goes straight to voicemail. Helicopters have been flying over the forest for two days, there's an APB out for him, and the deputies are using dogs to sniff him out. It's only a matter of time before he's caught.

I stare at the TV, transfixed as news coverage shows detectives swarming Luke's trailer and Drummer's house earlier today, pulling out sealed bags of evidence. Drummer has no idea how lucky he is that I burned his clothes.

My dad stationed a deputy outside his home 24/7, in case Drummer tries to return. Reporters harass his family, and *seven* past girlfriends have come forward to speak to the press. While they admit that Drummer never hurt them physically, a picture emerges of a handsome, reckless teenager who used girls for sexual pleasure and then dumped them. I can't exactly deny the accuracy of that.

The press, along with investigators, begins to scrutinize the Sandoval family, as if their wealth makes them somehow culpable in Violet's disappearance. Her parents retreat into seclusion as images of their lavish lifestyle take a dark turn, veering from Violet's girl-next-door activities, like riding horses, to pictures of her parents drinking cocktails in exotic locales, stepping in and out of limousines and private jets, and looking entitled, with their designer sunglasses and deep Caribbean tans, as they cavort across the globe *sans* Violet, leaving her in a dilapidated town with an eccentric grandmother and questionable local kids.

Lulu Sandoval doesn't flinch from the press. She holds court on her front porch as reporters surround her, and she vehemently declares Violet's special task force "an incompetent batch of idiots."

I'm supposed to leave for college in less than two weeks, but it's the last thing on my mind. All I want is to remember what happened that night.

The news cuts to other programs, and then there's a knock at my door. I'm not dressed for company, wearing cutoff shorts, an oversized Gap Lake T-shirt, and no bra. Thinking it's probably Mo, I throw open the door without looking out the side window first. Two clean-cut strangers stand on my porch, and even without an introduction, I know who they are.

They're the special agents from the FBI.

32

August 15

Days Violet has been missing: 13

Time: 7:05 p.m.

"Hannah Warner, I'm Special Agent Hatch and this is Special Agent Patel," says the taller of the two men. He holds out his badge. "May we ask you a few questions?"

I stare for a second as a thrill rolls through my body. *Holy fuck, the FBI is at my house!* "Come in," I say, inviting them into the kitchen. "Do you want some coffee?"

"No, thank you," Hatch answers for both agents.

I catch myself smiling at them—stop smiling, Hannah. These are *special agents*, not Disney princesses. I sit at the table with them, my knees bouncing. I feel as if I'm in a movie.

Hatch glances at the sling on my arm and the cuts on my face. "A bear, huh?"

My hands flap up to touch my wounds. "Yeah, comes with

living in the woods. They're pests, like raccoons, just bigger."
My laugh is too high-pitched, and I cut it off with a cough.

A smile flickers across Hatch's face as he opens his briefcase
and withdraws a notebook and pen. The other agent produces a
recorder. "Do you mind if we record this interview?" Hatch asks.

"Go ahead." My eyes flick toward the cedar box on the fireplace mantel, which is visible from the kitchen table. Violet's
necklace is there, mixed with Matilda's ashes. If the agents
knew . . . I turn to Hatch. "Does my dad know you're here?"

He folds his fingers together beneath his chin, making one
closed fist. "Ms. Warner—"

"Hannah. You can call me Hannah."

He nods and continues. "Hannah, we're acting in conjunction with the Gap Mountain sheriff's department in the search
for your friend Violet. Your father and his deputies are personally familiar with everyone involved in her case, and this . . .
subjectivity . . . can lead to false assumptions, case blindness,
and mistakes."

I breathe out. "Okay."

"Your father has empowered us to question all potential suspects and witnesses who are personally known to him or his
deputies."

I'm not sure if Hatch has directly answered my question,
but I nod because I want to hear more.

"May we begin?" Hatch asks.

"Sure."

He clicks his pen and poises it over the paper. Agent Patel
hits the Record button on the machine, and then Hatch's dark

272

eyes meet mine. "This is Special Agents Hatch and Patel speaking with Hannah Warner at her home." He rattles off my address and the date and time.

Then he looks directly at me. "I want you to know you're not under arrest or suspicion, Hannah, and you're free to end this interview at any time. We have a few questions you might be able to help us with, but you don't have to answer them. Do you understand?"

I start to fidget. As soon as someone says you're *not* under arrest, you feel like you are. "I understand."

"Are you willing to speak with us?"

"Yeah, okay." I notice that Hatch has immaculate fingernails and cuticles. I glance at my own, see they're chewed to shit, and hide them beneath my legs.

Hatch leans forward, his face shadowed by the dim light overhead. "We recently discovered a text sent by your friend Violet Sandoval on August second, the night she vanished."

Her pendant appears in my mind—V for *vanished*—and my knees instantly stop bouncing. My breath leaves my body in a small, unbidden gasp.

He continues. "The recipients of this text are Lucas O'Malley, Nathaniel Drummer, Maureen Russo, and yourself."

"Oh?" I keep my voice steady, my face still. I cannot react to this any more than I already have. My brain whirs fiercely.

Hatch continues. "This is the text's content. Would you read it out loud, please?"

He turns his pad of paper to me and points his pen at a

sentence. I squint even though I can see it perfectly. "Sure, uh, it says: *tomorrow I'm telling the police everything.*"

"Is this your cellular phone number?" He pulls out a new sheet of paper, a report that includes five cellular phone numbers, and points at one that I recognize as mine.

Every muscle in my body tingles. I realize these men are hunting and they're after me. "Yes," I answer.

"Did you receive this text from Violet Sandoval on August second at approximately eight-twenty-five p.m.?"

My gaze slides toward the mantel where Violet's necklace resides, and I willfully drag my eyes back to the kitchen. *Calm down, Hannah. They know you received the text, but they can't prove you read it.*

My mind recalls what it can about that evening. I ran over my phone right after the text arrived, and later, my dad found my phone and threw it away. My cell is long gone, buried in a landfill somewhere, and phone companies don't hold on to deleted texts very long anyway. These agents might be trying to trick me, so I answer the question as safely as possible. "No, I mean, I don't remember. I dropped my phone and accidentally drove over it. I'm not sure if I got that text."

Hatch sits back, studying me. Patel frowns and observes my face, my shoulders, and my posture.

I take a breath. They're fishing, that's all. By remaining silent, they're trying to get me to talk, to reveal.

After a solid minute, Hatch breaks first. He writes a note and changes tack. "Do you know what information Violet was referring to in her text? Do you know what she planned to tell the police?"

"I don't," I say, adding a shrug. "And I'd hate to guess."

Hatch's eyebrows knit together. "She's one of the monsters, correct? A group of friends known locally as Luke, Drummer, Mo, and yourself?"

"That's right." This agent has done his research.

"As best friends, did you five share secrets?"

My anger flares as I think about Violet and Drummer's secret relationship. "Not really," I answer.

Hatch looks surprised.

"Our group wasn't big on secrets," I explain.

"What do you mean by 'wasn't'?" he asks. "Has something changed?"

My voice warbles. "No—I mean, we know everything about each other."

I've lost my footing, and Hatch senses it. "Violet's text implies she had a secret, a big one, something that would interest the sheriff's department."

"Hmm," I say thoughtfully.

"You're her best friend, and you're telling me you have *no idea* what that was?" His face is incredulous.

"*One* of her best friends," I correct him.

He sits back and steeples his fingers. "Do you understand that we're trying to *find* Violet, Hannah? Anything you tell us could lead to her safe return."

Nice technique: make me think I'm helping while getting

me to implicate my friends or myself. "I know; I'm trying to help," I explain. "I just have no idea what she was talking about."

Patel clears his throat and peers at me harder. My mouth has gone completely dry.

Hatch asks another question. "Do you believe Violet had information related to the Gap Fire?"

"The fire?" I sputter, feigning surprise. "No. I mean, nothing police don't already know."

"Right," says Hatch, consulting his notes. "You and Violet were horseback riding in the forest when you saw the smoke, but you didn't see how it started. Correct?"

This is what I told my dad, so I nod. "That's right."

"Is it possible *Violet* saw who started the wildfire on July seventh?"

My answer is immediate: "No." He watches me and I force myself to take steady breaths. Whoever made up the English language did us all a favor when they created the word *no*. It's simple, direct, and hard to fuck up. It's perfect for lying.

Hatch clears his throat. "Yes, you stated that in your recorded interview, but Violet disappeared the evening before she was to give her official statement. Do you find the timing of that odd? Or the fact that she texted her friends and said: *tomorrow I'm telling the police everything*? What do you make of that, Hannah? Does it sound to you like she had information that some people might want to keep quiet?" He's barraged me with questions, and his eyes bore straight through mine as he waits patiently for a response.

My dad's old clock ticks on the kitchen wall like a heartbeat. I pull my hands out from beneath my legs and fold them. Okay, any reasonable person would admit that the timing of Violet's disappearance combined with her text is suspicious. "Yeah, I guess you could look at it as odd, but I don't remember seeing the text, so this is the first I'm hearing about it." Cold sweat rolls from my armpits in slow rivulets. I feel it and smell it.

Hatch glances at his paper. "Violet's grandmother reported her missing four hours after Violet sent the text. Three of the message's recipients are suspects in the Gap Fire arson case, and two of them are suspects in Violet's disappearance. Do you believe this is a strange coincidence?" He inclines his head.

"Yes," I rasp.

"I don't believe in coincidences, Hannah. To me, it sounds suspicious."

I don't respond and he doesn't wait, just plows ahead. "Would it be reasonable to conclude that everyone who received the text is involved in Violet's disappearance, including you?"

He's backed me into a corner, and even though I saw it coming, I squirm. "I mean, yeah, you could draw that conclusion, but it wouldn't be true." I shut my mouth. The less I say from this moment on, the better.

Hatch consults his pad of paper. "Your friend Maureen Russo is the only text recipient who has an alibi during the hours when Violet went missing."

I lean back, waiting for a question.

Hatch and Patel share a look. "Hannah, where were you on the evening of August second between eight-twenty-five p.m. and twelve-oh-one a.m., when your father found you hiding in the bear-proof trash can?"

I didn't expect the tables to turn on me this quickly. "I—I don't know. I can't remember."

Hatch releases his fingers and glances at his notes. "We don't know either, Hannah." He smiles a boyish grin that is incongruous with his hawkish features. "You're a difficult woman to track. Your car's been towed to a scrapyard, your phone thrown away, and CCTV footage has not turned up a sighting of your vehicle on any of the main roads in Gap Mountain, and yet you must have gone somewhere that evening if you drove over your phone."

I blink rapidly. "Is that a question?"

He grunts softly and Patel leans forward. They want to eat me alive, I fucking know it, but they're treading softly. My gut churns and my legs twitch. I pull on a lock of my hair. "I thought you said I'm not a suspect."

Hatch smiles again. "We're trying to rule you out, Hannah."

I smile back. *Sure, you fucking are.* As the sheriff's daughter, I know the game they're playing.

The special agents watch me another minute, and my knees start bouncing again. They're frustrated, which is good, but they're also very, very warm. I decide to offer an alternative theory. "Maybe Violet killed herself."

Both men lean forward, their eyes intense. Hatch searches my face. "You believe Violet is dead?"

"Oh, I—I don't know." Shit, what have I done? Why did I open my big mouth!

Patel jumps in. "We haven't said anything about the victim being dead."

"You just called her a victim."

Hatch tosses Patel an annoyed glance. "Why do you believe Violet might have killed herself, Hannah? Was she upset about something?"

I rub my face, feeling defeated and tired. I can't tell them why Violet was upset—that she couldn't live with her guilt. I can't tell them that she fought with Drummer. "I don't know why I said that," I admit to the agents. "It just—it had to be suicide or an accident."

"You seem quite certain Violet is dead," Patel says.

"What? No. I mean, she could be, but I don't know. I believe she's alive." I'm tripping over my tongue, sounding as guilty as hell. These agents are putting words in my mouth!

Hatch closes his notebook. "We operate on evidence, Hannah, not belief."

Blood glides to my cheeks. *I know that.*

"This concludes our interview," Hatch says, leaning back. "Thank you for your time, Hannah. Please call us if you remember anything helpful." He emphasizes the word *helpful* and then hands me his card. "Good night."

"Good night." I stuff the card into my back pocket, close the door, and inhale a deep breath. I feel dizzy and frightened, and I don't think I did well. I glance at Matilda's ashes, which are hiding the "victim's" necklace. The FBI agents were sitting yards away from some pretty crucial evidence and never knew it. The thrill returns, tingling my stomach.

I know I should have told them about the necklace—for Violet's sake—but I can't, not until I talk to Drummer, not until I understand how it got into my car.

33

August 16

Days Violet has been missing: 14

Time: 8:00 p.m.

The content of Violet's last text is released to the media in the morning. Reporters quickly identify the four recipients, and since Mo, Luke, and Drummer are also suspects in the Gap Fire, the media draws the same conclusion as the FBI did: that we're involved in a cover-up. Even though I haven't officially been named as a suspect, a compelling motive is established: *four desperate and dangerous teenagers murdered their best friend to shut her up.*

Gap Mountain residents line up to be interviewed, and our nickname, *the monsters,* takes hold in the public's imagination. Outrageous headlines follow:

MISSING GIRL MURDERED BY "MONSTERS"

SANDOVAL HEIRESS ROBBED AND RAPED BY ARSONISTS

MISSING GAP MOUNTAIN GIRL THREATENED TO SPILL ALL

TEEN "MONSTERS" SLAY RICH FRIEND
TO EVADE ARSON CHARGES

The only problem: there's no body. Divers have searched Gap Lake and found nothing, and the lake is too deep to drag.

Photos of us appear in the news—me, wrapped in bandages like a mummy; Mo, looking frail and frightened; Drummer, flashing his pretty smile that now appears malevolent; and Luke, a bruised, hollow-eyed seventeen-year-old with a shaved head, a serious face, and dark, empty eyes. We look desperate and mean and capable of murder.

Drummer's now been missing for three days. I text him nonstop: *Don't hide. Turn yourself in. Let me help you.* He doesn't respond. He probably destroyed his phone.

Mo calls and starts talking before I can say a word: "The FBI just left my house."

"Hello to you too."

"I can't believe this," she rants. "My parents are going crazy. My lawyer's bills are skyrocketing. Reporters are eating takeout on my sidewalk. Fuck."

"I'm sorry." My house is at the end of a mile-long gravel driveway in the woods. I'm not sure if this is why reporters are staying away, or if it's because my dad's the sheriff, because of aggressive wild bears, or because I'm the only monster (besides Violet) who hasn't been implicated in the Gap Fire.

I hear Mo shut her bedroom door. "The agents asked me what Violet was going to tell the police."

"Yeah, they asked me too." I lie on my sofa, surrounded by bags of chips and empty soda cans. My diet has gone to shit since all this started. On the mantel above the fireplace, the cedar box of ashes seems to throb at me, as if Violet is inside the box listening to us.

"Shit," I cry, flailing upright. "Hold on, Mo." Violet can't hear me, but that doesn't mean no one is listening! I quickly text Mo on her prepaid phone: *Don't say another word. FBI might be listening.*

Mo: *WTF is that legal*

Me: *with a court order, yeah, and you're a suspect. Come over.*

Twenty-five minutes later, Mo's Corolla pulls into my drive-way. I meet her outside. "Let's go for a walk."

She steps out of her car and follows me onto a trail that leads into the woods. It's several degrees cooler here. The stout evergreens stand like ancient chess pieces, frozen in place, stuck in eternal checkmate as we wander between them. "Did you tell the agents anything?"

She frowns. "No, but I'm not sure our silence is doing us any good anymore. Things are fucked up."

"They'd be worse if the police knew the truth."

"I guess. I can't believe they haven't found Drummer yet. Do you think he's okay?"

"Drummer has nine lives, I swear. They'll find him or he'll

come out soon. How long do you think he'll last without hair gel and a toothbrush?"

Mo laughs softly.

"When do you start school?" I ask, steering the subject away from Drummer.

"You didn't hear?" Mo pauses near a copse of fir trees and rubs her arms. "I officially dropped my classes for the semester. I can't concentrate, the commute would kill me, and every day I have less money for college." Her voice is throaty and raw.

"God, Mo . . ." She lost her home and now this. I don't know what to say. I've thought very little about college myself. I should be purchasing school supplies, not evading wiretaps.

Mo sighs. "It sucks, but I'm okay. I'm alive, right?"

"Yeah." I shiver. Has this become our new qualifier for a good day: the ability to breathe?

Mo lowers her voice. "Do you think Violet is really dead, Han? Could he—do you think Drummer killed her?"

"Not on purpose," I whisper.

Mo dissolves into silent tears and leans against me. I'm sad too, but I'm also scared. Sometimes I see Violet's body when I close my eyes—her bloodless skin, her empty eyes, her stiff fingers curled like claws—but then my mind zips away from that image and won't show me the rest. If I witnessed her murder, accidental or not, I can't let Drummer or Luke know I suspect them, and I can't tell my dad either, not without revealing the truth about the wildfire. I need to figure this out on my own. *When you finally remember what you saw, don't fucking tell,* Luke warned. God, I could be next.

In the distance, my horses whinny for dinner. "Let's head back, Mo. I need to feed the horses."

We say good night in the driveway, and Mo drives home. I trot to the barn, automatically holding the door open for Matilda, but of course she doesn't come, and fresh grief floods my heart. I let the barn door bang shut and plod toward the feed room.

Sunny nickers, tossing his head, and Stella pins her ears. Pistol trots from his pen into his stall and kicks the wall with his back leg. "Dinner is coming," I grumble.

I'm low on hay and make a mental note to buy more as I push the wheelbarrow toward the stalls. The horses watch me intently, growing more excited the closer I get. Sunny spins in circles.

Feeding them is over quickly, and my horses are happy, munching on hay, unaware of the greater world around them. They have no idea who the president is, or that a virus can shut down the world, or that Violet is missing, and I love them for it.

A shadow shifts behind me, and I flinch. A filthy hand covers my mouth. A man's voice whispers in my ear: "Don't scream."

34

August 16

Days Violet is missing: 14

Time: 9:15 p.m.

The hand over my mouth is hot and dry and covers half my face. I try to bite my attacker, and then the hand is gone. I spin around and come eye to eye with Drummer. "The hell, Drummer!"

"Sorry," he rasps.

I bend in half as if I've just run a marathon. "You scared the crap out of me."

Tears drip from his eyes, which are so dilated they look black. "I'm sorry," he repeats.

I grab him and hug him, and he leans heavily on me. "Where have you been?" He's wearing the same clothing I saw him in three days ago. He reeks of old sweat, and his hair is matted with grease and dirt. Dried blood stains his shirt from Luke's punches. Branches have left welts on his arms.

"I've been hiding in the woods and empty hunting lodges," he answers. "I can't go to jail, Han." His normally half-lidded eyes are round and desperate.

I smooth his hair, and my hand comes away oily. "I know and you won't."

He collapses on a wooden bench in the barn aisle. "We—" He covers his face, and his body starts shaking as words spill from his mouth. "It was an accident. Violet wasn't thinking straight, she was going to tell on us, send all of us to prison, and then we fought about you—about telling you we were dating."

I blink at him, shocked.

"I—I grabbed her wrists and she fought me. Look." He points at scratches on his arms that aren't completely healed, and I realize not all of them are from branches. Some are half-moon indents, like mine but deeper. I cross my arms to hide my still-healing scratches and stifle the ugly tremor that rolls through me.

He clutches his stomach, sinks to the barn floor. "She'll have my skin under her nails and bruises where I grabbed her. She thought I sprained or broke her wrist, and the worst part"—he heaves a breath—"I . . . she hit her head pretty bad. It split open; it was bleeding. She didn't look good, Han."

I sink down next to him. "Why did you leave her?"

"Yeah, that looks bad, doesn't it?" He wipes his eyes and

nose with his dirty T-shirt. "If I'd known I'd never see her again . . ." He leans into me, wetting my arms with his tears.

I stroke his back. "Did you take her cash? Was Luke there?"

He shakes his head. "I didn't take the money, and I don't know about Luke, but Han?"

"Yeah?"

Fresh tears leak from his eyes. "Where were you?"

I inhale sharply.

"Did you hide her for me?" He grabs my body and holds me tight. "You must have. No one else would help me, but you"—he strokes my hair—"you love me."

My head spins and I recoil, sick to my stomach. "I told you, I don't remember."

He pulls back and his eyes search mine. "I can't go to prison, okay?" He flops against me, crying harder.

"Okay," I tell him, but what am I agreeing to? My gut twists and screams, *This is wrong!* "You can't hide forever, Drummer."

He nods. "I know. I wanted these scratches to heal before the police saw them, but I'm so fucking hungry, Han, and it gets cold in the woods at night."

I read the misery in his face and can't help the tiny smile that curves my lips. If Drummer is anything, he's predictable. "Come on, let's get you something to eat. My dad's not home." I take his hand and lead him into my house. He's weak and feels as light as a child's balloon as I tug him along.

Inside, he collapses onto a chair and rests his head on the kitchen table. I heat a plate of venison, mashed potatoes, and a can of corn. My dad stocks Gatorade in the fridge, so I hand him one of those too. Drummer drinks the entire bottle in one gulp, and I hand him another. Then he digs into the venison.

"Don't eat too fast," I warn him.

"I don't care if I get sick," he says.

When he's done, I suggest he take a shower, and he lets me lead him to the bathroom. I disappear to fetch a clean towel, and when I return, Drummer has stripped off his shirt, pants, and underwear. He hears my footsteps and turns slightly. I halt and stare, my eyes traveling across yards of tight tan skin to the dark blond hair and pale flesh between his legs.

He lets me look, and I feel his gaze linger hotly on my face. Then he takes the towel and covers himself. "Thanks."

"Sure." I about-face and exit the room. My cheeks burn and my heart thumps. He does this on purpose! He gives me his affection, his trust, his beauty, his mistakes—everything except his love. He teases me and I follow him like a dog. It's sick. I'm sick.

I fall onto my bed and chew my nails, listening to the shower. Drummer gets off on fucking with me, and as my anger grows hotter, I grab my phone and pull up Justin's account. He has a new post—a picture of him riding a horse, a powerfully built pinto. Drummer's not the only hot guy in the world.

I scroll through my old messages and read the last one I received from Justin a few days ago: *Are you all right? I still want to make things up to you*

With a glare at the closed bathroom door, I decide to answer him. Maybe Justin and I could have a real thing. I text him: *I feel better. Are you free this weekend? I miss you*

As before, he's quick to answer: *yeah, I'd love that. I miss you too*

Justin is older but nice enough, I guess. *ttyl*

As soon as I slide my phone back into my jeans pocket, I feel confused and a little regretful. Am I ready for hearts and kisses with Justin? Then I remember that I lied to him about my age. Shit. I need to remedy that right away.

btw, have to tell you something. I'm eighteen. I didn't lie about SDSU, I am going, but I'm a freshman, not a junior. Sorry

A long pause and then his response: *18 is okay*

My face flushes and it strikes me again that I don't know his age. *How old are you?*

26

Every hair on my neck stands up. I knew he was midtwenties, but now that he's confirmed it, none of this feels right.

Drummer pops out of the bathroom with a towel around his waist. I quickly hide the phone under my leg. "What are you doing?" he asks.

"Nothing."

His expression hardens. "Did you just text your dad?"

"No."

He launches at me and grabs for the phone. "Hannah?"

"I didn't."

We wrestle over the phone, and his towel slips off. Drummer

pins me. His damp bare skin covers mine; his clean scent fills my lungs. I freeze and my breathing ratchets higher.

He pries the phone out of my fingers and unlocks it because, of course, he knows my password. Do I know his? No.

He reads the texts and slowly lifts his weight off me. His sharp blue eyes meet mine. "Who the fuck is Justin?"

I close my lips.

He scrolls and reads. "Is this the guy you slept with?" Drummer takes my silence as affirmation and huffs. "*Eighteen is okay*, what the fuck does that mean? This guy's a creep, Han."

I notice I'm trembling. "No, he's nice."

Drummer snarls, his face scrunched tight. "Oh, I bet he was nice."

"Give it to me." I reach for the phone.

"Wait," he says. He pulls the towel over his waist and snaps a photo of himself, wet and steaming from the shower. He texts the picture to Justin and writes: *i'm Hannahs boyfriend. stay the fuck away from her asshole.* And hits Send.

"Drummer!" I protest, but I start to laugh.

He puts up a finger and we wait. The gray dots show Justin reading the text, but he doesn't respond. "See, he's a creep. You'll never hear from him again." He tosses me my phone.

I wipe my eyes dry. "But he wasn't. He really wasn't."

Drummer sets his hands on his hips, in mothering mode now. "Do you want to keep seeing this guy, Hannah?"

I shrug one shoulder.

"Then I did you a favor." He relaxes and settles close to me on my bed, his thigh warm against mine. I lean against his bare chest and breathe in his scent. Another boy might kiss me right now, but Drummer won't. Maybe being best friends *is* better than being a girlfriend. Maybe this is enough.

"Can I sleep in your bed with you?" he asks, but his smile doesn't reach his eyes. He knows he's in serious trouble.

"Sure," I say, my voice husky. "But my dad will be home in about an hour."

Drummer nods. "It's fine, I'm done hiding. I just want to sleep for a while, with you. Lie down with me."

I hand him a pair of baggy sweats, which fit him since we're the same height, and my heart flutters as we slide beneath the covers together. "Roll over," he says.

I do as he asks, and he presses his body against mine. "You're so warm. I love you, Hannah Banana." He hugs me tight and falls asleep in seconds.

I realize he's saying goodbye, and my throat closes, my eyes burn with tears. I clasp his arms tighter around me, wishing this moment could last forever. If it were possible for Drummer and me to go to jail together, I might confess what I know, tell my dad everything! Drummer and I could be roommates, locked together in a cage. He wouldn't be able to leave, to get away from me. We could share a cot.

But it's not possible. He would live in a cellblock full of men—no pretty girls for miles. No Violet. At least I'd always know where he was. I smooth the sun-glossed hair on his arms. "I love you more," I whisper.

At ten-thirty my father enters the house. "Hannah!" he cries.

I slide out of bed and rush down to the family room. Dad's

face is an angry shade of red, and he's holding a pair of dirty Vans. "Are these Drummer's?"

My mouth falls open. Shit, Drummer must have slid them off in the kitchen when he ate the venison. Dad reads my expression and stiffens. "Where is he, Hannah?"

The jig is up. There's no hiding Drummer now, so I point upstairs to my bedroom.

"Did he hurt you?"

Not on purpose, I think. "Dad, Drummer wouldn't hurt anyone."

He pulls out his service revolver and stalks up the stairs. I follow and watch my father wake Drummer up and haul him away. And here we are again, my dad arresting someone I love—it's like a horrible experience repeated on a loop. Suddenly, I can't wait to move out of this house.

35

August 18

Days Violet has been missing: 16

Time: 9:30 a.m.

Drummer's arrest hits the news media machine like an explosion. His handsome senior photo contrasts dramatically with his bruised and battered mug shot, and his story feeds the media storm building in our town. The headlines are once again inflammatory:

SUSPECT ARRESTED IN MISSING HEIRESS CASE

AFTER THREE-DAY MANHUNT,
GAP MOUNTAIN SUSPECT APPREHENDED

TEEN ARSONIST & SUSPECTED RAPIST ARRESTED

GAP MOUNTAIN "MONSTER" CAPTURED

His DNA is collected and analyzed, and he's matched to the semen sample. To prove motive, forensic experts dig into his phone's GPS tracking, and it confirms he was at the *point of origin* when the Gap Fire started.

Meanwhile, the saliva taken from the pot pipe matches Luke's DNA, and a search of his house reveals a hidden bundle of hundred-dollar bills and his prepaid phone. Detectives send the money to the lab for fingerprint testing, but everyone believes it's Violet's. Drummer's prepaid phone has also been seized.

The world is certain now that at least two of the monsters attacked Violet so she wouldn't tell on them. It doesn't help that Drummer failed to delete a few damning texts to Violet on the prepaid phone, and these are released to the press: *i wish luke had never brought that damn pipe to the Gap. that fire fucked up my whole summer with you.* And: *I'm scared V. I don't want to go to jail.* And the worst one, sent to Violet on the night she disappeared: *do not talk to the police! i'm coming over.*

The media has tried Drummer and found him guilty. Reporters camp on his lawn, and his mild-mannered father goes into hiding while his mother takes her cue from Lulu Sandoval: she condemns the press and proclaims Drummer's innocence.

Traffic control becomes an issue in Gap Mountain for the first time ever. Between the tourists, the reporters, and the fire cleanup crews, the main streets are clogged. Sam's Market is doing huge business selling Gap Lake T-shirts and snacks. Mono County sends more deputies to help with traffic and nosy people, and Violet's family has their own police liaison, a female officer who stays at the Victorian estate and keeps the Sandovals informed about the search for Violet.

The arson cases against Luke, Mo, and now Drummer are fast-tracked and somehow, I'm the only one who is clean in this entire mess. Yes, I was under some suspicion due to being included in Violet's last text—*tomorrow I'm telling the police everything*—but not one friend has ratted on me, and there's no evidence linking me to the Gap Fire.

I can guess what's happening behind closed doors. Each monster will be offered a plea deal on the arson charges to turn state's evidence for the prosecutor. Whoever takes the deal first probably won't go to prison. They'll get community service hours and maybe a fine.

Luke's lawyer gets aggressive with her offense by suggesting that public-safety personnel are responsible for the deaths and destruction caused by the Gap Fire. She asserts that the county and the town did not employ a viable emergency evacuation plan or emergency alert system, in particular where the elderly and hard of hearing were concerned. My dad is as pissed as a wet cat about it.

I wait and wander, feeling lonely. As crowded as Gap Mountain is, I have no one to talk to. I jump at every noise. I miss my dog, I can't focus or complete my sentences, and my dad is suspicious. He doesn't push me, but I wonder how much he suspects. When I told him about the FBI visit, he was surprised. "They didn't tell me about it."

I know what this means: they believe his judgment is off, at least when it comes to me.

I book another appointment with my psychologist.

Later, I head into Gap Mountain and work a six-hour shift

at the Reel Deal. Kids and parents ask me how I'm "holding up," because they know Drummer and I were inseparable. Some ask if he "did it." I tell them to "get fucked." After two hours, Mr. Henley ends my shift early with a warning to "be nicer."

I don't want to return to my empty house, so I drive to Target in Reno to shop for dorm supplies. Sorrow has colored my whole world gray. My dog is dead, my Jeep is gone, my friends are facing criminal charges, Violet was most likely murdered, and I think I'm a witness—and maybe also an *accessory*. At least the Gap Fire is extinguished.

I shouldn't be shopping, I should be searching for Violet, but all the leads have dwindled. Last night, the news reported that imprints of Violet's heavy Gucci combat boots and several of her dark hairs were discovered near the lake where the scarf was found—indicating that her body may have indeed been dumped there. Where do people put things they want to disappear? Gap Lake.

I step on the gas pedal and make the long drive to Reno in silence. At Target, I yank a cart out of a line of red carts and push it inside. I get one with a wonky wheel but don't have the energy to return it. As I pass a mirror in Sportswear, I glimpse myself and pause. In my two-inch-heeled cowboy boots, I tower over the clothing racks. Even though I'm lean and tan, I don't look healthy. My best features, my large green eyes, are shaded with dark circles, and my face looks long and pinched. The healing scars create violent pink slashes across my skin. I'm a hulking, gangly, banged-up giraffe pushing a shopping cart.

I shove on, roll over a dropped hanger, and steer the cart

into the bedding department. I had planned to do this shopping with Violet and Mo. We were going to caffeinate at Starbucks, drive to Reno, buy our supplies at Target, and then eat lunch at Chick-fil-A. We were going to end the day at Dutch Bros for another coffee and then gossip all the way home—a perfect day.

Instead, I'm standing by myself in Bedding, staring at comforters and sheets in tightly packed bags. A lump fills my throat as I grab a gray-and-pink ensemble in size Twin XL and drop it into my cart. I move on and select towels, a makeup mirror, a power strip, a desk lamp, a pop-up laundry basket, and sets of hangers and closet organizers.

Afterward, I make my way to School Supplies and load up on binders, college-ruled paper, highlighters, pens, dividers, and spiral notebooks. I realize I'll need basics, like a stapler and a three-hole punch for my desk, and add those to my cart.

On the way out, I pass the pet department and stop to stare at the shiny food bowls, new leashes and collars, toys, and bones. I've never left Target without a treat for Matilda. Tears flood my eyes as I stand there sniffling. An older woman stops. "Oh honey, are you all right?"

"My dog . . ."

She doesn't know me, but she pats my arm. "They never live long enough, do they?" she murmurs.

I shake my head, sobbing in front of this stranger.

"What was your dog's name?"

"Ma—Matilda."

When I'm done crying, the lady looks directly into my eyes.

"Matilda was loved. That's all you can do, honey, love 'em, care for 'em, and let 'em go."

I nod and wipe my cheeks with the hem of my tank top. "Yes, okay, thank you."

"She's safe now. No more pain. No more worries." The woman strolls toward the cat aisle.

In a blur of tears, I go through self-check—to the annoyance of others, since I have so much in my cart. I swipe my dad's credit card and then load everything into his pickup. I leap into the driver's seat and start bawling all over again. But I don't think I'm crying about Matilda anymore; it's Violet. *She's safe now. No more pain. No more worries.* Is Violet truly gone forever? I should have told my dad about the necklace and the spots of blood in my Wrangler before it was junked. I shouldn't have burned Drummer's clothes, or mine. What have I done? Who am I protecting?

My head drops into my hands. "Remember, Hannah!" I shout. My head throbs and I smash my fist on the dashboard. "Remember!"

I was in my barn when Violet's text came: *tomorrow I'm telling the police everything.* I was angry; I remember that.

I clench my teeth. Telling the truth should have been a group decision. Who did Violet think she was to decide that on her own? Why would she send herself and her best friends to jail?

Rage and shock build inside me, exactly what I felt that night. I know why: because Violet can't take the pressure, she can't live with her guilt. But we can! We have to! We were born and raised in Gap Mountain. To confess is to lose *everything*—the trust of our town, of our teachers and friends and the citizens we've known our entire lives. We don't have six-million-dollar trust funds or nine-hundred-dollar-an-hour lawyers to fall back on. Violet is an outsider in every way. She's not a monster, not anymore!

I let out a stream of curses and beat my steering wheel. A family across the lot sees and turns quickly away. I slam the truck into reverse and peel out of the Target parking lot. My heart thuds and my anger flares bright red. *Violet, you spoiled brat, you brought this on yourself!*

Deep down, my brain knows exactly what happened that night. The trauma I'm hiding from isn't the bear attack; it's whatever I witnessed in that attic.

36

August 18

Days Violet has been missing: 16

Time: 9:05 p.m.

I run a red light and speed all the way home, just as the sun is setting in the west. Thankfully, my rage ebbs by the time I arrive, replaced by guilt that is as black and cold as my rage was red and molten.

I slam the truck door and enter my house in the dark. I need a shower. I feel dirty and sad and confused. I trip over a chair in the kitchen and wander into the family room feeling lost, devastated, alone. I stare at Matilda's ashes on the mantel and imagine the Tiffany necklace inside, surrounded by my dog's scorched bones. The box gleams and Violet's face appears in my mind, bloodless, her eyes blank. I touch the wooden container. "Why did you ruin everything?"

I decide not to shower—I don't want to see myself in the mirror—so I unload my purchases and then curl up in the recliner with my laptop. Logging into my SDSU portal, I make sure there's nothing on my to-do list.

Afterward, I browse news stories about Violet. She's trending again on social media: *#FindViolet #WhereIsViolet #MissingTeenHeiress*. Photos of her jumping her show horses, skiing in Switzerland, boating in the Bahamas—all featuring her charming dimpled smile and gorgeous body—have popped up in every story about her.

A clattering noise outside the house startles me, and I whirl, a scream rising in my throat. There's a figure in the back window! It's staring at me. God! I stagger for my dad's loaded rifle, cock it, and run outside, heart hammering.

"Hey!" I shout. "Who's there?"

The clattering sound comes again, and I charge toward it, rifle lifted to my shoulder. The night is inky black, the moon a dim crescent. "Hello?"

No answer.

"Drummer?" I call out. It could be him. He's out on bail. Maybe he's afraid I'll remember whatever it was he did and tell on him. Or maybe it's Luke, here to shut me up—*when you finally remember what you saw, don't fucking tell*. Did he do something to Violet that night, or was he just afraid to talk because he thought the phone line was tapped? I wish he'd answer my texts. Shit. "Who's there?" I call out again.

Slowly, I creep toward the noise as my breath stalls in my

throat. "Luke?" Something flutters and I shoot at it, hear the twang of the bullet striking metal. Fuck, I just shot our BBQ. "Calm down, Hannah," I whisper.

More deliberate now, I use the rifle's long nose to poke at the dark shrubs in case someone is hiding. I prowl toward the front of the house, where rustling sounds reach me from the driveway. It's a bear. It's got to be a bear.

Inching forward, I turn the corner and three black-eyed creatures zip past me: raccoons. "Holy crap!" I lower the gun, pause to breathe.

"Hannah?"

I recoil and fall backward, landing on the grass. It's Justin! "What are you doing here?" I grip the gun barrel tighter and stare up at him.

He's clad in a jeans jacket, cowboy hat, and boots. He spreads his hands, eyes wide. "Don't shoot me. I came to talk, that's all. You didn't hear me knock, so I went back and looked through your window."

"Talk about what?"

He narrows his eyes. "You have a *boyfriend?*"

I blink at him. What in the hell is he talking about?

Justin shakes his head. "He texted me his photo, on your phone, remember? Called *me* an asshole. What are you playing at, Hannah?"

Oh my god, he's talking about Drummer. I laugh. "I'm not playing. He's not my boyfriend."

Justin appraises me, his jaw circling. "So what is he? Another guy you lead on, like me?"

I push myself to my feet. "I—how did I lead you on? I slept with you!"

"Once," he says, lowering his gaze like a sulking boy.

"Wow," I sputter. "That's . . . wow." Since when is sex on a first date not good enough?

He shifts, adjusts his gigantic rodeo belt buckle. "Do you want to see me again or not?"

Oh, I get it now: his feelings are hurt. He either really likes me or he wants more sex, and he drove all the way here to feel me out. Well, I want someone I can't have too. It sucks. He'll get over it. "I'm sorry," I tell him.

He pulls a sharp breath through his teeth. "I won't ask you again."

God, I hope not. "Okay," I say contritely.

He backs away, stiff but trying to act casual. "Why are you out here with a gun anyway?"

"Because you scared me!"

He nods. "I thought maybe it was because of the missing girl. You oughta be careful." His gaze shifts and he stands taller. His eyes drift across my body, reminding me what we did in his car. I brace, wondering what he plans to do next, but the moment passes and he opens the door to his Altima, tips his cowboy hat. "Nice knowing you, Hannah."

As he rolls down his window and starts his car, I bend over, drawing a deep breath. When I glance up, I see the figure again, reflected in the window, and fall back. The figure also falls back. "Oh," I cry out. It's just me, not some killer. A high-pitched laugh pours from my throat as I hunch over, giddy with relief.

Of course it wasn't Drummer or Luke coming to shut me up. I stare at myself and begin to laugh. Once I start, I can't stop.

"Psycho," Justin murmurs as he backs down my driveway. Then he's gone.

When I'm done laughing, I flip the safety on the rifle and walk back inside.

—

After my dad gets home, we eat a late dinner in the kitchen. "Where'd you go today?" he asks casually.

"Reno. Got my dorm supplies."

He shakes his head. "College is coming up fast."

"Yeah, I leave next week."

"Oh, here," he says, handing me an envelope. "We got the payout check for the Jeep today."

"Thanks." Icy relief dribbles down my spine. "So it's really gone?"

"Yep." He stands, adjusts his belt. "I gotta tell you something, Bug. The district attorney wants to prosecute Drummer for Violet's murder. He's not cooperating or confessing or leaving the DA much choice."

I gape at my dad, noticing every silver-blond hair on his head, every tiny follicle of stubble on his cheek, every vein in his eyes, as my heart *thump-thump-thumps*.

He continues with a wince. "Thing is, I know Drummer, and he's a terrible liar. I don't believe he's innocent, and I don't believe he acted alone. I believe Luke helped him."

"How can they try Drummer without a body?" I blurt out.

He nods. "It's a long shot, and the FBI is not recommending it. A conviction would be tough, but the semen sample proves he was with her when she went missing, and the pressure is on. There's some legal precedent, I think." He picks at his nails. "If you know anything or remember anything, Hannah, you have to come forward."

"But no one has proved that Violet is dead," I point out. "And Drummer was dating her, which explains the sex. It doesn't mean he raped her or killed her."

My dad shakes his head grimly. "Absolutely no way to prove the sex wasn't consensual, so no rape charges. But Drummer, Luke, and Mo are arson suspects, and Violet threatened to confess something to the police that involved them. That gives all three of them strong motive for murder. Only Mo has an alibi."

My dad clears his plate and runs water over the dirty dishes, then sits down next to me. "Hannah, these are your best friends." His blue eyes search mine. "Now, I know you and Violet were riding when the wildfire started, but I believe you know more than you're letting on. You kids talk about everything."

I stare at my hands so I don't have to look at him.

He goes on. "I get it, policing your own kind sucks. I've been doing it my whole career. I—I had to arrest my own wife."

His voice grows thin, and I feel a lump form in my throat. "Please don't talk about Mom."

"Honey, the—"

"Law is the law," I finish for him, then lift my head. "Arresting her might have been the right thing to do as a cop, but not as my dad."

"Hannah," he scolds.

I stand up. "You ruined us."

"*She* ruined us," he rasps. His face turns red.

"No, it was your guilt!" I cry. "You never let it go, you never got me a new mom, you never looked at me without regret. I'll do *whatever* is necessary to keep my friends out of jail."

His fists shake by his sides, his flint-colored eyes narrow, cutting straight through me. "Like hiding a body?"

I gape at him.

"Drummer's car is clean, Hannah, no blood. The Sandoval vehicles are also clean. We believe Violet is in Gap Lake, but we don't know how Drummer moved her there. Tell me why that bear attacked your Jeep. Did it smell blood?"

My scalp prickles and my body goes preternaturally still. "It smelled beef stew."

My dad's stony expression cracks, and his face morphs into a clownlike grimace. He tries to hold my hands, but I won't let him. "I'm scared for you, Bug," he says. "I think Drummer used you and your Jeep to move Violet's body, and I think that when you remember, you're going to be very, very sad."

I step back, shaking my head.

"I'd like you to defer college and stay here, keep seeing your therapist."

A bitter laugh bursts from my lips. "Nope, no way. I'm going to college. You can't stop me."

"I'm not trying to stop you, I'm trying to help you. You aren't well." His voice changes, becomes soothing, gentle. It's how he talked to Mom when she was drunk.

I blink and hot tears slide down my cheeks. He's scared, that's all, and he's projecting. I disarm him by rushing forward and hugging him, which makes him cry. I'm stronger than he is, stronger than my mother was. "I'm fine, Dad. Don't worry."

He cries harder and I'm not sure if it's because he believes me or because he doesn't.

37

August 21

Days Violet has been missing: 19

Time: 11:15 a.m.

The next three days passed in tense misery as lawyers and prosecutors battled it out in conference and interrogation rooms over the arson charges. Mo was the first to crack, but the boys followed right after her. They each pled guilty to reckless arson, and their lawyers hashed out very different sentences with the judge.

Mo received community service hours and probation because she came forward first. Drummer was sentenced to two years, and Luke will serve four, since he brought the pipe and matches. Both boys were remanded to Wasco State Prison, where Luke, who was prosecuted as an adult, will continue to receive medical care for his TBI. All three claimed financial hardship and received fines of ten thousand dollars apiece.

The monsters stayed true to our pact, and none of them told on Violet or me.

The district attorney ultimately decided not to prosecute Drummer or Luke for Violet's murder. Without a body or any evidence that they removed her from the attic, a trial would be expensive and most likely unsuccessful. It should have been a happy moment for Drummer and Luke, but no one feels good about it, because Violet is still missing.

The extra law enforcement personnel who came to help my father while he was searching for Violet vacated Gap Mountain, and the special task force was disbanded.

—

Right now, I'm sitting in my family room, staring at Matilda's ashes and the secret buried inside them. The Gap Fire nightmare is over, at least for me. And my father's suspicions aside, I haven't been formally charged or accused in Violet's case either. I hear the old woman's voice at Target: *She's safe now. No more pain. No more worries.* I need to let Violet go.

My phone buzzes with a text. It's Mo: *Meet for lunch?*

I let loose a heavy sigh. She keeps telling me we need to talk, but I've been avoiding it, because suddenly, I want to get away not only from Gap Mountain but from the friends I've known most of my life. Mo was right: things will never be the same.

I text her back: *Sure. When?*

Now? Wildflower Café?

Before I head out to meet Mo, I open the cedar box on the

mantel, unfurl the plastic bag full of Matilda's ashes, root through them, and pull out the Tiffany necklace, shaking off the dust. It sparkles, so pretty in the sunlight, and feels harmless in my fingers, just an expensive piece of metal, not evidence of a crime or of a dead girl's last moments. I clip it around my neck and peer at myself in the fireplace mirror.

It looked so good on Violet, brilliant against her tan skin, swinging charmingly in her cleavage. It's not quite as pretty on me.

As I pose, remembering Violet, the door bangs open. "Want to have lunch?" It's my dad.

My breath hitches and I quickly flip the silver pendant around to hide the etched letter *V*. "Hi, Dad." Sweat prickles my scalp. I can't take the necklace off or hide it—he's staring right at me.

"What are you doing?"

My heart hammers. "Nothing."

He crosses the room, his eyes searching my face. "You thinking about Matilda?"

The cedar box is open on the mantel, the ashes revealed. "Uh, yeah, I'm kind of saying goodbye to her."

"I miss her too." He hugs me tight, squeezing the necklace between us. I don't dare breathe. "So, how about lunch?" he asks. Dad wants to spend all his free time with me before I leave for college.

"Can we do dinner instead? Mo just invited me to lunch."

His muscles stiffen at the mention of Mo's name, but then he sighs and releases me. "All right, dinner then."

He climbs the steep stairs to his bedroom as my breath rushes back into my body. I unclasp the necklace and let it slide between my fingers into the ashes. "Goodbye, Violet."

I shut the lid and glance at my reflection in the mirror, at the pink-tinged scars on my cheek, forehead, and arms. There's a patch of hair missing from the center of my eyebrow, but Mo was right, makeup fixes it. My green eyes are clear, and I'm wearing mascara today. I got my hair cut into shorter layers, a sassier style that helps hide the scars and the small areas where my scalp was shaved. If I smile big enough, I have a dimple too. I look pretty. I look ready for the rest of my life.

—

"You're brave to meet here," I say to Mo as we choose a booth at the café. Everyone in Gap Mountain knows that Maureen Elizabeth Marie Russo is: one of the Gap Fire arsonists.

Mo shrugs. "You know what, Han? I came clean and I'm serving my sentence. People will have to get used to me. And you know what else? It feels really fucking good."

"What does?"

She lifts an eyebrow. "Admitting what I did and paying for it. It's freeing. I can hold my head up again, and besides, not everyone hates me. Some people understand. It's not like we did it on purpose; we were just fucking around, being stupid. The church is holding a special service for Gap Mountain teenagers, and they asked me to speak. I'm going to share about the danger of bringing fire into the woods and the importance of telling the truth." She cocks her head; her hazel eyes bore straight into mine.

Thankfully, Omar arrives right then to take our order. He's distant but polite. We order BLTs, fries, and chocolate shakes.

I change the subject. "What about college?"

She plays with her knife, spinning it in circles. "I'm conditionally admitted for next year, assuming I complete all my community service hours. I had to write one hell of an essay to convince the dean."

"I'll bet."

She nods. "I equated my arson conviction to a plot point in Irving's *The World According to Garp.*"

I laugh out loud, drawing frowns from the other diners. "How in the world did you do that?"

Mo flashes a grin that reminds me of happier days. "I theorized that I've been 'predisastered,' like Garp's house in the book. Remember? He wants to buy a house, and then a plane hits it, so he figures it's safe forever. I mean, what are the odds of another disaster, right? They're astronomical."

"Right," I say.

"So I told them I've been predisastered, and they can count on me to never make an awful mistake like that fire again, and it worked."

"You're clever, Mo."

Our food arrives and she dips a French fry into her ketchup. "I try."

We dig in and eat in companionable silence. I miss hanging

out and having fun. It's familiar and nice and gives me hope for my future in San Diego. I swallow and ask Mo what I want to know in a quiet voice: "How come you guys didn't include me when you confessed about the fire?"

She swallows, picks at her food. "That's what I wanted to explain, because I figured you would wonder." She glances up, her eyes a bit colder than I expected. "The truth is, we lied for Violet, not for you."

"Oh?" My cheeks start to burn.

"Yeah. Our lawyers don't know it, but we consulted privately. Everyone believes that you and Violet were riding horses together when it happened; you were her alibi. If we told the truth about you, it would implicate her."

I stare at my hands.

Mo sniffles. "Violet's dead, she has to be, and we want her to rest in peace. We won't smear her name. It was Drummer's idea, actually."

Tears roll down my cheeks and splat onto my fingers. My friends weren't protecting me at all—just her, the girl who has everything (well, had everything). I push my plate away. "Yeah, that makes sense."

"Are you *angry?*" Mo asks.

I glance up and she recoils at whatever she sees on my face. "No," I say, wondering what the hell is wrong with me. "I'm grateful. I am."

"You should be." Mo leans forward with her butter knife clasped in her fist. She points it at me. "You're as guilty as we are." Her voice is tight and controlled. "If anything, you're guiltier. You're the one who grabbed Luke's arm. He was stupid, yeah, but you were the reckless one."

The word hangs between us: *reckless*.

"We saved your ass," Mo adds.

"No, you saved Violet's ass."

She stands up, throws down ten bucks. "You're fucking welcome." And she stalks out of the café, to the shocked stares of the patrons.

I wait until she's long gone, and then I pay the rest of the bill and leave. I don't need this drama. It's over. I'm leaving and never coming back.

In the morning, my dad drives me to Southern California. As Gap Mountain vanishes in the rearview mirror, I release a long, pent-up breath. Finally. It's over.

38

Turns out, I hate dorm life. I haven't made a single real friend. My floor is loud, and kids party until 3:00 a.m. most nights. I can't study, can't think, and no one here gets me. When I'm in a mood, no one understands how to tease me out of it—they don't even realize it's a mood! They know me as the tall, quiet girl who leaves any room as soon as it gets crowded. They leave me alone, but I want to make friends, I do.

I miss the monsters.

Right now, my roommate is down the hall, throwing up in the bathroom, still sick from last night. If it were Mo or Violet, I'd be with her, rubbing her back. We used to share our miseries. Obviously, that changed when some of us went to prison and I went to college. What did I expect? I'm free. I just never imagined I'd be free all by myself.

I'm studying a textbook on socioeconomic factors as they relate to crime when my phone rings. I don't recognize the number, but I'll talk to anyone who isn't my roommate. "Hello?"

"You have a collect call from Nathaniel Drummer, an inmate at Wasco State Prison. Will you accept the charges?"

The room shrinks and my chest tightens. I'm not sure what she means by "collect call," but I don't care—it's Drummer. "Yes, I'll accept!" We haven't spoken since his arson sentencing, though I've written plenty of letters, begging him to call me.

The call is put through, and the connection is quiet except for Drummer's breathing. When he speaks, his voice warbles. "Hey, Hannah."

"Hi! How are you?" I cringe. What a stupid question.

"Not good," he answers. His playfulness is gone. His voice is deep and rumbling. "I miss her, Hannah."

I pull a breath. God, did he call to tell me that? "I miss her too."

Another long silence. Then, "The food here sucks."

I laugh, feeling awkward, and try to relate. "Here too! And my room is *tiiiny*. I might as well be in prison—I mean, except for the parties and the homework."

Drummer sucks in a breath. "Not the same, Han, not at all."

"Right, sorry."

I hear him fidget. "It's—I wanted to tell you something about Violet."

I close my eyes and he goes on. "She was a good person,

Han. She wanted everyone, you and the monsters and her grandma, to know we were dating, to come clean about it. She hated secrets."

Sure she did, I think.

Drummer cries quietly on the other end of the line. "I refused because I thought you'd be really pissed, and I left mad. Now I've lost you both."

His words shatter me. "You haven't lost me, Drummer."

His tears turn to bitter laughter, and then his voice sharpens. "Hannah, my girlfriend is dead because of what we did."

My stomach clenches as my breath leaves my body. "I— don't say that."

"I just—I don't know where she is, or if I accidentally killed her. I don't know if someone covered it up for me." His tone is raw, accusatory. "And I'm not sure I want to know."

I'm breathless; I can't speak.

He's silent a full minute. Then he releases a long, heavy sigh. "I called to tell you we're done, Hannah. I'm sorry. I'm really fucking sorry, but we're not good together. I have a counselor and he's helping me set boundaries and believe in myself. Our friendship is over."

"Drummer—"

"Hannah, it's best for both of us. Okay?"

I dissolve into a fit of coughing and crying. "Okay. I'm sorry."

A long pause and then Drummer says, "I'm the one who's sorry. It's all my fault, Han."

My stomach drops. "What is?"

"You and me—us. I liked having a smart, pretty girl like

you on the hook. I never wanted to lose that, but when I get out of here, I want a real relationship. I don't want to use girls anymore or run when things get hard. I've gotta take care of myself."

I swallow my tears. It feels good to hear him admit he understands how we were—together but not together. It makes me feel less crazy. Our relationship was real, just real bad.

He clears his throat. "Take care of yourself too, okay?"

"I will."

"It's not all bad here," he says. "Luke and I are talking again, and we joined the inmate firefighting squad. We'll be putting out wildfires, Han. Fitting, yeah?"

I hear pride in his voice and let out my breath. The boys' futures aren't destroyed; they're just not what any of us imagined. "That's great, Drummer."

"Have fun studying," he says, and we both laugh. "Goodbye, Hannah."

"Goodbye." After I hang up, I flop onto my bed and sob.

39

September 14

Days Violet has been missing: 43

Time: 2:30 p.m.

It happens in my Introduction to Criminal Law class. The two FBI agents who interviewed me in Gap Mountain stride through the lecture hall door just as class begins. They're tidy and well groomed, wearing suits, and my heart dips into my stomach.

The professor halts midsentence. "Can I help you?" she asks.

The lead agent approaches. "I'm Special Agent Hatch with the FBI." He shows his badge.

I grip the sides of my desk with one thought pounding in my head: *it's not over.*

Our professor offers a half smile and glances at her students, looking bemused.

Snickers roll through the lecture hall. It's a criminal law

class, so this feels like a joke. The students settle, waiting to see what happens next. I don't believe a single one of them would be surprised if the agents produced a wireless speaker and started stripping.

Hatch lowers his voice and whispers to the professor. Her face changes, growing serious. She checks her class list and nods. "Yes, she's my student."

My chest squeezes. The room blurs. Briefly, I wonder how fast I can run.

Hatch gazes across the hall. We're spaced far apart, and his eyes bounce from student to student until they land on me. "Hannah Louise Warner, come forward, please."

Quiet laughter erupts and students peer at one another, leaning forward and whispering as they search for Hannah Louise Warner.

My eyes dart to the exits, and the special agents notice this and begin to move. My entire body is clenched tight; my feet are rooted to the floor. Hatch marches toward me, his gun briefly visible inside his jacket, and the students catch on that this is not a prank. Their smiles change to frowns. Those closest to me move away. Static fills the air as kids realize this might get ugly.

I'm poised to bolt but force myself to face what's coming as Hatch makes his way through the rows and Special Agent Patel stands beside the main exit. Students ease away from their desks and line the walls.

"Remain calm," Hatch warns as several students rush out of the hall. He finds his way to me. "Hello, Ms. Warner."

My eyes swallow him—his suit, his power, his surety.

"We need to speak to you." He's neither rude nor polite.

"Why?" I croak, my throat tight. "Am I under arrest?"

He releases a sigh that says, *You want to do this right here?* "You are not, but I have a search warrant that requires you to come with me now." He shows me his papers.

"Oh," I say breathlessly. The warrant gives him the right to search my dorm room, my belongings, my phone, and to collect my DNA and fingerprints. "What's this about?"

He lifts one thick eyebrow. "This is about the alleged murder of Violet Sandoval. We have some questions for you, Ms. Warner."

His warrant trembles in my hands.

"We'll walk you to our vehicle now. If you resist or struggle, I will handcuff you. Do you understand?"

"Yes." My heart kicks, and my blood speeds through my veins.

Hatch and Patel lead me out of class, to the shocked stares of my classmates. As soon as I'm out the door, their energy erupts behind me in excited exclamations. The professor tries to calm them down. Someone says, "I think I've heard of Violet Sandoval. Isn't she that missing heiress?" Then utter silence. I imagine fingers tapping on phones and laptops, searching. In a minute, they'll know.

The agents' unmarked car is parked in a tow-away zone in front of the Sciences complex. They usher me to it and help me inside.

They drive me to a field office, where my fingerprints are

taken, my DNA is collected, and my phone is confiscated. Next, they lead me to a chilly interrogation room that holds a desk, several chairs, a box of tissues, and a pitcher of water. There's a two-way mirror on the wall behind me. "Wait here," says Hatch. He and Patel move to leave.

I reach for Hatch's arm and stop just short of touching him. "I don't know anything. I have amnesia."

I don't begrudge him his smirk. "If you truly have amnesia, Ms. Warner, you're in for quite a shock." He shuts the door behind him.

I shiver and my guts twist. Maybe they found Violet's body. Maybe they located my salvaged Jeep. I stare at my arm, where the half-moon indents were before they healed—*angry voices, blood on white carpet, a hunched figure in the window.*

My mind reels, and I feel suddenly sick because the truth is—I know *exactly* what happened to Violet Sandoval. Yeah, my memory came back the night Justin scared me and I ran outside with my dad's rifle. It happened when I saw my reflection in the glass—it all came rushing back, and now I wish it hadn't. In fact, I'd leap into the jaws of another fucking *bear* if it would make me forget.

The question is—do these agents know what I know?

40

September 14

Days Violet has been missing: 43

Time: 4:14 p.m.

The special agents return with a thick manila folder and a recording device. A third agent follows and stands against the wall.

Hatch sits across from me and places the folder squarely in front of him. He considers me for a full minute, and I stare right back. He knows I remember, I can see it in his eyes, and he hopes to trip me up. But from the day we started the wildfire, my goal has been to survive, and that hasn't changed. Knowing full well I'm walking into battle, I swallow my fear, find the flat, calm center of my soul, and surprise the agents by speaking first. "You said you had some questions?"

Hatch's boyish grin flickers across his face. "Ms. Warner,

you asked me once to call you Hannah. Is that still your preference?"

"Sure, that's fine." It's always felt good to cooperate with authority, a little too good. I shift in my seat and remind myself we're on opposite sides. He is my enemy.

"Hannah, you're not under arrest, but we have a few more questions about your whereabouts on the night of August second, the evening your friend Violet Sandoval went missing. I must warn you that you have the right to remain silent, and anything you say can and will be used against you in a court of law. You have the right to an attorney and if you can't afford an attorney, one will be provided. Do you understand what I've said?"

Before I can remind him of my amnesia diagnosis, Hatch raises one manicured finger and adds, "I know you have a medical condition, but this new evidence might help you remember. It might help us find Violet."

My legs stop bouncing. So they haven't found her body, which means they still don't know what happened to her, which means they're still fishing.

Hatch nods to a telephone mounted to the wall. "You can call your father if you want, but he won't be allowed in the room. He's an investigating officer in this case, and he cannot be present during the questioning of his adult daughter. Do you understand your rights?"

I cross my arms. "I didn't ask for my dad."

Hatch peers harder at me. "Would you like professional

representation, Hannah?" He fusses with a cluster of photos, and I glimpse images of my bedroom, my house, and even my dog.

I sit up straighter, curious. "No, I'm good. I want to help."

He and Patel exchange a glance, and Hatch settles back into his chair. From her place against the wall, the third agent shifts her feet. All three are armed, and the room is quiet and sterile. I pour myself a glass of water to interrupt the silence.

Hatch finally opens his manila folder. "Hannah, during our last interview, on August fourteenth, you failed to provide an alibi for the evening Violet disappeared." He produces a photo of a dented car. The tires and some other parts are missing, but I recognize the general shape and color of my Jeep. What the hell? I thought it was gone. My knee bobs and I force it still. *Don't react, Hannah.*

Hatch continues. "After the interview, we issued a search warrant for your vehicle. It took us some time to track down the Jeep, and much more time to analyze the fluids and hairs inside."

Oh, crap.

Patel pushes the search warrant toward me with a terse smile. I glance at it and nod to indicate I accept it. After my Jeep was salvaged and towed away, I never thought I'd see it again.

Hatch hands me a sheet of paper full of numbers and strange diagrams. "Our forensic experts identified DNA belonging to a *ursus americanus*—"

"A what?"

"A black bear," he explains. "DNA belonging to a black bear. They also found the remains of beef stew, and human blood belonging to Violet Sandoval."

His lips part into a smile, as if he believes this proves something, and I wonder if he understands *anything* about living in the woods. "So?"

Hatch tilts his head.

I uncross my arms and lean forward. "My blood is in there too. Do you know how many times I've cut myself fishing and hunting? And Luke's, from that time he fell out of the tree and cracked his head open, and Mo's. She gets bloody noses every winter. Violet's probably the most careful, but she sliced her foot open on a rock last year and I drove her home."

I'm lying, of course—no one's allowed in my Jeep if they're bleeding—but the words ring true to Hatch.

Disappointed with my answer, he moves on. "Hannah, we were able to extract your Jeep's GPS tracker. On the evening of the second, you drove directly from your house to Ms. Sandoval's home. An hour later, you drove to the Gap Lake trailhead overflow lot. Your vehicle remained there for approximately seventy minutes, and then you drove home. Upon arriving home, the black bear attacked you. Your father found you hiding in your bear-proof trash container at twelve-oh-one a.m." He thrusts a map at me, depicting each of my stops and the timing.

My head begins to throb. I forgot about the GPS. I blink at the agents, my mind whirring. "How do you know I was in the Jeep?"

Patel's eyes slash toward Hatch, and he swallows hard. Hatch ignores him. "We don't know, Hannah. That's why we're asking."

I nod and suppress a smile.

Hatch steeples his fingers, something I've noticed he does when he's thinking. "Is it possible Drummer borrowed your car?" he asks.

"I told you, I don't remember anything. I don't see how I can help."

Special Agent Hatch gives a small shake of his head. "He's not trying to find Violet; he just wants to arrest someone. His gaze sweeps my face; his hooded eyes flicker. Hatch has more to show me, a lot more. He hands me another paper. "After finding Violet's blood in your vehicle, we wrote a warrant to search your home and cell phone records."

I lean back as my guts coil and thrash. Sweat instantly collects on my scalp. "That seems excessive. Does my father know about this?"

"He's been informed," says Hatch. He then produces a round of photos—more images of my wrecked Jeep, including close-ups of the blood spatter, photos of the bear's dead body, images of the Gap Fire, and photos of Gap Lake. Each one strikes me like a punch, and I force deep, slow breaths.

Hatch walks around the table carrying his chair and sits beside me, leaning close, eye to eye. "We're trying to help you remember, Hannah."

No, you aren't, I think. *You're trying to make me confess.*

Then he introduces a series of photos in rapid succession,

lining them up in front of me. Heat rushes to my cheeks as I observe images of my personal diaries and hundreds of photos of Drummer. "You've been obsessed with Violet's boyfriend for years, haven't you?"

"No." I wipe my face, try to compose myself. Drummer is not an *obsession*. I love him.

"Were you stalking Drummer that night, Hannah?"

"No," I bluster. "I wouldn't do that."

"You weren't implicated in the Gap Fire, but you had a compelling motive to make Violet disappear, didn't you?"

My body braces. I shake my head.

Hatch continues. "You were jealous, weren't you, Hannah?"

"N-no," I stammer.

"You applied to Stanford University and got rejected. But she was accepted, wasn't she?"

I feel my cheeks color. I can't believe they contacted Stanford about my rejected application.

Hatch's smile turns cruel. "Violet could afford private college while you planned to sell your car to pay for a public university."

My anger flares. "So?"

He doesn't flinch. "Violet was beautiful and an accomplished equestrian. She was valedictorian of her class, and she had the one thing you always wanted: she had Drummer."

I leap from my chair, suddenly furious that he's using Drummer's nickname, as if he knows him. "So what? Is that a crime? Do you think *I* killed Violet?"

Patel breathes faster too as Hatch slides his dark eyes to mine, a twisted smirk playing on his lips. The room goes deathly quiet as he produces a see-through evidence bag. Inside is a Tiffany necklace with a circular pendant inscribed with the letter *V*. "Look at this, Hannah."

My eyes roll toward the pendant, and the air rushes from my lungs. How in the hell did he find that? It was in my dog's ashes! I grip my hands together to hide their sudden trembling.

"Do you know who owns this necklace?" he asks.

"It looks like Violet's," I respond, my heart bounding like a rabbit. *Okay, Hatch, enough with the games,* I think. *Just fucking arrest me, get it over with.*

"Here's a question," says Hatch. "How did Violet's necklace get mixed in with your dog's ashes?"

He slides a photo of bright-eyed Matilda in front of me, and anger shoots through me like a bullet. How dare he use my dog against me! I lift my head, meet his triumphant gaze, and stare him down. My hair is loose, hanging in my eyes, and my body is coiled like a spring. Hatch flinches away from me. That's right, I think, now you see me. I decide I have nothing to lose by telling the truth. I take a long breath and sit back down. "I found it in my car."

"Why did you hide it from the authorities?"

Again, I answer honestly. "I don't know."

"Do you believe you're involved in Violet's disappearance, Hannah?"

I lean back in my chair. "No." There's that word again, the best friend of liars.

He steeples his fingers and studies me for a good long time. The clock on the wall ticks, Patel takes quiet breaths, the agent against the wall clears her throat, and the truth bubbles inside of me. A part of me wants to let it out, to fill the void, make everyone happy, solve the case, but it won't bring Violet back, so I swallow it.

Hatch is full of swagger as he sits on the table, leaning over me. "Have our photos jogged your memory, Hannah?"

I realize he's being tactical. He's jarring my brain with information and images from that night, trying to force me to remember, and he doesn't give a damn that a psychologist might consider that dangerous. What a bastard. If I hadn't remembered on my own, I'd be dust right now.

Patel slams another photo onto the table. "Do you recognize this?"

I nod. It's the glass unicorn I gave Violet for her tenth birthday.

Hatch leans in, eyes blazing, lips tight. "We believe it's the murder weapon." He passes me a crime lab report. My throat knots up. They are getting warmer.

Patel studies me. "We reexamined the sheriff department's evidence collected from the attic and discovered a microscopic fragment of Violet's scalp and blood on one of the hooves."

A genuine shiver rolls down my spine. "That's awful."

"Any of this ringing a bell?"

I cross my arms, refuse to answer.

Again, Hatch breaks first. "Hannah, do you believe Violet Sandoval is dead?"

I allow real tears to flow, because I miss my friend. "You said *murder weapon*, so yeah, I guess so."

A frown curves Hatch's lips as he turns to me. "Our primary suspects are Nathaniel Drummer and Lucas O'Malley. Would you characterize them as your best friends?"

I don't like where this is leading. "Yes, I would."

"Are you romantic with either boy, or both?"

Heat floods my cheeks, but I refuse to drop my eyes. "I'm not."

"But you're loyal to them." I nod once. "Loyal enough to help them hide a body?"

I glare at him, my fury rising.

Hatch shifts and attacks me from a new angle. "Or are you afraid? Is it possible you're covering for Drummer and Luke out of fear of retaliation? Because we can protect you, if that's the case."

Am I afraid of Drummer? Never. Am I afraid of Luke—strong, powerful, angry Luke? Sometimes. I lean forward, tired of these questions. "I don't remember anything. Why are you asking me?"

Patel sits taller as Hatch adjusts his tie and presses on. "Because we need your help," he admits, and just like that, the power in the room shifts back to me. "We can't charge either boy with murder. The evidence is circumstantial, and we don't have a body. Proving in a courtroom that Drummer or Luke killed Violet would end in defeat. We need more—we need an eyewitness confession."

I nod. That's what I thought all along: they're fishing. They're not even positive Violet's dead. My fluttering pulse slows to a steady beat.

Hatch frowns. "We know your Jeep drove to Gap Lake, where we believe the victim's body was disposed of, we know she bled in your car, and we know you hid the necklace she was last seen wearing. What we don't know is who was driving. This case isn't closed, Hannah, and I believe you're an accomplice. If you give evidence against the boys and tell us where to find Violet's body, I can offer you full immunity."

Full immunity. My lips close. My pulse thrums. What Hatch doesn't understand, and what Violet never understood, is that monsters don't rat on monsters.

"Hannah, your father's a sheriff, and he tells me you're studying criminal justice at college and that you might go into law enforcement yourself." Hatch's eyes harden to steel. "What I don't understand is why a woman with your background and career goals would hide evidence."

My hands scrunch into fists. My *background* is that my father sent my own mother to prison, where she later died.

Hatch spreads all the incriminating photos in front of me, including the photo the journalist took of Gap Lake with red sunlight spilling down its center. "If you want to solve crimes, Hannah, why not begin with this one? I'm going to ask you one last time: Who murdered Violet Sandoval, and where is her body?"

The three agents in the room go quiet. The familiar urge to cooperate pulls at me. Hatch leans forward and waits, his thick brows pulled tight.

I can no longer hear the murmured conversations outside the door or the air-conditioning blowing. I know who killed

Violet, but if the agents think I'm going to tell them, they're fucking crazy.

I meet his gaze. "I don't know."

Hatch's left eye twitches. "That's your official statement?"

"Yes."

Patel slams the manila folder shut and curses beneath his breath. Hatch gathers his jacket, moves to the door, and turns to me. "We will never close this case, Hannah. We won't stop investigating until we prosecute the person or persons responsible for Violet's disappearance to the fullest extent of the law." He strides out of the room.

My admiration trails him. I would expect nothing less from the *Federal Bureau of Investigation*, Special Agent Hatch, nothing fucking less.

41

The agents drop me off on campus, and I cannot believe I'm still free. Somehow, like a cat, I've landed on my feet, but it's not just good luck. Even before my memory returned, my instincts were in high gear, protecting the monsters and myself. I made a few mistakes, but not enough to get any of us arrested.

As I pass the Student Union building, I catch my reflection in the shaded window and stop cold. I shift and step back to observe my backlit image. *The hunched figure in the window* was me—was always me. After returning from Target and hearing raccoons rustling outside and then talking to Justin, I caught my reflection in the glass and I remembered everything. But the memories did not bring relief as I'd hoped— they brought terror.

The special agents have it wrong. This is what really happened to Violet Sandoval.

———

Six weeks earlier

At 8:25 p.m., Violet sends a group text to our nonburner phones: *tomorrow I'm telling the police everything.*

I drop the manure rake I'm holding. My heart stalls.

Luke: *WTF! You cant*

Mo: *what do you mean by everything?*

No answer from Violet. No gray dots, nothing. I dial her phone, and the call goes straight to voicemail. I dial Drummer, my hands shaking. He doesn't answer either.

I pull up the location-sharing app. Shit. He's already there, in the attic! He went to her house without us. Fucking Drummer. He can't handle Violet on his own, not about this.

I rush out of the barn to my car and text Luke and Mo on our prepaid cells: *meet at the attic. Now.*

Luke: *10-4*

Mo: *I'll try*

I crawl into my Jeep and feel my regular phone slide out of my pocket and shatter on the ground. Shit! I can't think, can't breathe.

I slam the Wrangler into gear and spin the tires, throwing rocks into the shrubs as I fishtail onto the main road. My boxy Jeep leans precariously around the bends, but I don't care. I just drive.

We have to fix this together; we have to change her mind. And if Violet's so hell-bent on telling the truth, she *and* Drummer can start by confessing to *me*, and I don't mean about the fucking fire!

That was the last thing I remembered, but when the rest came to me, it came all at once, like water from a broken dam. . . .

———

My tires crunch across the Sandovals' crushed-stone driveway. Drummer's Impala is already here, parked out of sight of the house. I glance up and see a light on in the attic. Slowly, I back my Jeep between two large pine trees so I can sneak up on Violet and Drummer.

I slide quietly out of the Wrangler and scoot through the darkness toward the back of the house. Lulu habitually forgets to lock the back entrance, because it's the door the poodles use to go in and out all day. I test the knob and it turns. The door creaks. I push it gently open and step inside the house.

A television blares in the family room, and delicate snores emerge from a body on the couch. It's Lulu Sandoval; she passes out each night after her evening glasses of wine. I leave the door ajar and shuffle toward the back staircase, which is narrow and steep and leads to the third floor.

Stepping carefully, I reach each tiny landing, turn, and climb higher. The stairs are made of cherry wood, and they're old. They moan and bend beneath my feet, but the house is noisy like that, and the stairs' complaints meld into the various other sighs and creaks of the old home. At the top, the attic door is closed, but there's a giant antique keyhole. I sink to my knees and peer through it.

I recoil at what I see: Drummer and Violet kissing on the red sofa. My heart wallops. They're fully clothed but her top is pushed up and her eyelashes are wet with tears. So are his. Their kisses are deep and passionate, as if they're starving for each other, and their faces are scrunched. They're trying to be quiet, stifling their soft moans.

Drummer adjusts his jeans, slides up her skirt, and then thrusts. She clutches him, gasping, and I realize they're having sex. God!

I jerk away from the keyhole and cover my ears.

When it's over, I scurry back and watch them. Drummer pulls down his shirt. They're both flushed and rumpled and gorgeous. I chew my lip, listening.

"That was the last time," Violet says to him, catching her breath. "Until we tell the truth about the fire, it's over."

"Doesn't feel over," Drummer teases, his lips wet from kissing.

Violet sits taller and adjusts her top, artfully reties her scarf, and straightens her short tweed skirt. "I don't want to see you anymore if you can't be honest—about the fire or me. I don't like secrets. We never should have lied. *I* never should have lied to Sheriff Warner," she amends.

He grabs her shoulders and makes her look at him. "Please don't tell, V. I'll say I started it, if you want. But don't tell on the others."

Her mouth pops open, and her dark brows knit together.

"That's not fair. We did this, all five of us, and we need to face it. That's the point. We need to clear our consciences."

He shakes his head.

She scowls. "It's not fair that just Mo and Luke are in trouble."

"I know," he agrees, still shaking his head. "But like Hannah says, telling won't change anything. It'll just ruin all our lives."

"They're already ruined," she whispers. "That's what none of you seem to get. We know what we did—*we* know—and it will haunt us forever. Don't you feel awful?"

He sucks in his lower lip. "Yeah, I do."

"If we confess and pay our dues, we'll feel better. As soon as I decided to tell, I felt better."

Drummer grips his head in his hands. "Everyone in Gap Mountain will hate us."

"I don't care. I hate myself."

"Yeah, but we grew up here." He sighs. "I won't do it without talking to the others."

Violet's expression hardens. "You mean without talking to Hannah, don't you? That's the other thing, Drummer: you need to tell her about us."

My heart flutters in my chest.

"You're both going to college soon. Why tell her now?" he asks.

Violet squints at him. "Because it's another secret."

He turns his eyes toward her, and they're so full of misery

and love that I lose my breath. "It will crush her, V. We're her best friends. I can't hurt her like that."

"Because she's in love with you?"

He shrugs.

Violet's body goes stiff. "You like leading her on, don't you?" she accuses. "You tease her and keep her on the hook. You go to her with all your problems. Maybe you like her and just can't admit it."

My blood pumps faster. Humiliation pins me to the floor.

Drummer laughs, as if an attraction to me is ridiculous. "I don't like her that way. Don't worry."

"Hannah's pretty," Violet argues.

He shrugs again.

My hands clench into fists, and my fingernails dig into my palms.

"If you don't tell her about us, I will." Violet's tone grows demanding, and Drummer balks.

"No," he says, growing petulant. I see that Violet is getting territorial, and her demands on Drummer are only going to increase. Their relationship is doomed, and I smile.

Violet crosses her arms. "What do you mean, *no*? I'm not hiding this anymore. I'm done with all the lies."

He stands. "Don't tell me what to do. Hannah's my friend."

"No, she's not." Her voice rises to a whispered shout; her lips tighten and thin. "She's your back-burner girl, always ready when you need her. Have you slept with her yet?"

"God, no. She's like my sister."

Violet lifts her chin. "That's a lie. If she were like a sister, you wouldn't hide our relationship from her."

I watch them through the keyhole, my eyes volleying from one to the other as they fight about me, my anger simmering.

Drummer glares at Violet. "You're hiding me from Grammy."

Her voice becomes tremulous. "That's different."

"It's not. You don't want her to know you're fucking a local boy, and I don't want Hannah to know I'm fucking one of her best friends. You're such a hypocrite, V."

Violet lowers her voice. "Get out of here, just go."

Drummer backs away and puts on his shoes, shoving his feet in and strangling them with his shoelaces. "I don't *use* Hannah."

"Then tell her about us, put her out of her misery. She loves you, you know."

He yanks his car keys out of his pocket and glares at her. "Why do you want to fight? Why can't you let all of this go?"

"Because you're a coward and Hannah's your puppet. It's sick. You're both sick!"

My fury ignites as Drummer snatches Violet's wrists and yanks her off the sofa, dragging her to eye level. "Take that back."

Violet digs her fingernails into his arms. "Or what?"

He gives her body a hard shake. "Take it back."

"I can't believe you're defending her!" Violet thrashes like a hooked fish, leaving long red welts on Drummer's arms. She frees a hand and clocks his jaw with it. He curses, wrenches her wrist, and tosses her aside. Violet's back slams into the writing desk, and she lands beneath it, faceup. I watch, breathless, as the solid glass unicorn I gave her when she was ten wobbles side to side and then falls, striking her temple with a sickening thud.

Violet screeches and cradles her head, eyes wide and filling with tears. Blood wells and oozes down her face in a long stripe. Red droplets soak into the white carpet. "You hurt me!" she cries.

"Fuck, I'm sorry!" Drummer rushes to her side, but she shoves him away.

She gapes at the blood and her reddened injured wrist. "Go, just get out of here."

Panic flickers across his expression. "No, let me help you." He picks up the unicorn, wipes it clean on his shirt, and puts it back. Straightens the desk. Tries to check her wound.

Violet rises to her full five-foot-one-inch height and faces him, her voice flat and edged in ice. "Leave now or I will fucking scream."

Drummer's lips tremble, but he turns away and sulks out of the room, taking the main stairs down to his car. In the distance, I hear his Impala start and drive away.

Violet lets out a low, frustrated growl and staggers into the wall. She slides down it and sits, leaning back, holding her head. Blood drips between her fingers, and the droplets splat onto the floor. She pulls her hand away and watches the red liquid slide down her arm. "Oh . . . oh no," she moans. Violet can't stand the sight of blood, never could. She blinks rapidly and slumps over, unconscious.

My feelings spin out of me as I stand up on the landing. Shit! This is bad! I start to open the small attic door but hear a skittering sound on the other side of the house, a sound I know well. When we were younger, fourteen and fifteen years old, we used to sneak in and out of this attic through the window. We climbed up and down using the trellis that leans against the house.

Right now, someone is climbing up.

42

August 2

Days Violet has been missing: 0

Time: 9:10 p.m.

God, if anyone sees Violet like this, they'll blame Drummer. I rush into the room, lift her light body, and carry her into the small back landing. After propping her against the wall, I run back in and toss a throw pillow over the blood smeared on the white carpet.

I sneak out, close the door, and peek through the keyhole, holding my breath.

Strong male hands appear in the window and force it open. Then Luke crawls through, pulls out his prepaid phone, and starts texting. Shit! He might be texting Violet. Sure enough, her phone pings from her purse on the writing desk. With a heavy sigh, Luke lifts out her phone and then puts it back, muttering, "Fuck me, where are you?"

He waits a moment, cracking his knuckles, and then curses again and pulls out her wallet. Shocked, I watch as he withdraws all her cash and shoves it into his pocket, creating a thick bulge. Then he turns and exits the way he came.

I let out my breath and turn to Violet, but the sight of her steals my words. When I set her down, she twisted forward and landed on one side of her face, like a broken doll. Her skin is pallid, and her lips are colorless. She looks *dead*.

"Drummer, you asshole," I whisper. He made a mess and ran away, like he always does. But Violet's not dead, she just fainted. The slow, steady puffs of her breath tell me that. Still, if I don't pacify her when she wakes up, who knows what she'll do—accuse him of assault and then rat on us about the fire? Everyone will end up in prison because of Drummer. *I'll die if they put me in a cage*—his words prompt me. I have to fix this.

Violet moans and shifts. Good. I'll take her to the hospital.

I slip back into the room, retrieve her phone and prepaid cell from her purse, slip them in my pockets, and then return to tug on her arm. "Come on, V, get up."

She grimaces and tries to stand, but like a newborn colt's, her legs slide out from under her. She completely missed the point of her combat boots, I think as I help her up. If she'd kicked Drummer with them instead of pulling away, she wouldn't be hurt right now.

Propping Violet up with one arm is easy for me, because I'm so much taller. She starts to revive as I awkwardly help her walk down the back staircase to the first floor.

As we pass the family room, Lulu flips over, but her breaths remain deep and steady, her snoring peaceful. We move past her and out the back door, around the side of the house. A motion sensor light turns on, and I startle when a person appears. No—it's not a person, it's *me*. My backlit figure reflects off the window and, in the dark, with my hair disheveled, my posture hunched, and a semiconscious girl in my arms, I appear hulking and monstrous. I look away.

We reach my Jeep, parked in the shadows, and Violet's head lolls against my chest. I don't think she can sit up, so I lay her across the backseat with the leftovers and then climb into the front, turn over the engine, and press on the gas.

As we roll away from the house, I catch up to Luke, who's departing on his bicycle. He stops and waves me down. *Shit*. I roll my window open a crack, hoping V doesn't wake up.

"Have you seen Violet?" he asks.

I swallow. "No, have you?"

He frowns. "No. Drummer must have gotten here first. Maybe they went somewhere." He rubs his head. "Look, after her text about the police, she called and told me to come over and get some cash and not to let Grammy see me, but she didn't unlock the damn attic window. If you see her, tell her I got the money."

"Okay, but why is she giving it to you?" I'm surprised because, generous as she is, we don't borrow money from Violet. Monster pride, I guess.

He flushes. "It's just to help me out until I can move back home. She insisted."

Swallowing thickly, I say, "I'll tell her." Then I close my

window and speed past him before he asks for a ride or notices Violet lying on my backseat.

As we hit the main county road, the color returns to Violet's face. "Hannah?" Her eyelids flutter as she sits up and tries to focus on me.

I release a huge breath. "You scared me for a minute. You hit your head."

"Drummer . . . ?"

"Shhh, he's gone. Just lie down and I'll take you to a doctor."

"God, what's that smell?" she asks.

I laugh. "Your grammy's beef stew leftovers."

When I reach a split in the county road, I roll to a stop. Straight ahead is the hospital. Violet rubs her forehead and sees where we are. "I'm fine, Han, really. I don't need a doctor."

"You sure?"

"Yes. Where's my phone?" While she feels around the backseat for it, I turn the wheel and accelerate. I'm glad she's okay, because we need to talk about her police interview tomorrow, somewhere private.

"Where are we going?" she asks.

I smile. "To the Gap, where else?"

43

I drive the back roads to Gap Lake, because I don't want to get pulled over by one of my dad's deputies, not with a bleeding, slightly confused girl in my backseat. As we roll past trees that stand like ancient sentries beside the road, Violet climbs into the front seat. Her face and scarf are stained with blood. "Why are we going to the lake?"

"To talk."

"Seriously?" She rubs her injured wrist, growing distracted. "Drummer pushed me, can you believe it?"

If I remember right, she was insulting *me* when he got mad, but I shake my head.

At the trailhead, I park in the overflow lot and peer out the windshield. It's a beautiful evening. The moon flocks the pines needles in silver light, as if it just snowed, and starlight sprinkles the night sky. The wildfire smoke is gone. I step out of the Jeep, inhale the warm musk of the forest, and wonder what San Diego will smell like. Will I miss the woods, I wonder?

Violet groans. "Hannah, I don't feel good."

"You need fresh air." I lean in and pull her out, notice droplets of blood on my backseat, but she looks much better. I set her on her feet. "I got you."

She tilts her head, and the moonlight illuminates her face. The gash across her forehead flaps open, but head wounds always looks worse than they are, right?

"Where's Drummer?" she asks, looking groggy.

"I told you, he left. He hurt you and left." Maybe she'll start to understand that he's a coward and she's too good for him. "Come on, V, let's get to the water and clean you up."

Violet nods, gains control of her feet, and we hike to the western shore of the Gap and park ourselves on a stone mesa overlooking the lake. A steep cliff slides straight down from the edge and meets the water about five feet below. Kids like to dive off this flat rock, because there's nothing to hurt you, no submerged rocks or shoreline, just two thousand feet of cold water. There's no beach here either, no way to climb out without help.

The lake spans beyond us, dark except for the moonlit surface, and deeper than any secrets Violet and I have between us. "Give me your scarf, okay?"

She obediently unwinds the expensive silk from around her neck and hands it to me. Her mascara is smeared from sex and tears, and I bet I could smell Drummer on her if I got any closer. This is a sobering thought, and I look away, toward the woods where Luke lit the pipe. I have to stay focused on why I'm here—to make Violet change her mind. I dip the scarf into the water and gently clean her wound.

She offers a weak smile, and her dimples form two dark points on her heart-shaped face. Everything about Violet is pleasing, from the husky timbre of her voice to her artful hands to her expressive lips—I realize I'm staring.

But just like Drummer, she blooms under attention, and she stares back, blinking her long-lashed eyes. Then she reaches for her pendant and startles. "Oh no, where's my necklace?" She lurches into motion and crawls around the rocky plateau, feeling into the crevices.

I hunch over and help her; we search everywhere. "It's probably at your house."

"I better not have lost it," she says. After a minute, Violet pauses to rest, and her eyes sweep the flat, mirrorlike lake and the woods beyond. She hums a few bars of a song and motions toward the Gap. "The stars are in the lake and the lake is in the sky. Everything is reversed. Do you see it?"

"I just see water."

She laughs. "No, it's the reverse world, where everything is opposite. Where we didn't start the fire."

I'm glad she brought that up. "I don't see that, V, I see *this* world, where we *did* start the fire. We need to talk about it. You can't tell the police what happened."

Her fingers curl like claws. "It was an accident, Han." Her sharp chin juts toward me.

"God, you still don't get it." I shake my head. "It's a crime, people died. We'll go to prison, not college. Do you want your grammy to know you lied? And what about your parents? Do you want them to know you helped start a fire that killed ten people and then lied to the sheriff about it?"

She scrunches her face. "Hannah, stop. Getting caught or not getting caught doesn't change anything. We know what we did."

"It changes everything!"

"I've made up my mind."

Hot tears well in my eyes. "How can you send yourself and Drummer and all of us to *prison*? Luke's lawyer might even get his charges dropped."

"That's not the point. It's better to tell than get caught. Please take me home. I told you I don't feel good." She wipes the dust off her skirt, swaying on the rock that overlooks the water.

"We all have to agree," I mutter.

"You mean we all have to agree with *you*. This is fucked up, Hannah. Mo called tonight and yelled at me, Luke begged me to keep quiet, and Drummer offered to take the blame for everyone, but none of you care what *I* want."

I stand next to her. "I thought you wanted to go to Stanford? If you tell the police, they'll charge us with felony reckless arson and probably murder. Your money might buy you a good lawyer, but you'll never live down a murder charge, V. How are you the only one who doesn't get that? And you can bet Stanford will rescind your acceptance."

Violet arches a brow. "You forget how rich I am, Hannah. I don't *need* college."

"But I do," I rasp, my breath coming faster. "Don't be an asshole, V."

"Why are you studying criminal justice if you don't care about the law? Do you realize what a hypocrite you are?" Her body becomes stiff, and her face twists into an imitation of mine. She speaks robotically: "I'm Hannah. I want to fight crime like my dad and I don't care how many laws I have to break to do it." She laughs so hard she starts hiccupping.

My face turns to stone. My fists clench. My voice shifts and deepens. "Everything I've done has been to protect us."

Violet sneers, her patience gone. "No, you're protecting yourself." She sees I'm upset and digs in deeper. "Maybe you monsters can live with the police breathing down your necks and ten murders on your heads, but I can't."

"You're not better than us," I sputter.

She slinks closer, her pent-up feelings finally breaking free. "I'm not coming back after this legal shit is over. I'm spending next summer in Europe. I'm done with you, and I'm done with Gap Mountain."

Done with Gap Mountain? I blink at her, feel the heat bubbling in my gut. The pine trees blur. "What about Drummer? I know you two are together."

She steps back, startled. "He told you?"

"No, he didn't fucking tell me, it's obvious. Plus, I heard your fight in the attic. I'm not his 'back-burner' girl."

She inhales sharply. "You were *spying* on us?"

I ignore that. "If you loved him, you wouldn't turn him in."

Her brown eyes bore into mine as we circle each other on the plateau. Her words howl like a storm: "I do love him, and I know what's best for him. He needs to come clean, and then he needs to get the fuck away from *you*."

I can't speak. My body goes rigid. Tears spill from my eyes. "You're obsessed, Hannah."

"No!" I cry, drawing closer to her. "Drummer loves me. He's already getting sick of you."

I'm not sure this is true, but her furious expression is worth it. I can't think, can't see anything except Violet's doll-like face: perfect long lashes, high cheekbones, dark dimples, and plump lips. She suddenly looks . . . unreal.

"Did you bring me here to yell at me?" she asks.

I step closer, my hands balling into fists. "Promise me you won't tell and I'll take you home."

"It doesn't work that way," she says, crossing her arms. "Anyway, I made my decision."

I grab her arm. "Think of someone besides yourself."

She gasps. "I am! I'm thinking of that firefighter we killed. She had *children*, Han!"

I drag her closer, tower over her, my muscles quivering. She widens her eyes and begins to shrink. My tone is clipped; my words are stony. "You told the first lie, Violet. You started this."

She stares up at me, her pupils getting rounder and darker. "Because I was high and stupid and because no one had died yet. Now the police are all over us, and Luke drove off a cliff, and Mo can't afford college." She stands on her tiptoes, and her lips twist into a cruel smile. "What *you* don't understand, Hannah, is that I can do whatever the fuck I want!" She inhales. "And I want to tell."

I gasp. I've never seen her so mean, so heartless.

She flashes her dimples in triumphant fury. "And *you* can't stop me."

It happens in an instant. I lift my hands and shove her so hard she flies backward.

Her eyelids flip wide. "Hannah!" Her arms slice the night air, pinwheeling in a perfect arc. She falls off the flat rock and into Gap Lake with a loud, echoing splash.

44

August 2

Days Violet has been missing: 0

Time: 10:40 p.m.

My breath catches as I lean over the edge and watch Violet thrash and sputter. She lifts a hand toward me. "Pull me out!"

I squat onto my heels. "No."

"Hannah!" she shouts. "It's cold." She paddles hard and claws at the rock wall that edges the fathomless pit we call a lake. Her blue-polished nails chip against the stone. She resumes paddling, fighting against her heavy boots and water-logged clothing.

I cross my arms. "Promise you won't tell."

Her face pales and her teeth begin to chatter. "That's not fair. Help me out." She lifts one hand again, instantly sinks, and then fights her way back to the surface. "Hannah, please. This isn't funny."

"You're right, it's not funny, it's our fucking lives," I rasp, thinking of the monsters. "You threatened us, V. You have to take it back." Her legs kick; her breaths become labored. I imagine those expensive Gucci combat boots filling with water, becoming anchors. Violet will give in. She has to or she's going to drown. "Promise me," I repeat.

She shoots me a look of pure hatred and glances at the beach two hundred yards away. "Fuck you." She swims toward it.

I release a breath. God, she's stubborn.

Violet paddles, maybe twenty feet, before sinking again. She fights her way back to the surface, and her hands slap the water. She's struggling but quiet. "Violet?" I call out.

She opens her mouth, but before she can speak, she sinks again. Her black hair waves like seaweed.

I watch, waiting for her to pop back up. She's so dramatic.

A minute passes, or maybe it's just seconds, I can't be sure. "Violet?" I lean farther over the edge. "Hey, Violet!" Fuck! I yank off my shoes and dive in. The water hits my chest in a cold burst. I swim deep, eyes open, searching for her. There are no plants, no gentle slopes, just an inky darkness.

I kick deeper into the black water, reaching, hunting, until my lungs burn. Shit, shit, shit! I aim for the surface, take a huge gulp of air, and then dive back under. The chill seeps into my skin, and my heart slams my rib cage so hard it hurts. I swim until my ears clog and sharp pain rockets through my skull.

Then I see her in the depths, reaching for me, her arms like tentacles.

I kick harder until our fingers touch and our hands lock

together. I try to swim, to pull her up, but Violet's boots and clothes make her heavy and we shoot down together, sinking, falling, my lungs throbbing.

Her mouth opens in a silent scream. She claws at me like she's trying to climb up my arm. Her fingernails dig into my skin. Panic floods me. We're both going to drown.

No! I can't!

I grab her fingers and pry them off my arm. Bubbles rise from her lips as we plummet toward the bottom of Gap Lake. One hard kick and I free myself from her grasp.

I'm sorry, I think as I paddle wildly toward the surface. A glimpse back shows me black hair waving, contorted lips, and terrified eyes, and then the darkness swallows her.

I dog paddle to the surface, coughing and spluttering. The cliff she couldn't climb mocks me, because I can't climb it either. I'm trapped, but unlike Violet, I'm not wearing combat boots or hoping someone will rescue me. I make the long swim to the beach and flop onto the rocky shoreline.

I lie on my side, my stomach heaving, my breath coming in ragged bursts. She's gone—gorgeous, funny, brilliant Violet. God, she has two thousand more feet to fall before she hits bottom.

I flip over and stare at the moon, realize she's never coming back. A keening sound erupts from my throat and morphs into a wail. An owl hoots and coyotes yip in the distance, a timeless eulogy.

I lie there, immobile, for a long time, my mind blank, my hair and clothes drying in the wind. After a while, I get up, retrieve her two phones, and toss them into the lake. After that, I find my shoes and drive home in a daze, taking the back roads.

At the house, I park in my driveway and sit in my Jeep, trembling and crying. Just as I decide to go inside, the bear that's been nosing around my property rushes out of the woods and gallops toward me, its saliva dripping—sniffing beef stew and blood.

I run—the worst thing to do. It catches up and swipes me with a gigantic paw, throwing me against our side fence. I curl into a ball as its teeth pinch into my skull. I scream and scream for help. Then I hear Matilda's ferocious bark. This is truly the last thing I remember.

45

Sunlight flickers across my eyelids as I remember where I am—at college, staring at my reflection in the library window. I glance around, notice a few kids watching me, curious. How long have I been standing here? I tuck my chin and stride across the grass as if I have somewhere to go.

There is some relief in understanding what it all means— the angry voices, the blood on white carpet, the hunched figure in the window—but there is no relief in understanding that it's my fault. The boys didn't kill Violet, I did. And I got my dog killed too.

I see Violet in my mind's eye—her wet hair plastered to her head, her eyes round and frightened and angry, her voice— *Hannah, please. This isn't funny*—and I wonder if I waited too long to save her *on purpose*. Am I a murderer, *just like my mother?* Tingles rush across my scalp. No—I didn't, I wouldn't—but I was so angry, so *hurt*. Violet said she was done with Gap Mountain, which meant she was done with *me*.

My throat tightens and tears blur my vision. Maybe I could forgive her for telling about the fire, and maybe I could forgive her for loving the same boy, but I'm not sure I could forgive her for abandoning me. I miss her, I do—but Violet was wrong. She'll never be done with Gap Mountain.

Digging my nails into my palms, I think back to how it all started. How we five became best friends because no one wanted to play the human in a summer play. Perhaps that wildness—our attraction and relation to monsters—is the same wildness that tore us apart.

The only thing I know for sure is that when the news breaks that I hid Violet's necklace, my friends are going to hate me. Drummer hurt her, true, but he didn't kill her. Luke took her money, yes—and I understand why he was afraid of the police finding out about that—but I believe his story, that Violet gave it to him. And none of the monsters ratted on Violet about the wildfire. They loved her as much as I did. They tried to protect her. What will they do to me if they ever find out the truth? God.

I don't know where I'm going, so I just walk. As I pass the student center, thinking hard about everything, I remember that I have an ethics paper due tomorrow. Ethics, shit—which side of the law am I truly on?

I reach for my phone, remember that the FBI agents confiscated it, and discover a piece of paper lodged in my back pocket.

It flutters onto the concrete and I bend over, pick it up. It's Special Agent Hatch's business card. I study both sides. It's not too late. I could call him, confess . . .

But I worked hard for this—to stay out of prison and start college, to survive—and I'm alive, still free. As I squint at Hatch's card, I realize that if I tell the truth about Violet, no one will believe it wasn't murder. Between her bloodstains in my Jeep, her scalp fragment on the unicorn I gave her, my car's whereabouts that night, and the fact that I hid her necklace in my dead dog's ashes—I can't prove Violet's death was an accident. Besides, the truth would have to include her involvement in the wildfire, and that would tarnish her image. No one wants that.

A surreal feeling washes over me. Birds chirp, leaves brush against the wind, and students pass like schools of fish, parting and re-forming around me. It's a beautiful day in sunny San Diego, and I'm finally here, at college, studying criminal justice, just like I wanted.

I miss the monsters and our lazy summer days at the lake. Things were about to change between us, sure, but they hadn't yet. The hours were golden and warm, dappled with laughter and soaked with hope. And then the five of us made a big fucking mistake.

I no longer hear the bikes and skateboards speeding past, the murmurs of conversation, and the laughter of my fellow students. My heart rate spikes, and my knees tremble. My future spans before me, beautiful and unknowable. I inhale and let my breath go.

I am the Gap, I realize. I am the swallower of secrets. I did my best to protect the monsters, just as I promised. I tried to protect Violet too. I warned her not to tell the truth, that it would do more harm than good, but she wouldn't listen. We're not criminals because we did something bad; we did something bad because we were reckless. It's not the same.

I crumple up Hatch's business card and throw it away. I believe in the law, I do, and it's the law's job to catch me. This is Hatch's problem, not mine; I'm just a student. I vow right then that if I ever make it into the FBI, I'll be a much better agent than Hatch. I sling my backpack over my shoulder and head to the dining hall.

In the end, Violet raised her hand. She decided to play the human. Walking across campus, I imagine her black hair waving, her graceful hands reaching, and I hope she sank all the way through the Gap and emerged into the mirrored world she envisioned on the other side, a world where we live opposite lives—where we tell the truth, where fires cannot burn, and where monsters do not exist.

A Note from the Author

Thank you for reading *Lies Like Wildfire*. While I wrote this story to entertain readers, it is inspired by my personal experiences with wildfire. The story is set in the fictional town of Gap Mountain near Yosemite National Park, but the real-life events occurred over two hundred miles away in Sonoma County, California.

My first experience with wildfire occurred on October 8, 2017. A tiny spark on private property grew into the Tubbs Fire, which roared over the foothills toward my community, gobbling everything in its path. It destroyed more than 5,500 structures, many of them private homes, and scorched over 36,000 acres. Powered by dry brush and winds reaching sixty miles per hour, the Tubbs Fire cost $100 million to suppress, caused

$1.2 billion in damage, burned for 23 days, took 22 lives, and was, at the time, the most destructive wildfire in California history (the Camp Fire surpassed it the following year). This fire became quite personal to me due to the many close friends who lost their homes.

The idea for *Lies Like Wildfire* was born in 2019 while I was hiking through a county park near my house. I stopped at a lake, thinking it would be fun to write a thriller because I love reading them so much. I imagined five teens enjoying a hot summer day by the lake and then doing something very, very bad—accidentally, of course. Instantly, I knew they would start a fire. There are few things more terrifying, out-of-control, or destructive than wildfire. Also, it's a crime to start one, even accidentally.

When I returned from the hike, I began to write, and all the horror my community and I had experienced with the Tubbs Fire came alive on the page, but I realized I needed more detailed information. I contacted Matt Gustafson, the Sonoma County Fire District Deputy Chief. We met at a coffee shop, where I interviewed him about wildfire, arson, teen perpetrators, fire investigation, fire laws, fire suppression, Red Flag warnings, and his personal experiences with wildfire. I'm so grateful to Mr. Gustafson for his time and expertise! I added what I learned to the novel.

But I wasn't finished. As you know, this book is about more than wildfire. After Violet went missing, I knew I needed to learn about police procedure and investigations. I contacted Lessa Vivian, an investigator for the San Francisco District Attorney's office. She was also incredibly generous with her time and expertise and thoroughly answered all my questions. I added that information to the novel as well.

Wherever I got things wrong regarding the wildfire or the police/FBI investigation, I either took creative liberties or just plain misunderstood. All mistakes are mine.

Once the novel was completed, I emailed a draft to my literary agent, Elizabeth Bewley of Sterling Lord Literistic. Not long after I hit send, Nixle alerts began pinging on my phone as another massive wildfire started on October 23, 2019: the Kincade Fire. This time, my home was in its direct path.

While my agent was reading *Lies Like Wildfire*, I loaded my horses, pets, and family into trailers and cars and evacuated. CAL FIRE's computer modeling predicted that my house and town would be destroyed, and our mayor was told to prepare to lose the community. Almost 200,000 people across multiple towns were asked to flee, and 90,000 structures were in danger. Wind gusts hit 93 miles per hour and the fire burned for 13 days. It was the biggest wildfire ever to hit Sonoma County and burned over 77,000 acres.

Thanks to an incredible show of spirit, 300 fire departments, operational areas, and protective districts from across the nation banded together and beat back the Kincade Fire, and no lives were lost. Against all the odds, they saved my town and my home from destruction. Once the county park reopened, I returned to the lake where I'd first imagined my story. The entire area was scorched black; everything around it had burned.

While *Lies Like Wildfire* does not feature first responders, they are the real heroes in the fight against wildfire, and that includes the inmate firefighting squads who also risk their lives. I'm forever grateful for their efforts! The emotional, physical, and financial details in the novel are drawn from residents' experiences, and I want to thank the people of Sonoma County who shared their personal wildfire stories with me or with the media. Our community slogan became *The love in the air is thicker than the smoke. #SonomaStrong*

Though inspired by real-life events, please understand that *Lies Like Wildfire* is a work of fiction. This novel's purpose is to entertain, but I hope it also educates about the dangers and traumatic aftereffects of wildfire. Thank you for reading!

Acknowledgments

I thoroughly enjoyed writing *Lies Like Wildfire* and want to thank the book's first readers, two children's book librarians— Sheila Nelson (my mom!) and Tiffany Bronzan. They were quick to read and give feedback and were quite helpful when I wrote eight different endings and sent them a new one each morning. I'm grateful for their unrelenting enthusiasm.

Special thanks to my second reader: my agent, Elizabeth Bewley. She instantly connected to *Lies Like Wildfire* and had ideas on how to improve the manuscript. With a talented and steady hand, she guided the book—and me—through the submission process to publishers. Since then, I've come to rely on her incredible eye for story and voice. I've been blessed with stellar support in this industry over the years, and I'm proud and pleased to add Elizabeth's smart and thoughtful advocacy to my experiences.

I was thrilled when Wendy Loggia, Senior Executive Editor at Delacorte Press, acquired *Lies Like Wildfire*. The whole process was a whirlwind, and very exciting. Our first chat included everything from our love of dogs to our love of true crime and thrillers. I knew my book had found the best home, and as we dove into edits, that belief was confirmed. Thank you, Wendy, and Alison Romig, Editorial Assistant, for helping me uncover the story beneath the story. And much gratitude to Beverly Horowitz, VP and Publisher at Delacorte Press, for her quick and ongoing support.

Bravo to Casey Moses for designing the cover! She commissioned original artwork from an innovative, passionate artist named Mishko. The flame lettering is gorgeous and hypnotic on a background speckled with ashes. I love it! Much appreciation to Andrea Lau for using the cover's design elements to craft a compelling interior with special features for the nixle alerts, texts, and press conferences. It's a joy to see the work come to life.

Huge thanks to Carmen McCullough, Editorial Director at Penguin Random House Children's Books, who acquired the book for the UK and sent me the most enthusiastic email! I am so excited for *Lies Like Wildfire* to publish overseas with such an amazing team.

Many more thanks to Szilvia Molnar, Foreign Rights Director, and Danielle Bukowski, Foreign Rights Manager, at Sterling Lord Literistic for their dedication to placing *Lies Like*

Wildfire in foreign markets. Special gratitude to Pedro Almeida at Faro Editorial, who acquired the book for the Brazilian market. I cannot wait to read a Portuguese translation of the monster's story. I won't understand it, but that's okay; I know how it ends.

I'm also thrilled to work with Berni Barta, agent at CAA. She's so smart and creative and immediately had a strong vision for adapting *Lies Like Wildfire* to the screen.

Thank you to my fellow writers. No one gets this process like you do. When I'm freaking out over a plot hole, a terrible first draft, or monstrous self-doubt—you've got my back! Rather than miss anyone in this far-ranging group, I'll thank the writers I speak with weekly: Natasha Yim, Shirin Yim Bridges, Robyn T. Murphy, Jennifer Gennari, Shells Legoullon, L. B. Schulman, Merriam Sarcia Saunders, and Nikki Garcia.

I am eternally grateful for my best girlfriends—you know who you are! You keep me connected to the real world, cheer me through my personal ups and downs, and join me for adventures. The writing life would be quite lonely without you.

And finally, thank you to my family. Sometimes you get the last piece of me, but the truth is, none of this means anything without you. I love you. Special gratitude to my husband, who encourages me through good times and bad. We all need someone who believes in us, especially when we don't believe in ourselves. And last but not least, much love to the pets that inspire my animal characters. Thank you.

ABOUT THE AUTHOR

Jennifer Lynn Alvarez earned her B.A. in English Literature from the University of California, Berkeley. She is the author of two middle-grade fantasy series, The Guardian Herd and Riders of the Realm, and she's the Sonoma County Coordinator for SCBWI. Jennifer also supports public libraries by volunteering for her county's Library Advisory Board. *Lies Like Wildfire* is her debut young adult novel and her first thriller. Jennifer lives on a small ranch in Northern California with her family, horses, and more than her fair share of pets.

jenniferlynnalvarez.com